The Dirty Bitches MC

Season One

Avelyn Paige, Winter Travers
Geri Glenn, GM Scherbert

Editor – Rebel, Edit and Design

Proofreader for Avelyn – Nikki Reeves

Cover Designer – Wicked by Design

Format by Brenda Wright, Formatting Done Wright

Dedication

To the women who together will become more. More independent. More loving. More resourceful. More diverse. More daring. More explorative. More explosive.

Table of Contents

Livin' on a Prayer

By Avelyn Paige
AKA Rogue

Wedding Day, 2008

"Lawd have mercy. It's hotter than two rabbits screwin' in a wool sock out here. Did ya have to have an outdoor wedding in August, June Bug?" My Uncle Max remarks, tugging at his tie like it's a noose around his neck. "Y'all don't have a lick of sense to be holdin' this weddin' in the summer."

I smile back at him over my shoulder, as I adjust the thin piece of my tulle veil over my face, thinking over his words. He's not wrong about picking the worst time of year for a wedding. Alabama summers are probably the closest thing to an earthly experience in Hell as you can get. The hot, sticky air clings to your skin like a wet blanket. Just walking outside can be an Olympic sport, if you aren't in good health. And if the heat isn't enough, the mosquitoes and tornadoes will have a weaker person packing their shit and moving up north with the Yankees. My granny used to tell me that it took a special kind of person to choose to live in a place like Alabama, and she wasn't kidding.

"You know, Uncle Max, I would've picked a winter wedding if I could have. Lachlan's grandparents were dead set on us being married, if we wanted to live together, while he's in college. They wouldn't have it any other way."

Well, they would if they could've forced us apart, but Lachlan stood his ground against them and his parents. If they wanted him to go to college, so he could run his daddy's sugarcane business in New Orleans, he would do it only if I was with him. My presence in his life is non-negotiable. Either I went, or he didn't. It didn't take his family long to realize that the two of us came as a pair, and they weren't ever going to change that fact, even if they held their breath and stood on their heads.

"College? Bah. That boy's grandmama has her nose so high in the air that she could drown in a rainstorm," he declares, fidgeting with the tie again. "He can run that damn place just fine without a fancy college degree."

"We know that, but it's family tradition that all the Lee men go to the University of Alabama, before starting in the family business. You know Southerners don't care one lick about anything else, when it comes to upholding their traditions."

"The Lees have Alabama, and the Ryders have incarceration and early pauper graves. That's our tradition."

"Hush, Uncle Max. Not all the Ryders are like Grandpappy and Granny."

"What about your Mama and Daddy?" He fires back.

I huff in response. Mentioning their history is a low blow, even for him.

"You didn't turn out like them, and neither did I."

Thank the good Lord for that. After Grandpappy and Granny burned down the church, with a homemade moonshine still they'd built in the basement, I didn't think our family history could get any worse. But my Mama and Daddy decided to 'kick it up a notch,' as that famous chef on television used to say, by burning down the new church they had built in its place a few years later, doing the exact same thing. If there's one thing you don't mess with in the south, it's God and His house. Unfortunately for this town, the Ryder clan seemed to specialize in terrorizing the Lord and Reverend Davis.

"Why do you wanna go marryin' into the Lee family anyhow? They aren't like us, June Bug. That boy's family thinks they're shittin' in high cotton."

I turn on my heels and slowly pad my way over to him, offering my own sad attempt at a Windsor knot at his Adam's apple. The cheap, slick material glides under my fingers, as I try to sort out the mess he's made of it. At first, he'd refused to wear the suit I'd laid out for him because in his words, "It makes me feel like a stuffed sausage at the pork processing plant in Orestes." It took a little convincing, and a plate of Granny's old-fashioned oaties to finally bring him around.

"You can't pick who you fall in love with," I state, as I make the final loop through the knot. "I love Lachlan. His family just comes as a bad booby prize."

My uncle's worn, leathery hand gently grasps my chin, pulling it up to meet his gaze.

"That boy doesn't deserve you, June Bug. Never has and never will."

I smile up at him, pressing my face against his warm hand.

"You know his family might be telling him the exact same thing right now," I mutter under my breath. And it's a thought that scares me to death, if I'm being honest with myself.

A grimace forms on my uncle's face, as his hand falls away. He turns to look in the direction of the other tent, where my future husband stands ready for our wedding with his family at his side. A family that very much wanted him to pick another as his wife, and someone more respectable than an orphan girl raised by her uncle and his motorcycle club. In their eyes, I'm the girl every parent warned their rich sons about. The mile-long prenuptial agreement was proof enough. If we divorce, I won't be touching a lick of the family money. They made sure the only assets I can walk away with are what Lachlan and I have together. It's their insurance policy that a piece of white trash like me can't leave with half of their fortune, despite the number of times I've told them I don't want their money. I just want the love of their son and grandson.

But Lachlan doesn't see me like his parents do with their misguided, old-fashioned views. I'm just a girl who fell in love with a boy that just so happens to come from a wealthy family. A family that this entire town idolizes, while they all cross the street to avoid getting the Ryder taint on them, like we are contagious.

The Lees are old money, and they make sure that everyone in town knows it. Every single Lee, until Lachlan, walked around with the biggest chip on their shoulder and thought the sky was blue because they decreed it. They have more money than Moses, and each one lives a lifestyle that most of us only dream about.

Big houses.

Fancy cars.

And a misguided sense of an inflated ego.

The Ryders, on the other hand, are the exact opposite. We grew up poor and died poor. My Mama and Daddy weren't any exception to that rule either. They squeezed quarters so hard the eagle would scream, but in the end, the only thing they met was the bottom of a six-foot deep grave, after overdosing on cheap heroin they'd bought with Daddy's disability check. I should've been sad when they died, but there was a part of me that was relieved. I didn't have to live in fear that I would come home and find that they had abandoned me.

No, their deaths were a gift because it put me into my uncle's care. I was safe with him and have been, until this very day when I asked him to give me away to a man he didn't think deserved me. Uncle Max loved me like his own daughter and had never treated me any differently. I think a part of him regretted that I was raised around such a rough crowd, as the Descendants of Destruction Motorcycle Club, but I wouldn't change it for a single second. Life was exciting, and I never felt unsafe. It was like living with fifteen uncles who would never let anyone or anything harm me, including Lachlan.

Every time he came around, one of the guys would pull him aside and give him the rundown of what would happen to him, if one hair on my head was harmed, or if he made me cry. I shudder just thinking about what they might have told him. Lachlan of course, abided by every single one of their rules they had told him, and he never revealed to me their demands.

That's when I knew he was it for me.

Lachlan saw past the dirt poor, white trash reputation of my family, when he didn't have to. He had money, and could have had any girl in town that he wanted, but he chose me. A girl who could never live up to the high standards of his family.

"June Bug?" My uncle interjects, effectively bringing me back to reality. "Are you alright?"

"I'm fine." I smile. "Just thinking about today and how we got here is all."

"Today's just the beginning for you. You may think that marryin' that boy is gonna make your life easier, but it won't. That little band around your finger is gonna be more trouble than what it's worth."

"Is that why you never jumped the broom, Uncle Max?"

"Damn straight. I'm not the marryin' kind of man. Too stubborn for my own good."

"Pretty sure that's where I get it from," I tease. He laughs, knowing it's true. The Ryder family's stubbornness gene is strong in both of us.

"Ornery never looked so pretty. Give me a twirl," he requests.

I oblige, grasping the edge of my A-line skirt and spin twice on my tiptoes around the tent. The light catches the pearlescent beads and sequins, glittering on the white walls of the tent surrounding us.

"Your Mama and Granny are smilin' down from heaven on you today, June Bug. I don't think I've ever seen somethin' as pretty as you in my life. Not even a brand new Harley with extra chrome and ape-hangers."

"Well, when you put it that way…" I laugh, staring into the mirror at the stranger looking back at me. Lachlan's mother and sister spent hours pinning and tucking my long blonde hair into ringlets around my face. Like a debutante for her debut to society, followed by a heavy layer of beauty queen makeup. My reflection wasn't that of a poor eighteen-year-old girl. No, it was of a woman about to marry the man of her dreams and chase after her happily ever after.

My uncle sidles up beside me, beaming like a proud father.

"It's time," the wedding coordinator says, as she pops her head into the door of the tent.

I take one last good look in the mirror and sigh.

This is it. This is the last time you'll look into a mirror as Dixie Ryder. You're gonna walk away from the alter as a Lee. I hope you're ready for that.

My uncle steps aside, as I turn and head out the door of the tent with him in tow. The bright summer sun beats down on me, and a bead of sweat drips down the open back of my dress.

Lord, just get me through the ceremony, before I sweat clean out of this dress.

Uncle Max steps to my left, offering me his arm. I take it and wrap mine around his to steady myself.

"Bride is on the move," the coordinator barks into the microphone strapped to the side of her face, alerting her assistants that my impending arrival is near.

As we approach the crowd of people seated in white chairs, under the shade of the Lee Family Willow Tree, my uncle chuckles.

"What's so funny?" I question.

"It looks like a biker rally next to a garden party," he laughs.

I peer up at the crowd and laugh myself. On the left are my uncle's club brothers and their old ladies dressed in leather and black. On the right is Lachlan's family and friends in their Sunday pastel finest with large hats atop their heads, like this is some kind of English royal wedding.

"Last chance, June Bug. We can still make it to my bike if we run now," Uncle Max teases one last time.

"Not a chance." I smile back.

The string quartet begins to play, as we make it to the back edge of the guest seating. The preacher asks for the attendees to stand, and then all eyes are uncomfortably on me, as we pass each and every row of familiar and unfamiliar faces.

"Gold digger," a voice whispers, as I pass by Lachlan's side of the family.

"A pity he picked that one," a feminine voice responds back.

"That dress is so tight that you can see her religion," another voice echoes. "How shameful."

Though their words hurt, they do not surprise me. I was a Ryder and a black sheep who was about to join the high and mighty Lee family. But I won't give them the satisfaction of seeing how it hurts. Every inch of this wedding, from how I look to the kind of cake being served at the reception, was going to be under scrutiny. It's just how it goes with Southern high society. You will be judged, and you will learn to live with it without one ounce of protest. Lord help these women if they catch me on a bad day. I reach down deep, mustering up every ounce of strength I have inside of me to block them out, focusing on what's ahead.

Lachlan.

He stands tall to the left of the minister in a dark gray suit and cream tie. His lean frame fills out the suit much more than his usual button-down shirt. Lachlan is by no means skinny in any way thanks to good southern cooking, but dressed up, he looks so different. His brother, Lukas, stands behind him. The two of them could be twins with the exception of Lukas's dark hair to Lachlan's light, sandy blond.

He smiles as we inch closer.

My uncle stops at the mark just as we'd practiced the night before, and the preacher begins the service. I peer to my left and frown, knowing that I'll find no one behind me that loves and supports me like Lukas does for Lachlan. My uncle and his club brothers are all I have in the world, except for Lachlan, but his grandmother refused to allow me to stand-alone. It wasn't fitting she had said, and her grandson's bride would have a bridesmaid, even if it meant that the woman standing behind me was none other than my rival for Lachlan's affections, his childhood best friend, Ashley Monroe-Buchanan.

Ashley is everything the Lees wanted in a daughter-in-law. She's a tall waif of a girl, with glittering blonde hair, and a wardrobe straight from Fashion Week in New York City thanks to her daddy and his family's oil money. I tried to like her, until she began to interfere with mine and Lachlan's relationship once things became serious. She wanted what I had and made no bones about it, when it was just the two of us around, but as soon as Lachlan entered the room, she was all syrupy sweet.

To him, she was harmless.

To me, she was the wrecking ball I was dodging to stay alive in our relationship.

I sneak a peek over my shoulder and spy Ashley's fake, one-hundred-watt smile aimed not at me, but at Lachlan. No doubt she's imaging herself in my place, daydreaming of a life with him, and me out of the picture. She catches me looking over at her, and instantly diverts her gaze to mine with a solemn grimace.

Yeah, that's what I thought. He'll never be yours, sugar, as long as there's air in my lungs.

"Who gives this woman away to this man?" The preacher drawls with a booming voice.

"I do," my uncle proudly states. "On behalf of her mother and her father."

Uncle Max untangles my arm from his and takes a step closer to Lachlan, craning down to meet him face-to-face.

"Take care of her, boy," he warns in a whispered tone. "You know the consequences if you don't."

"I will, sir," Lachlan's deep voice affirms.

Satisfied with his answer, Uncle Max turns back to me, kisses my cheek, and places my hand into Lachlan's before taking his seat in the front row next to his club's president, Magnus.

The preacher begins his sermon, and we go through the motions, until at last Lachlan's lips descend upon mine. The act of a man claiming his wife in front of all of our witnesses.

"You're mine now, Rogue. No one is ever going to tear me away from you."

Three Years Later

"Another round, sugar?" I question the man leaning against the wooden bar top of my Uncle's dive bar, Grease Monkeys.

"I'm good," he replies, waving me off.

"You let me know if you need anything else." I grab the discarded towel I use to wipe down the bar and head towards the other end. One of my regulars, Tommy Jenkins, is lying lazily with his head in his hands. I start to ask him if he wants another round, but when he raises his head, the glassy haze of his eyes gives me the answer I need.

It's last call for him. After as many rounds as he's had, it's a damn miracle he's able to keep his balance on the barstool. One more would surely have him slipping off the side, possibly landing him in a drunken heap on the floor.

"How about I call Mr. Beuford to give you a ride home, Tommy? It's about time for you to scoot on out of here and sleep off that hangover you're working on."

"I ain't done," he snaps, reaching over the bar top to grab me. His calloused hand grips my wrist tightly, just as my eyes connect with Uncle Max's, when he walks out of the office upstairs.

"I'd let go, Tommy, before my uncle jerks a knot in your tail."

"I ain't doin' shit, until you get me another drink, bitch. And I ain't afraid of that bastard neither."

Tommy yanks on my wrist, nearly dragging me over the bar with his brute strength, but before he tries it again, Uncle Max is at his left with his hand clamped around his throat. Tommy lets go almost immediately.

"What did I tell you about touching Dixie, *boy*?" My uncle says, growling in a low voice. "She's off-limits to the likes of you."

Tommy tries to talk, but my uncle's grip tightens around his throat. He wasn't exactly looking for an answer from him. He was making a statement that his niece isn't a plaything, especially in his bar and under his care.

"I told you the last time it was your final warning. Do you have cotton in your ears, *boy*?"

Tommy fights against his grip, but it was a lost battle, before it ever began. My uncle has nearly one hundred pounds on him and an iron-like grip. Tommy wasn't going anywhere, unless Uncle Max made that call.

"You ain't coming back again. Are you, Tommy?"

He bobs his head up and down in agreement. Uncle Max is satisfied with his coerced 'yes,' so he lets him go, sending Tommy sliding off the stool and straight to the floor in a gasping heap.

"You apologize to Dixie, then get your fuckin' ass outta my bar."

My uncle looms over him, watching his every move. He struggles to pull himself up on his own, but Uncle Max leans down, grabbing him by the collar of his shirt, and jerks him upright, moving him at a faster pace.

"Apologize," he orders.

"Sorry, Dixie," Tommy chokes out. "I didn't mean it."

The tone of his voice says the opposite. He isn't sorry this time, nor has he been sorry the last two times it happened, when I cut him off. Tommy was just doing what he needed to do to stay alive.

"You and me, son are gonna have a little chat outside, while Dixie calls your ride."

Tommy's eyes flash with the fear of not knowing whether the chat will be in words, or my uncle's fist. If I'm being honest, the latter is more than likely the case with a repeat offender like Tommy, but for his sake, I hope a discussion will be enough.

I watch as my uncle damn near drags the man out of the bar with his heels scuffing up the old wood floor, as they head towards the exit. As they disappear, I turn to grab the phone off the wall and make a quick call to Tommy's grandpappy to come get him. He answers almost immediately, as the result of having had to come get Tommy in recent weeks. He used to be a good kid, but tough times had hit our sleepy little southern town. Stress and hardship changes people, and Tommy is no exception.

Businesses were closing up shop, as the factories nearby began to close. With no work, the townspeople were leaving in droves, and the ones who stayed behind were pissing away what little money they had on booze and drugs to kill the pain. It was sad to see Magnolia Springs sinking to an all-time low, but that's what happens, when you take the boom out of boomtowns.

A short while later, Uncle Max emerges from the front. My eyes immediately go to his clenched hands at his hips. There isn't any blood, or the sound of an ambulance pulling up. He strides up around the bar top and motions for me to follow him.

"Lola!" He yells out to the other girl waitressing. "Watch the bar!"

"Sure thing, Buzzard," she replies, using his nickname from his motorcycle club. Most of the girls who work here are either old ladies or patch pussy for his club. Myself being the only exception to the rule, since I'm family and in a bad way myself. Uncle Max helped the club and the women associated with it any way he could, especially in times like these.

Following my uncle back through the hallway, to the stairs that lead to his office upstairs, I silently think on what he wants to talk to me about. If it was about Tommy, he'd have done it at the bar for the entire place to hear as a warning. *No.* This is about something else. Why else would he be dragging me up these rickety ass steps for the sake of a private conversation?

Something has to be wrong.

The steps creak under his weight, until we finally hit the landing where his office sits, and his breathing is audible from the exertion. My uncle may not be an old man, but his life has taken a toll on his body a lot more than he'd like to admit. He slides around his desk, plopping loudly into the seat. I choose to stay standing, leaning against the wall rather than sitting down, like a student about to be lectured by their teacher.

"We need to talk," he grumbles. "About your living situation."

Here we go again. It's the same argument we've been having, since Lachlan and I moved back home with our tails tucked between our legs. His grandparents cut him off financially, when he dropped out of school, leaving us with nothing, but my nighttime waitressing job. We tried to make it work, but we had no other choice than to come home. The recession and the lack of jobs made our hard situation impossible, until my uncle and his club stepped in to give me a job, while Lachlan looked for work. Unfortunately, the only job he has been able to find is working for Ashley's father, putting him right back into her crosshairs. It's the last thing I want him to do, but we are in a desperate way. Money is money, despite the fact that I hate where he is getting it from.

"We've been over this already. Lachlan and I are fine living at Mama and Daddy's trailer."

Anger flashes across his face at the stubbornness that flows through both of our Ryder family veins.

"You need to move in with me, June Bug. That trailer park isn't safe for you, when Lachlan's working night shifts on the new highway."

"I'm fine," I scoff. "I have a shotgun."

"That shotgun ain't gonna do squat, if you can't get to it. Take my offer. Besides, I already cleaned out your old room for the both of ya."

"I wish I could, Uncle Max, but Lachlan doesn't want to take another handout. He says he's lived too long with other people's generosity."

"That boy is a damn fool. He needs to get his head outta his ass and learn to shove down that rich pride of his, when it comes to your safety," he growls. "Your life should mean more than that to him. Seems to me I need to have a 'come to Jesus' meeting with your husband."

"Like you did with Tommy just now?" I spitefully fire back. "You can't solve every problem with a punch to the face, Uncle Max."

"Sure seems to have worked with Tommy. Lachlan won't be any different."

I shove off from the wall, sidling up right next to my uncle's seated position, sitting down on top of his desk.

"Please, let me handle Lachlan. I know you're worried for me, but we're going to make this work. The trailer is temporary, until his checks start coming in, and when they do, we're going to buy a little house here in town."

Uncle Max's large hand grips mine tightly. His loving gaze gives me comfort, telling me that he won't force his way into the situation. At least not yet.

"I hope that happens, June Bug, but y'all don't have a pot to piss in or a window to throw it out of. Just move in with me, and give this ol' man some peace of mind that you're safe."

I pause, quietly considering his offer. With no jobs, folks are beginning to get desperate for money, even if it means stealing to get it. The drugs and drinking problem has only escalated the situation more. Maybe he's right.

"I'll talk to Lachlan, but no promises," I offer him, as an olive branch.

"He'll see reason. Any man worth his salt would see it. Now, you get on home and talk to him. I'll get going myself and get supper started, before we go get your things," he retorts, releasing his grip on my hand. Pushing himself up out of his chair, he stalks around me, heading to the door.

"You lettin' the grass grow under your feet, girl?" He teases, as he reaches the door. "Get goin'. You've got a husband to convince."

"I'm goin'. Good Lord," I laugh. Sliding off the desk, I stalk towards him and pause. He leans down and kisses the top of my head, like he does every night, before I head home.

"Love ya, June Bug," he calls out, as I step through the doorway and start down the stairs.

"Love you, too," I call out, just as I hit the bottom step. I make a quick stop by the bar to grab my purse, before heading back down the hallway that leads to the exit. The hot summer sun wraps around me, like a heated blanket in a heat wave.

"Sweet Jesus. You'd think that I hadn't grown up in the southern pits of Hell," I mumble under my breath. The chrome handle of my truck burns my fingertips, as I touch it.

"Christ on a cracker," I exclaim, quickly reaching for it again, and fast enough to keep from frying my fingers to a crisp.

I take a deep breath and dive into the sweltering temperatures inside. Thankfully, I had the foresight to put down that old towel on the leather seat, or my ass would be as red as cherry tomato in an old widow's garden. I make quick work of getting my truck started, and the windows cranked down to find relief from the heat. Backing out of my spot, I head home.

The drive from Grease Monkeys to our trailer is short, only about ten minutes, if I time the lights and the train right. And tonight is my lucky night. I make it home in record time, pulling into the grass next to the broken-down trailer I call home sweet home in all its rusted glory. Without paying any attention, I slide from the truck and head for the door, only to stop, when I notice a familiar BMW sitting next to Lachlan's sedan.

Ashley's fucking here, and for no good goddamn reason to my knowledge. Lachlan would have told me she was coming over, if this was planned. It has been a few weeks, since I'd last found her darkening the door of my home. I had hoped deep down that it would be the last I saw of her now that Lachlan was working for her daddy.

Deep breath, Dixie. She's his friend. Don't go getting yourself riled up, until you know what's going on.

I walk briskly to the door of the trailer. As my hand reaches for the latch, I pause, as their voices come through the paper-thin door.

"I wish you would've let me talk to her first, before we did this, Ash," Lachlan's low southern voice drawls.

"Lach, you didn't have a choice. We both knew this was going to happen eventually."

Wait. What? No. Please God, no.

"I know, but it still doesn't make telling her any easier. This isn't what I wanted for her."

Tell me what? That he fucked her? I'm going to be sick.

My stomach clenches at the thought, but before I can empty the meager contents from my lunch at the bar, her shrill voice rings out again.

"Sometimes, you don't always get what you want in life," Ashley coos sweetly, as her heeled shoes clack past the door that I stand on the other side of, listening to my life as I know it implode. "Lachlan, you had everything you could've ever wanted, until you married her. Now look at you, living in a rundown shack, barely rubbing two pennies together. What we did will change all that and give you back the life you deserve."

I'm going to tear every fucking artificial blonde hair out of her head. I'll give her what she deserves.

Without thinking about how I'm going to handle this, I throw open the door and charge in. Lachlan stands in our kitchen, a glass of water in hand. He stops dead in his tracks, and the glass falls from his hand, shattering against the floor. My eyes quickly divert to Ashley who stands in our little living room in a skin-tight dress and high heels that no doubt cost more than this trailer did. Her eyes go wide, when she catches sight of me.

"Oh shit," she squeaks.

"You *bitch*!" I scream. It takes three steps, before I cross the room and find myself nose to nose with her. She tries to backpedal away from me, but I get ahold of her wrist, cementing her in place. I won't let her run from this. "Did you fucking plan this?"

"I d–didn't plan anything, Dixie. It's not what you think," she stutters, as she trembles in front of me.

"Shut it! I know what I heard outside about how this was always going to happen!" I yell, motioning between her and my husband who stands silently behind us. "For years you wanted him. You pined over a man you couldn't have. So what did it take? Did you dangle the old money back in front of him again?" I look over at Lachlan. "Or is her pussy just that good?"

"Now hold the fuck on here, Rogue. That's not what this is," he interjects, stepping between us. "It's nothing like that at all."

"Don't you dare call me that right now," I sneer. "Not when you're destroying our relationship for this bitch."

"Just calm down. I can explain," he offers in a deliberately calm tone, like he's trying to talk a person down from the ledge. *Nice try.* Diffusing the situation has long since passed.

"Calm down? You've got a snowball's chance in hell of that happenin' right now."

"Dixie, please. Just let me talk."

His cool blue eyes soften the longer I look at him. The guilt he refuses to admit is clear as day on his face.

"Let Ash go, and we'll talk. All three of us."

I consider my options. I could let him speak, taking the chance of him breaking my heart in the process, or I could end this now, sparing my heart. Either way, I will be the one hurt in the end. This is how it was always going to end.

"You've got five minutes, before I haul her ass out of here by her hair and you behind her." I relent, letting go of Ashley and stepping away from the both of them. My arms cross against my chest, as I look at them.

"We—I mean, I have some news," he starts, carefully choosing his words. "I joined the Army this morning."

My jaw drops. "You what?"

"We can't keep living like this. We need money, insurance, and a real home. Not this dump."

"Dump?" I question. "Living here is only temporary. We've talked about this a million times. We had plans, Lachlan, and they didn't include you running off to join the Army."

Ashley nervously shifts next to him.

"Don't think I forgot about you, homewrecker. Where does she come into this?" I coarsely mention, making for damn sure she knows I see right through her feigned innocent act.

"She's going with me."

"You've gotta be fuckin' shitting me! She has all the money in the fucking world, and I thought that the one thing she couldn't buy was you. I guess I was wrong."

"You don't understand," Ashley interjects, but I place my hand on her face, shoving her away. "He's sav—," she starts, but I cut her off.

"No, you don't understand. Your time to talk to me was before you both made this decision."

Silence fills the room, as my body shakes. There's only one move to make, and it will be one that haunts me for the rest of my life.

"Get out of my house, and take your blue-blooded bitch with you," I order with a straight face, despite the hurricane of emotions swirling inside of me.

"You don't mean that!" Lachlan cries out in shock.

"You made the decision, when you chose her over me."

Lachlan stares at me in complete disbelief with Ashley at his side.

"I guess you win after all," I say flatly, as I stalk to the door, holding it open for them both. "Get out."

Lachlan looks to Ashley, and then to me before turning on his heels and stalking towards me and the door. Ashley rushes out, but he stops in front of me.

"I love you, Rogue. Just remember that. I'll give you tonight, but tomorrow, you and I are going to talk again, once you've cooled down. This isn't the end of us."

He walks out of the door, stopping on the step and peering up at me one last time.

"This ended the minute you made your decision," I retort, and then slam the door between us closed for the last time. I fall to a heap on the floor, as soon as I hear his footsteps crunch on the ground and his car start, as well as hers. The moment he pulls away, the dam holding back my tears cracks, and they stream down my face like raging rapids.

I cry for our relationship.

I cry for myself.

But mostly, I cry for my stupidity, and for thinking this would ever be a happily ever after, like in the story books Mama used to read to me as a kid.

Happily ever after's don't exist in real life, and it's high time I understand that.

The minutes tick by, until I have no more tears left to cry. The silence envelops the room, until the sound of the house phone rings on the wall in the kitchen. I force myself up from the ground, wiping away my tears, as I walk over to the phone.

"Hello?" I answer, my voice hoarse from crying.

"Dixie, baby. It's Magnus. You need to come to the bar. Somethin' has happened."

Three

Present Day

"It's been a few years, hasn't it?" I whisper to the silent gray stone in front of me, bearing the name of a man I miss every day of my life. A few sprigs of early spring flowers are poking through the dirt around the stone at my knees. I don't care that my jeans are getting dirty. Cleanliness isn't the reason I'm here—he is. Just like last six years, today is about him. His life, and his legacy.

"I brought you your favorite," I tell him, as I sit a bottle of Johnny Walker Black against his headstone. "Now, don't go drinkin' all of it in one night."

The sound of a car's tires crunching on the driveway near his final resting place pulls my attention away. The green sedan quickly ambles by, and I bring my attention back to him. The man who saved my life, when his ended.

"I gotta tell you, Uncle Max. I thought you were going to live forever. Guess the jokes on us, right? Tommy Jenkins is still missing.

Although, I think we both know where he ended up thanks to your brothers," I quietly admit.

I think back to the scene from the night he was murdered on the steps of his own bar. The lights and sirens of the police cars lit up the street like the 4th of July. His club brothers surrounded the front entrance, but I managed to push my way through them. Uncle Max's body lay still on the sidewalk, like he was asleep, but with the exception of the single gunshot wound centered in his chest, and the pool of blood underneath him. Tommy killed him that night because Uncle Max laid hands on him. A dozen or so witnesses saw him pull the trigger and snuff out an innocent man's life before running. The statewide manhunt came up empty, but I knew the truth. Magnus and the Descendants of Destruction MC took care of him. They never said a word, and they didn't have to. I just knew.

A beep from my phone snaps me back to reality. It's time to head back.

"I better get goin', Uncle Max. I suspect you'll be getting lots of visitors today. I love you, and tell everybody up there, wherever you are, that I miss them, too."

Without another word, I turn and walk away on another year that I didn't have Uncle Max in my life. Each time the calendar rolled around to this date, I felt the sense of dread because not only did I mourn his passing, but it was also the last time I saw Lachlan. His promises to talk the next day never came, and shortly after I put my uncle to rest, a solicitor showed up at my door with divorce papers. Though I'd given up first, I had hoped deep down that he would still try to fight for me. Call it little girl idealizations of romance, but I still hoped.

The gleam of my bike reflects into my sunglasses, as I stalk towards her. The sleek chrome and red of the gas tank on my Harley Softail Cross Bones, who I named Bad Bitch, glimmers under the late afternoon sun. She's a smooth ride of pure mechanical perfection thanks to my club's garage, and my VP, Stiletto's careful eye.

I slide over the smooth, black leather seat and flick on the ignition, letting Bad Bitch rumble between my thighs, as I toss on my helmet. With it fastened securely to my head, I pop the kickstand and head towards my uncle's old bar that is now mine. Grease Monkeys is my legacy and payment on his promise to always protect me. Even though I'd rather have him, than the deed to the bar.

The ride is a bit chilly, but my cut keeps me warm. In the wake of Uncle Max's death and the demise of my marriage, I needed stability back in my life, while I picked up the pieces. That solution came in the form of my sisters in the Dirty Bitches Motorcycle Club. We are a sisterhood of no bullshit, a love for bikes, and stirring shit up with the locals. My sisters gave me a piece of my life back that I greatly needed. *A support system.*

The bar comes into view a few minutes later, and the crowd is one for the record books tonight. Rebranded DB's Saloon, in honor of my sisters, the bar is my baby. I've spent thousands of dollars, over the course of the last few years, fixing up the place with a new security system, kitchen, and remodeling of the office upstairs to include an apartment. I've only just scratched the surface of what I have planned. While I don't use the apartment much with living full-time in Uncle Max's old house, it is nice to know that it is there, when I or any of the DBs need it.

As I pull into my spot around back, I notice the prospect I'm sponsoring, Shotz, helping one of the liquor distributors carry in the order I placed a few days ago, including the case of the special reserve moonshine I'd ordered from Gatlinburg. *Perfect timing.* I'll be cracking one of those jars open later tonight.

"Everything okay?" I inquire, once Shotz slides the case inside the back door.

"All booze ordered and accounted for, Prez. I'll take your order upstairs, after I get this last case of Bud in the cooler."

"Sounds good. The girls here?"

"Waiting on you in your office."

I thank her, sidestepping around the stack of beer cases in the doorway and head up the stairs to my sisters. A loud burst of laughter fills the room just as I hit the landing, and I find the three of them crouched around Titz, my road captain, and her phone.

"Y'all know if you keep watching that fetish porn shit that she likes, you'll go blind, right? "I joke, as I enter the room.

"You don't know what's good for you, Rogue. Try a little weird."

I plop down in my desk chair, kicking my riding boots up on the desk before responding.

"You have your kink, and I have...not that. I'm fine."

"You say that now, but there's a box with your name on it in the closet at the shop. Got it just for you. A little early birthday present," she says with a wag of her brows. "Something you're gonna love."

She flashes her phone to me with a photo of what I can only describe as the scariest vibrator on the planet plastered on the screen. It has more knobs and switches than most electronics in the bar. Stiletto peeks around and smiles wide, when she sees the screen.

"You didn't!" Stiletto chimes in. "The clit swizzler 1000? I thought you said those were on backorder. I told you I wanted one."

"I'm not hearing this right now," I groan, rubbing my brows with my fingers.

"It does this really special flick and swish shit that apparently feels amazing when you..." Links, our club enforcer, trails off before she notices the look on my face.

"You about done?"

"Not in the slightest," Titz gleams back. "I'll bring over your gift later."

"How about you say you did and don't. Give it to Stiletto. She seems to wanna take the clit...what the fuck ever 1000 for a ride."

"You bet your sweet ass I do," she interjects. "I'm claiming it. Dibs. Dibs. Dibs."

The three of them burst out into laughter again, but I can only shake my head at the shit I put up with. I hear a set of footsteps heading up the stairs, and Shotz appears in the doorway with my case of moonshine.

"Where do you want it, Prez?" She asks.

"In her ass," Titz cackles. The three of them burst out into laughter, while Shotz looks on in confusion.

"Over there." I nod at the closet in the corner. "I'll put it away later."

She does as I ask, before heading back down to the bar, reminding me that I should probably make an appearance tonight with it being the anniversary of Uncle Max's murder. His club, like every year since, will be here to honor his memory.

"Well, as much as I would like to play sex toy bingo with the three of you, I better get downstairs and check in. Y'all coming?"

"Not yet, but after a quick run over to the shop, we will be," Titz fires back.

"I fucking give up with the three of you tonight."

"Come on, Rogue. Don't you want a little buzz bliss tonight? It'll turn that frown on your face upside down," Stiletto adds. "Hell, it might even loosen those britches up a bit."

I throw up my hands, as I trot down the stairs with the three of them hot on my heels. We enter the busy bar area and disperse. I spy Stiletto bee-lining off towards our local sheriff, Pryor Jones. No doubt to goad the man not making her latest brush with the law easy, trying to reform her ways yet again. As many times as they've crossed paths, you'd think her photo would be up at the sheriff department's wall of infamy. Links and Titz sidle up next to one of the guys from our brother club, Southern Lords.

I notice Shotz out of the corner of my eye, getting overwhelmed by orders at the bar, so I decide to step in to help her. It doesn't take long to catch up the draft and mixed drink backlog to the point she'll be fine on her own. I start to head back to the main area from behind the bar, when Magnus, my uncle's old club president, corners me.

"You go out there today, Dixie?" He inquires.

"I did. Doesn't seem like it's been that long."

"Time creeps up on you the older you get. You need anything, you know who to call."

"I know, Mag. I appreciate it."

He slaps his hand to my shoulder, bringing me in for an awkwardly rough hug. Mag may have been my uncle's president, but we were never really close in my time with him. He steps aside, and I go about my business with checking in on the customers and the other clubs. The DoDs are huddled into their normal corner, while our brother club is in the other. The blood isn't bad between them, it's just best not to have two brooding groups full of alpha male biker testosterone mixing in one area. They're usually civil, and today especially.

"I'm heading upstairs to get a cash drop ready," I tell Links, as I pass by. "Be ready in fifteen to follow me down to the bank."

"Just grab me, when you're ready," she replies, before turning her attention back to the VP of Southern Lords.

Night's like this is where we made our bread and butter for the month. On a good night, DB's brings in a cool grand or more, but tonight will more than triple that, which only means that I will need to keep a closer eye on the cash on hand. I wave to Shotz from the crowd to signal her that I'm taking the drawer, and just as I get back to the bar, Richter, one of the DoD's, grabs me and pulls me onto his lap.

"You ready to marry me yet, Dixie?" He teases, as usual.

"The answer is always the same. Hell no, old man."

"Come on. Make an old man smile."

"Richter, I wouldn't marry you if you stood on your head naked and did the Macarena."

"I may be an old man," he laughs, "but don't tease me with a good time, doll."

I hear a thud below us, as he toes off one of his boots.

"Keep your clothes on, or Sheriff Jones will be haulin' your ass outta here for indecent exposure again," I caution.

Richter smiles and laughs, as I pull away. He's a harmless old man, but he's creative, I will give him that. Maybe one of these days, I'll accept his proposal just to see him squirm a little.

As I pass by the bar, Shotz meets me at the corner, sliding the drawer into my hand. She heads right back to work, and I go about my way, trudging upstairs to do the count in peace. It doesn't take long to neatly stack the bills in order and in the same direction. I tally up the total, and then slide the deposit slip into the bank bag with the nearly two thousand dollars in cash already. It's gonna be a good fucking night. My phone dings with a message from my enforcer. *Time to go.*

I grab my leather jacket from the back of my chair and stuff the bank bag inside, before zipping it up. While most people in the town know not to fuck with the bar or us, you can never be too cautious with this kind of cash out in the open. It's better off safe and secure at the bank in the DBMC account. I close my office door behind me, making my way back down the stairs, finding Links waiting. She follows me outside both of us heading to our bikes, but we don't get far, before Shotz comes yelling out the back door.

"Prez, we got trouble. You better get in here."

I look to my enforcer, and we both bolt for the door. She slides her hand down her back, pulling the handgun she tucks away on night's like tonight from its hiding spot, just as we get back into the main area of the bar. My gaze settles on several of the DoD's huddled together, while Magnus beats the shit out of a man who has his back towards me. Mag throws a left hook and connects with his jaw, sending the man stumbling back.

"What the fuck do y'all think you're doing in my bar?" I yell out. "Knock it off!"

Sheriff Jones is already in the middle of the fight, before I can shove my way through the crowd of men.

"I told you to stay away, boy," Mag yells, as Pryor drags him away from the fight. "She doesn't need you here."

Jones shoves Mag back towards the door and follows behind him. Let's hope he can sweet-talk his way out of this one, but I highly doubt it. He's been kicking up too much trouble lately with that mess with the zoning board about the new addition he wants to add to the DoD clubhouse. I would bet you anything that Pryor is going haul his ass in for a night in the gray bar hotel just for the ruckus they caused at the last town board meeting. It was front-page news, and an embarrassment for law enforcement around these parts.

"Last call!"

A collective groan flows through the crowd, but I can't keep serving, when shit goes sideways like this, especially with Pryor's ass here. I don't need the law breathing down my neck. The bar begins to clear out, leaving only myself, the DBs, and few drunken stragglers, waiting for their rides home. It's funny how fast this place can clear out, when the bar closes for the night, or the police show up.

While the sheriff deals with Mag, I turn my attention to the man on the other side of the fight. I shoot a glance back to Stiletto who's flanked by Links and Titz on either side, before walking up to the man who just had his ass handed to him.

"You alright, sugar?" I ask, reaching out to touch him on the shoulder. He spins on his heels and the breath gets sucked straight out of my lungs, when I see his face.

Lachlan fucking Lee is in my bar.

Four

Fuck! Shit! Fucking Shit!

Why is he here? Am I dreaming? Did I take a blow to the head in the fight, and this is some fucked-up version of my subconscious messing with me right now? This can't be real.

On the count of ten, you're gonna wake up, and he's not gonna be standing in your bar.

One. Two. Fucking ten.

I open my eyes, and there he is still looking at me, like a starving man finding out the mirage of McDonalds is actually real.

God-fucking-dammit. This really can't be happening on today of all days.

Oh, how he's changed, since the last time I saw him. His lean body is now large and muscular, like one of those men from the superhero movies that seem to play around the clock on cable. Two full sleeves of tattoos run up and down his arms, where his perfect tan skin used to lie naked. But it's his fucking beard that sets my dormant arousal on fire.

Goddammit, he knows what beards do to me.

Southern boys and beards. My two weaknesses currently wrapped up into a sexy as sin bundle that is my ex-husband who's standing in front of me, staring at me like I've gone off the deep end. Maybe I should call in a prayer request to Reverend Davis. This time I'm going to actually need it.

"Aren't you gonna say hello, Rogue?" He quips. "Or did you forget how to do that?"

Big girl panties, Dixie. Pull 'em up, before it's too late.

"Hello, Lachlan," I coolly respond.

Good job. Keep going.

"I see the welcome wagon around here's still friendly," he remarks.

"You're implying that you're welcome here, which you're not by the way," I inform him. "Exit is back the way you came."

He steps closer, as his large body dwarfs my petite frame a lot more than it used to. The Army clearly turned his lean body into a hard one made up of more muscles than I can count. He has always been bigger than me, but at five foot five, just about everyone is.

Stop looking at his beard. I'm talking to you, hormones. You're making this worse.

"You changed your hair," he drawls, stepping close and running a finger through a stray piece of the pixie cut purple and pink hair near my face. "Suits you more than that bottle blonde did back in high school."

His touch sends a shockwave to my core. Just like it used to, before he betrayed my trust and made decisions without me. Something I would do good to remember, despite the fact that my body keeps responding to his. *Fucking traitor.*

"I've changed a lot of things, since you've been gone."

"I can see that," he notes, as his eyes scan my body. "Like the tattoos."

The urge to cover my exposed skin hits hard, but I push it down. Playing it cool is the only line of defense I have against his presence, and he damn well knows it.

"Why are you here? I doubt you came here lookin' to walk down bad memory lane."

"I made a promise that I didn't get to keep, and I aim to pay up, even if I'm a little late."

"A little late? Try seven years late."

"I know, and I'm sorry."

"Apologize to someone who cares, Lachlan, because I sure as shit don't. You had your chance, and it left, when you did."

A murmur from the peanut gallery reminds me that we have an audience, watching this all unfold. *Just fucking great.* This isn't a conversation that I want to be having at all let alone in public. The last thing I need is for the old lady gossip mills to get started about Lachlan coming back.

"Is that?" I hear Titz whisper behind me.

"Oh, yeah. That's him all right," Stiletto responds.

"He's hot," Links adds.

"Not helping, ladies," I murmur over my shoulder.

"Right," Links declares. "We don't like him. But look at those arms."

Lachlan must take notice of our audience too, because he sidesteps past me with his hand extended out to greet my sisters.

"Care to introduce me to your friends?" He says over his shoulder.

"Why bother? You won't be around long enough to get to know them," I answer back.

I shift my stance, turning to face him and my sisters. Titz is looking him up and down, while Links eyes him like a predator sizing up her prey. I notice out of the corner of my eye that Shotz is standing directly behind where I keep the shotgun under the bar. I shoot her a look, and she moves away. As much as I would love to take a shot at Lachlan, jail and the bloodstains on my newly finished floors isn't worth it.

"This is better than Jerry Springer. There's no way in hell we're leaving yet. The fight bell might ring, and we'd miss it," Titz jokes.

"Y'all seriously need to get a hobby. Go home already."

"And miss the show? Not on your life. Shotz, get the popcorn," Stiletto orders. She starts to move, but I stop her, before she can even take a step.

"Don't you dare, prospect. You get them popcorn, and you'll be kissing your patch goodbye."

"Spoilsport," my VP argues. "Can we at least stay? We'll be quiet."

I face palm, before sliding my hand off in an exaggerated manner. This is getting out of control fast.

"This isn't daytime television. All of you out, now!"

Shotz walks away from the bar and flips the sign on the door to read closed. She sashays over to my sisters and falls in line with them.

"Y'all can go on now. I have this handled."

"You sure?" Stiletto asks. "We can stick around if you need us, and without popcorn if you'd prefer."

"He won't be staying. Go on. You too, Shotz. I'll close up tonight, and I'll see you all at church in the morning."

Links keeps her eyes glued to Lachlan, as they start for the back door. He doesn't say another word, until he hears the back door click, leaving us alone for the first time, since that night exactly seven years ago today.

"Dixie, I…" He starts, but I cut him off.

"I meant what I said, Lachlan. You're too late. Nothing you can say to me would change a damn thing. You made your decision, and now you have to live with it."

He moves closer to me, but I back up, keeping the distance between us. He lets out an exasperated sigh, clearly frustrated that I didn't just fall back into his arms, like a wilting little debutante on the eve of her ball, and the first male suitor asks for her hand. I wasn't the young and stupid girl I was, when we got married. I'd seen the world for what it is. A dark place in a pit of despair ready to suck down anyone who gets too close for comfort.

"I admit that I should've done things differently, but I would've still went into the Army. It was the only option I had."

"You had more options than that, and you damn well know it. You could've talked to me, and let me in. You had a job and a wife, but it wasn't enough for you, and that blue blood of yours."

He growls at the mention of his past, and the word that I angrily threw at him that last night. A word that describes him and his family to near perfection. He was the golden boy, and I was white trash. It was like trying to force oil and water to mix.

"That's where you're wrong, and why I came back. I walked out of our house seven years ago, thinking you needed time to cool down and to see why I did what I did, but you just walked out of my life and never gave me that chance to explain," he snaps with the first hint of rage flicking across his face.

"And you didn't think when you enlisted. As your wife, I should've been the first person you talked to. Not that fucking bitch."

"Leave Ashley out of this."

"Why? She stuck her nose in it, and now she's a part of it. Surprised she's not here, since she got everything she wanted, when she got you. Bet you put a ring on her finger, before the ink was even dry on our divorce papers."

"Fuck no, I didn't marry her. I married you and only you. Stop trying to deflect it onto her."

"Even now, you're still to blind to realize what she did. She wanted what I had, and she took it the only way she knew how."

"She didn't get me, Dixie. She never has and never will. Ashley didn't want me. She wanted the lifestyle my family's name could give her because hers was flat broke."

"Bullshit. The Buchanans are loaded, and they are almost as rich as your family."

Lachlan sighs heavily and drags me by the hand over to the bar top, plopping me down on a stool, before he speaks again. I can't help but notice the way his shirt ripples against the movements he makes.

Stop it, brain. He looks good. We get it. Not the fucking time.

"They were deep in debt. Her daddy sunk everything he had into that construction company, after their wells dried up. It went belly up the minute the state pulled their contract for the highway because of budget cuts."

"Why are you lying to me? Everyone in this town knows that The Buchanans moved down to Texas to be closer to their oil rigs."

Does he think I'm stupid? If The Buchanans lost their asses, then the entire town would've been talking about it. Secrets that big are cannon fodder around here. The widow's trade secrets like kids trade Pokémon cards.

"They didn't move, Dixie. The bank was about to take their house. They live with one of her aunts in the guesthouse, and are as poor as church mice, living on their hospitality."

I eye him, watching for his tell where his nose twitches, when he lies. Either he's practiced to hide it in the years he's been gone, or he was telling me the actual truth.

"That's why I joined the Army, Dixie. Same for Ashley. We were trying to protect ourselves from the fallout, and I was trying to protect you."

"Where is she?" I ask, before I can stop myself. Please don't say she's here. I really don't want to have to face her and apologize for what I said before, if the tale of their fall from grace is true.

"Last I knew, she was in Germany with her husband and three kids."

What in the ass did he just say? Married with kids?

I've never felt smaller than I do right now. I sit in silence, not really knowing what to say. I want to believe him, but he had so many chances to tell me this long before tonight. The swirling conflict inside of me is on the brink of implosion, if I don't get away from him, and think this out on my own.

"I know that look, Rogue. I can see the wheels turning in your head, and I know what that means. I think I'll head home. We can talk more tomorrow."

"Who says there'll be a tomorrow?"

"I think once you really think about this, you'll understand more than you think you will."

He starts to walk away, before he quickly turns back and reaches into his jacket, pulling out a stack of papers bound together with a thin piece of twine.

"I almost forgot." He says, placing the thick stack into my hand. "Read these, and when you're ready, call me. I'm staying over at my parents' house."

He doesn't say another word, as he walks out the front door and down the sidewalk, leaving me sitting at that bar frozen in place with the papers still in my hand. I peer down at them and realize they're letters. My fingers trace the edges, counting them. There are nearly three-dozen of them stacked neatly in the bound bundle. The one on top has my name listed in Lachlan's thick handwriting.

"Fuck. I can't do this right now," I exclaim, throwing the letters to the bar top and walking away. I try distracting myself by cleaning up around the bar. I put the chairs on top of the tables, sweep and mop the floors, and wipe down all the table surfaces, but all I can think about are those damn letters.

Not today, Satan. Not today.

I stalk over to the light panel, flicking off all the main bar lights, but leave the few security lights on. Remembering the deposit still nestled inside the pocket of my jacket, I head for the door, firing off a quick text to the DBs group chat, letting them know I'm heading to the bank in case the money or myself goes missing.

Titz: Did you fuck him?

Stiletto: Ditto that question. Deets please.

Links: Do I need to hide his body?

I fire back a quick response, letting them know that no, I didn't fuck him and didn't plan to, and that there was no body to hide yet, leaving all three of them greatly disappointed. I nearly make it out the door, before I stop, realizing the letters are still there on the bar.

"Goddammit," I exclaim into the silence. Turning back for them, I tuck them into my jacket pocket opposite of the nightly deposit. I may be taking them with me, but it sure as fuck didn't mean I was going to read them. At least, that's what I'm telling myself for the time being.

I stared at those letters the entire night and didn't get a lick of sleep. Am I curious about what the contents hold? You're damn right I am, but I'm still not sure if I'm ready to open that can of worms just yet. I'd spent years closing off my heart to him. A long seven fucking years, and one brief moment with him, has me ready to jump back into his arms without a second thought.

"Get it together, Dixie," I berate myself, staring at the letters again. "He's just blowing smoke up your ass to get back into your pants."

But was he really?

The Lachlan Lee that I knew as a child was about as blunt as a person could get. His mouth didn't come equipped with a bullshit spewer, unlike the rest of his family. He wasn't the snake in the grass that everyone thought he was with the Lee name. His daddy was known for his ability to sweet talk the devil himself into giving him a dollar. My Uncle Max used to tell me all the time that if a Lee's lips were moving, then they were lying. He hit the nail on the head, when it came to the rest of Lachlan's family, but I never believed it about him. Well, not until the night he destroyed our family that is. I guess even the blind can see through the bullshit, if they try really hard.

Maybe God didn't give me the sense that he gave a goose, but a part of me still wanted to know if Lachlan really was telling the truth. Hour after hour, I've debated on reading them, and when I finally work up the gumption to do so, the alarm on my phone begins to ring. It's almost time for daily church at the clubhouse with the DBs. The letters will have to wait just a bit longer.

I leave them lying on the edge of my nightstand, before I head into the shower. The hot spray drives the tension out of my shoulders and neck, but not completely. There is only so much a shower can fix. The mess I'm currently in is more of a quart of moonshine level problem. A night of no sleep isn't going to make the day ahead of me any easier either.

Quickly dressing in my normal cut-off shorts, old concert T-shirt, and my riding boots, I grab my cut and keys, as I pass the kitchen island, heading out the door. I pause before stalking back in after those letters. I'm not willing to take a chance on the house burning down and taking them with it, before I have a chance to read them. Not that I expect the house to burn down, but luck isn't exactly something I have a large amount of.

Bad Bitch sits idle in the garage next to my old pickup truck, which is in dire need of a wash. I make a note to do just that later, as I slide onto BB and pop open the garage before leaving for the clubhouse. The spring air is chilly against my skin on the ride, but the scenery is beautiful. The grass is just beginning to turn green again, and the magnolia trees, that made Magnolia Springs semi-famous in our little piece of small-town Alabama, are beginning to bud. In just a few short weeks, the bloomers, as we like to call them, will flock into town to see the rows and rows of blooming magnolia trees in all their splendor, filling the air with their sweet fragrant blooms. It's the time of year that's great for all aspects of our club's businesses because of the increased tourism money lining our pockets. Regulars of Titz's tattoo shop have booked months in advance for a few hours of her time while here. Soon she will be slinging ink long into the night for those seeking to take a permanent piece of the south home with them, but at a higher than normal cost of course.

Just as I pass the small local church on the corner of Main Street, the clubhouse comes into view. The dark paint on the exterior of the clubhouse, my bar, and Titz's tattoo shop stick out like sore thumbs against the old-school brick façade of the other local businesses nearby. The location of our clubhouse and businesses are a thorn in the ass of many because of the old church biddies who often take to complaining to Mayor Myers about getting us out of their prim and proper little town. Their complaints always fall on deaf ears thanks to the favor we did for the mayor, regarding his daughter's little piss-ant boyfriend who thought it was funny to call her a slut. Little fucker shit his pants, when we rolled up to his house for a little chat about how to treat ladies.

I swing out, before walking my bike back into her spot in front of the clubhouse. Two more bikes sit neatly in a row outside already. Swinging my leg over, I unfasten my helmet, slinging it on the handlebars, before stepping onto the sidewalk, directly in front of Mrs. Montgomery, one of the church ladies that may just despise us the most. She walks past me with her purse clutched tightly to her chest, scowling at me.

"Bless your heart!" I yell to her, as she disappears out of sight, likely on her way to the local café to meet the other blue hairs for breakfast. I laugh, as I walk inside and find Titz and Stiletto already sitting in our meeting room, engaged in a deep conversation. Links is nowhere to be seen as usual.

"Morning, Prez," Titz gleefully greets. "Torturing that Montgomery woman again I see."

"Meh. Just givin' them biddies another thing to wag their tongues about at breakfast. It wouldn't be a good week, if they weren't all praying for us at the weekly church prayer circle."

"Ain't that the truth," Stiletto laughs. "Rough night?"

"You could say that," I offer up, as I plop down in my seat at the head of the table.

"How was he?" Titz inquires with a look of pure, deviant pleasure. "Was it a good fuck down memory lane?"

Stiletto instantly looks up, as Titz's wild imagination runs amuck over me being alone with him. Though I hadn't fully regaled them with all the stories of mine and Lachlan's life before the divorce, they knew enough to understand that him being here wasn't good for me, or for the dam I've built to keep him out, if he ever did show back up again.

"Didn't happen. I kicked him out, after y'all left and went home."

"Alone?" Stiletto asks with a wag of her eyebrows.

"Yes. Alone."

Titz grumbles in dissatisfaction. I don't know what she dreamed up, but apparently, the lack of any kind of physical contact between Lachlan and I was ruining her day. Too bad for her, I was going to keep on ruining it.

"Seriously?" She sighs. "First, you don't want my gift. Now, you won't hop on his dick for me. Some friend you are."

"Jesus, Titz. When and where I use my pussy is my own decision. It's not up for a club vote."

Her eyes grow wide, and I instantly regret what I just said, but before she can reply, Links comes flying into the door, like the devil's chasing after her soul.

"Glad you can join us," I tease, as she takes her seat. Her chest heaves up and down, as she tries to catch her breath.

"Sorry," she mutters under her breath. "Pryor pulled me over on the way here, and he wasn't taking the 'Dixie doesn't like tardiness' excuse. He said hi by the way."

"I see. Maybe I should start tellin' you an earlier time just to make sure your ass gets in its seat on time."

"Ha ha. Funny. What did I miss?" She asks, looking to the other women sitting around the table.

"Someone's salty that Dixie didn't get laid last night, and we were about to put it to a vote of who gets to control her pussy, I believe."

"The hell we are," I fire back. "Like I would let the three of you have control of that. I'd be the damn town bicycle, if Titz had her way."

"Damn straight."

We all bust out laughing, and it takes several minutes, before we finally settle down. Our meeting is a quick one because we don't have much to discuss. Titz tries to interject Lachlan back into the conversation, but I shut it down quickly. There's no need to talk about him, until I'm ready to decide what, if any, role he's going to have in my life in the future. We quickly adjourn, scattering into our respective roles for the day and leaving me with one last duty, before the letters hit the top of my to-do list.

I make a quick stop by the bar, checking in on Shotz, before mounting my bike again and heading off to the one place where I can read the letters in peace. *Links' garden.* A place of solitude that is both beautiful and peaceful. Some people just don't understand how awesome a garden can be, when you need to think.

After a few quick turns, I pull into the driveway outside of Links' modest house. The smell of her garden wafts around me, as I slide from my bike and head towards the back gate. Grimm, her Great Dane, barrels into me with his favorite stuffed chicken that has one eye flopping around in his mouth completely covered in sloppy drool.

"Hey, buddy," I say, rubbing the top of his head that comes just above my waist. He lets out a happy moan, before following along behind me with the chicken still in tow. The beautiful colors of her garden are nearly to peak bloom, as I settle down into the small bench she has cornered away by the clematis vines. I pull the letters from my inner pocket and gently place them on my lap. Grimm looks down at them, giving my hand a lick, before plopping down hard on top of my feet, pinning me in place.

"Titz has got to stop feeding you those treats. You're crushing my feet," I mutter, as his weight settles on top of me. He looks up with a puzzling glare, before settling back down again, leaving me alone with the decision of whether or not I'm really going to read these damn letters. On one hand, it could bring us back together again. The other is far more sinister and heartbreaking. The cool summer breeze whips through the garden, while I think. Finally, I come to a decision.

I need to read them. My fingers slightly tremble, as I pull the first loop of the twine binding them, and then the other. The bundle shifts and slides into a pile on my lap. I pick up the first one, gently thumbing the lip of it open, and pull out the first letter. The paper is thin, and the ink has bled through to the backside, and I sigh, as I unfold it.

Dear Rogue,

I don't know how to start this letter. Words have never seemed to fail me, until I think about our last night together. It's something that I do often out here in the desert, when my shift ends. It's a lot like Alabama with sand and scorpions, instead of crunchy grass and mosquitoes. Actually, it's worse than home because you're not here with me. I hate what I did to us. It's something that I will regret every day of my life. You didn't deserve it, and I hope that one day you'll let me make it right. Only seven more months, before my tour ends, and I might get to see you again. If something happens to me before that, I just want you to know how much I still love you. I never stopped and never will.

Love,

Lachlan

A few tears begin to dot the page, as they fall from my face and onto the letter in my hands. I open the next, and within a few hours, I've read them all. Each one making me cry even more. His sadness lingered on every word written in his heavy script, during his time in the desert. He

49

wrote about his regrets, his decisions, and the future he didn't think he wanted to live in without me. I sit quietly, before I notice a rustling noise coming from the front gate of the garden. Grimm bolts from my feet and greets his owner, who notices me sitting in her sanctuary.

She continues down the steps, before settling in next to me. Without a word between us, I hand her the stack of letters. She reads a few of them, before setting them back down on my lap, as I stare off into space.

"You know what this means, don't you, Dixie?"

"I do."

"When a man loves his woman with this much passion, despite the distance, you can't take that for granted. I think you need to talk to him. And by talking, I mean fuck him first, and then talk to him after."

I shake my head, as I laugh. Her priorities are a little more backwards than mine, but she's right. Lachlan and I do need to talk. I'll worry about the other part, after I hear him out. I shove off the bench, gathering my letters and retying them back together.

"You going?" She asks.

"Better now while I still have the nerve."

Links nods her head, before I walk away back towards where I came in, and where my bike still sits.

"Do you need a condom?" She yells out from her perch in the garden. "Got some new ones from Titz that make you tingle."

"You need Jesus," I fire back.

"And you need to get laid."

Lord have mercy. Her neighbors are probably adding us to their prayer lists as we speak. I love my sisters with all of my heart, but the mouths on them would make Reverend Davis cuss up a storm.

I mount my bike and take off towards the one place I never thought I would cross the threshold of ever again.

My luck failed me again, as soon as I hit the red dirt road of the Lee's home. I should have known better than to expect anything less than this from his mother. Welcome wagons to people like me weren't covered in debutante school apparently, as I stand before her with my hands in the air in a white flagless sign of surrender at the sound of a shell being racked into the chamber of a pump-action shotgun. She must have missed that particular lesson.

"Hi, M–Mrs. Lee," I stutter out.

I'm going to get my ass Swiss cheesed for just trying to apologize to her son. Lachlan Lee, you better be worth all this trouble.

"Get your pink-haired, Ryder white trash ass off my porch," Lachlan's mother, Meredith, screams at me with the shotgun aimed straight at my head. It was as if she knew I'd be coming, and she had been keeping watch for my bike or truck coming down the long winding lane to the front porch of their expansive home, nestled in the heart of the biggest sugarcane farm on this side of the Mississippi. On second thought, she's probably been waiting out here because of the rumor mill spinning about our little rendezvous at the bar earlier in the week. I probably should have called first.

"Mrs. Lee, could you put down the shotgun, please?" I ask, laying on the thickest layer of sweetness I can muster, when it comes to her. I'd be lying if I said my relationship with my ex-mother-in-law had ever been cordial. "I just need to talk to Lachlan for a hot second. I'm not here to start any trouble."

"Trouble follows you Ryders wherever you go," she hisses. "The only way this gun is lowering to the ground is when your ass leaves my property. I'm going to give you to the count of ten, before I pepper your hide."

"Lachlan, I swear to God your ass better be down here, before your mother shoots a hole clean through me!" I scream up to the second floor, hoping that he's actually home right now.

"Don't you go talking to my boy, trash. He's none of your concern anymore. Thank the good Lord for that."

Mrs. Lee nods her head in satisfaction at her declaration, and then butts the gun farther into the crook of her shoulder. I watch, as her finger inches closer to the trigger, just as the heavy front porch door swings wide open with Lachlan bursting through it in a pair of jeans and nothing else. His eyes go wide, when he assesses the situation. His mother and his ex-wife are in a Mexican standoff with me at a great disadvantage, being the unarmed party.

"Mama, what the fuck are you doing? Put that damn gun down," he orders, as he stalks closer to her, but her eyes stay locked on me.

"She's trouble, Lachy. I don't want her here."

High time she finally came out and said what she really thinks of me, but the timing is shitty at best. I'd much rather have this lively discussion without the threat of death.

"Mama, I'm not gonna tell you again. Put down the damn gun. You don't want to do this."

She scoffs, and then briefly looks over at him, before taking a step closer to the edge of the porch and me.

"I've been dreaming of doing this, since the day you brought her into this house and gave her our last name."

"Mama, please," he tries again, reaching out his hand towards the gun. He pads closer to her, snatching the gun away in one swift movement. I never thought I would ever say this, but thank you Jesus for him going into the Army. I may not have survived this, if he'd gone to cooking school.

"Go inside now, Mama. It's time for your medicine," he orders. She looks up at him with tears streaming down her cheeks. "Come on, now. I'll go in with you and get you settled down."

Reluctantly she relents, and shuffles back towards the door with him at her arm. He helps her inside, but quickly looks back at me.

"Don't move. I'll be right back."

Lachlan disappears back inside the house for several minutes, before returning to find me sitting on the edge of the porch, trying to settle my nerves. He grips a T-shirt in his hand, as he settles in next to me. His muscles are on full display, and I fight to keep myself from reaching over and tracing them with my finger. *My how the years have changed us both.* The boy who left me was as skinny as a rail, but this man is now nothing like the boy I married. Where Lachlan had been soft, now he was hard.

"You forget how to put on a shirt, Lachlan?" I tease in a feeble attempt to cut the tension. He smiles back at me, before slipping it over his head and broad shoulders.

"Better?"

I nod a quick yes, resuming our awkward silence.

Think of something quick, before this gets any weirder.

"Any more of your family members gonna come out after me with a shotgun?"

He grimaces at my ill-timed joke, and his gaze falls to the ground between his feet.

"I'm sorry about Mama. She should've been napping. She didn't mean what she said."

"I've always known how she, and well, everyone else in your family feels about me. Only you seemed to be oblivious to it."

He sighs and shuffles closer to me. The earthy scent of his cologne wafts over the closer he gets. The hints of sandalwood lure me in, daring me to snuggle in close to him.

Why does he have to smell so damn good? Heaven help me, he's distracting.

I should be mad as a hen, but the closer he gets to me, the more my mind goes into the gutter at what we could be doing, instead of having this talk. How his hard body would feel against mine, as he threw me over his shoulder and carried me inside, squealing all the way to the bedroom.

Stop it. Focus, Dixie. Priorities.

"I always knew, but I didn't care," he starts. "It's just worse now with the Alzheimer's taking her mind. It's bringing out the meanness in her. She threw the urn full of my grandfather's ashes at my dad last night."

My stomach drops at his revelation. Alzheimer's is a horrible disease that takes loved ones away twice from their families. Once when their minds go, and then when their bodies do. It's terrible, and despite my past feelings about his mother, my heart goes out to them.

"It's not a consolation for what she just tried to pull, but I wanted to you know that she's not in her right mind."

I peer over my shoulder back towards the house, thinking about what they must be going through with her right now. Maybe this isn't the right time to be talking to him after all. He's got enough on his plate as it is. I shove off the porch and start walking towards my bike, when his hand grabs my wrist, spinning and pulling me flush against him.

"Let me go, Lachlan. I shouldn't have come."

I try to pull away again, but his grip only tightens more around me. I peer up at his blue eyes, as he smiles down at me, and the coarse hairs of his beard brush against my forehead.

That fucking beard. Kill me now.

"If I'd known all it was gonna take to get you back into my arms was my mama holding a shotgun, I would've invited you over sooner," he jokes.

I punch him lightly in his chest, breaking free from his grasp.

"That's not funny."

"Too soon?"

I glare at him. My hands fall to my hips, as he takes a step closer to me.

"Sorry. You're right," he admits. "Will you still be my friend?"

I shake my head, quietly laughing at his stupid joke. How I fell in love with this man all those years ago was lost on me, but dammit, if those feelings weren't still there, when the real him shined through the cracks of his Lee exterior. Lachlan takes one more step closer, gently wraps his hand around mine, and drags me back to the porch, motioning for me to sit down.

"This is a bad idea," I warn him.

"Just sit your boney ass down on this porch, and then you can decide whether or not this is a bad idea."

"It's my funeral. Literally," I sigh, while sitting down next to him. We sit in silence for few minutes, before his voice rings out again.

"Do you remember when we were in high school, and we tried to climb that tree over there?" He asks, motioning to the old oak tree near the edge of the driveway to the left of us.

"I remember you falling out and breaking your hand," I recall.

"That would be the part you remember."

"Some things stick more than others. What can I say?" I shrug and smile.

"Broken bones aside, that was the exact moment that I realized how much I loved you."

My heart stops dead in my chest. I wasn't as prepared for this, as I thought I was.

"We spent that entire summer, chasing after each over all over God's green acre, but when I saw you climbing down after me when I fell, I knew. You were my girl, and I was never going to give you up."

What do I even begin to say to that? My mouth is failing me, while he's here pouring out his heart to me. *Think of something, stupid.*

"I read the letters," I interject, stopping his trip down memory lane.

"You were never one for letting me finish things, Rogue." He smiles over at me and wraps his arm around my shoulders, bringing my head to rest on his. "I know you did, or you wouldn't have come here. I meant what I said in them. Every single word. I was a fool for not coming after you sooner, but the Army kept me away."

His touch is so soothing against my coiled nerves. If you'd asked me a few days ago where I saw myself today, I would have never guessed sitting on this porch with him. Life has a funny way of directing you exactly where you're meant to be at just the right time. And that time is right here with him, healing old wounds.

"Why didn't you send them to me?"

"I did. I sent them, but every single one of them were returned."

Confusion floods my mind. *Returned? Did he have the wrong address?* To be honest, I didn't even look that closely at them to check. That's when it hits me. It wasn't a bad address. It was a group of meddling old men who thought they were protecting me.

"The Descendants," I offer. "They returned the letters."

Lachlan pulls me closer to him, kissing the top of my head.

"That was my guess, too. I don't blame them, Dixie. You'd just lost your uncle, and I'd taken off. They were just protecting you."

Something he says spurs a question that has long been unanswered.

"Why didn't you come to the funeral?"

"Same answer as the first. Magnus made it clear that I wasn't welcome around you anymore. I tried to get in there, but much like last night, he was in the way. I just learned how to get around him and fight back, since the last time I tried."

I curse under my breath. Magnus and I are going to have a talk about where and when he gets to have a say in my personal affairs. Protecting me was one thing, but this? It was overkill.

"I can see those wheels of yours turning again," he murmurs against the top of my head. "Don't blame them. Magnus was doing what he thought was right. I'd have done the same thing in his place."

I shift my head from his shoulder, peering up at him. The magnetic pull of our closeness brings his lips within inches of mine. The tingling sensation of his warm breath tickles my nose, but a loud crash from inside the house snaps us apart. He releases me, jumping up from the porch and looking through the door. The moment between us is over, before it ever started.

"It's my mom. I should probably go."

I pick myself and my broken pride up off the porch, stalking to my bike once more. The light footfalls from his steps behind me makes me stop and turn to face him again.

"You and me. Dinner tomorrow night," he orders.

"I can't. I have to work at the bar."

"Give me a night then. This isn't over between us, Rogue. Not even a little bit. I'm not going to lose you again. Promise me dinner."

"Fine." I smile. "How about Wednesday night? I can get someone to cover my shift."

"Wednesday at seven o'clock. I'll pick you up," he calls out, as he turns to run back to the house, after another crash reverberates from inside. I can't help but smile at the thought of seeing him again. It's a smile that doesn't leave my face for a second the entire ride home.

Livin' on a Prayer

Seven

The days fly by in an instant, until the day of our date finally arrives. After working the early afternoon shift at the bar, I quickly run back home to shower. What I didn't expect was to find all three of my sisters sitting on my bed, waiting for me, when I exit with a towel wrapped around me, barely covering my lower bits.

"Don't y'all knock? You damn near gave me a heart attack," I cry out, desperately trying to get my towel wrapped tighter around my body. I'm not shy by any means around these women, but I do have to draw the line somewhere. Nudity being the number one item on the lines we do not cross list. The second item being not to open that sex toy closet at Titz's shop. The things you find in there will scar you for life. Like the too-close-for-comfort-looking rubber sex doll someone had ordered from her. Creepy as fuck, let me tell you.

Titz eyes me, and nods her approval. "Good idea shaving your wookie bush. You don't want Lachlan to have to break out the hedge trimmers, before he goes down on you later."

"I'm keeping that one for later," Links remarks. "Pretty sure I might be able to use that one again."

"You're all nuts," I declare, as I try to step away from them, grabbing a bra and pair of panties from the top drawer of my dresser, before darting into my closet to dress in peace.

"Need some help?" Stiletto calls out from my bedroom. "I may just have a pair of heels that could take that ass and make it clap."

I take a deep breath before answering.

"Thanks for the offer, but I think I'm going to pass. I'm not a heels kinda girl like you. I prefer my feet firmly planted on the ground."

I search through my closet, looking for something comfortable, and find an old black shirt I haven't worn in years. The thin lace that dots the arms, as well as the necklace, looks fancy enough to pass, if Lachlan takes me out somewhere a little more upscale. Pairing it with a pair of dark skinny jeans, I slip them over my thin hips, buttoning them quickly, before pulling the shirt over my head. The full-length mirror to my left taunts me, causing me to second-guess my decision.

"You coming out? I wanna see a fashion show," I hear Titz's voice call out. "Better be sexy, or I get to pick what you're wearing tonight."

"Naked is not an option," I holler back.

"The hell it isn't," she snaps.

I take one last look in the mirror, before I step out to catcalls from the DB peanut gallery.

"I like it. Shows just enough skin, but doesn't scream 'I'll drop my panties for you without any work,'" Stiletto remarks.

"Ha! Not enough skin if you ask me. She needs to get laid. Not try and play hard to get," Titz retorts.

Links remains quiet, as she analyzes my outfit, motioning with her finger for me to spin in a circle. I flip her off, before I do, and she nods her head in satisfaction. I complete my outfit by slipping a pair of black sandals on my feet.

"That'll do, Prez. That'll do," she remarks with a knowing smile.

"Do you think he'll write you another sappy letter, after you fuck tonight? An ode to your pussy, maybe?"

I turn to Links, giving her a sharp look. *She blabbed.* Dammit all to hell. I'll never hear the end of this now, and neither will Lachlan, if this works out.

"Sorry." She shrugs. "They were going to find out one way or another."

She's right. I would have told them about the letters eventually, but much, much later, after things settled down, between Lachlan and I. Despite our history, what was about to happen is so new that I don't want to risk scaring him off.

"Just don't mention them to him, if he's around, please."

Titz jumps from the bed and pulls me into a tight hug.

"Don't worry, Prez. I won't say a word, until he pops that pussy again. After that, it's game on."

I hug her back, as we both laugh.

"I wasn't kidding when I said that y'all need hobbies other than playing paparazzi to my love life."

"Oh, paparazzi. Can I watch then? I'm great with pointers."

"No!" The rest of us answer in a collective response.

"No fun," Titz whines. The arrival of a vehicle pulling in the drive sets off the motion sensor that Links installed for me a few years back, when I moved into Uncle Max's house full-time. Life on my own wasn't easy at first, but the security system helped.

All three of them rush past me to peer out the window, after we all hear the sound of a car door shutting.

"Say, Dixie," Titz starts, "if you don't want him, can I play with him for a bit?"

I shoot her a glare.

"Just kidding." She smiles. "Too clean-cut for my tastes."

His heavy footsteps echo off the newly cemented sidewalk, stopping just short of the front door. The four of us leave my room to meet him all while they whisper out orders to me on what to do on the date.

"Push your tits up higher."

"Rub one out for him under the table. They like that."

"Call me if you need to hide the body later."

"Shh," I plead. "I think I can handle one date. Now scoot, before he sees you."

The three of them dash back to my room, no doubt with their faces smashed against the window, craning for a good look. The doorbell rings, and I wait a few seconds, before opening it.

This is it. My chance to find out where this will go. Don't fuck it up.

I open the door to find Lachlan dressed in jeans and a button-down flannel shirt.

Shit. Did I overthink this? I feel so overdressed.

He leans forward with a smile and kisses me on the cheek.

"You look fine, Dixie. Perfect in fact. So, stop overthinking this."

"How did you…"

"Wheels in your head," he replies, reaching down and taking my hand in his. I quickly turn to close the door behind me, noticing the three faces of my sisters watching from my bedroom window. Titz gestures with her hands about how she expects this night to end. Unfortunately, Lachlan catches her mid-finger thrust.

I use my free hand to cover the blush on my face, but Lachlan pulls it away and pulls me behind him, making sure to shoot Titz thumbs up, as we pass.

"Stop encouraging them."

"It's nice to see you squirm."

"Ass."

They scramble away from the window, like they were never there, and reappear at the corner of the house, as Lachlan opens the door of his truck for me.

"She's in good hands, ladies. No need for a bunch of chaperones. I'll bring her back in one piece," he tells them, as he secures me inside.

"Try not to bring her back at all, lover boy!" One of them calls back.

He opens the door and slides inside, smiling at them.

"Some friends you got there. I'd like to hear about how you met them on the way to dinner."

He starts up the truck, pulling away from my house. Making a quick turn north, Lachlan drives as I tell him about how the Dirty Bitches MC came to be. He laughs at the story, only making a few comments here and there.

"I'm glad you have them in your life. It's good to see how happy having a club of your own makes you. It makes me even happier you took my nickname and used it with them. It suits you."

Shit, he noticed. Come on, brain. Give him an excuse that makes sense.

"I couldn't think of anything else."

Smooth. Real fucking smooth.

He just laughs, knowing damn well that I'm lying through my teeth. Damn him, and his mind reading skills. You'd think after so many years, he wouldn't be able to do it, but damn it all to hell, that skill of his seems better than ever.

Before too long, he pulls into a familiar spot, and it's a spot that we used to frequent in our early teenage years. *The Slop Bucket.* It has to be the worst name for a restaurant in the history of restaurants, but they serve the best chili dogs in the state of Alabama. Lachlan quickly parks under the awning, and a waitress skates over to us, just as he gets the window down.

"What can I get you, sugar?" She drawls, while pulling out the pencil tucked behind her ear.

"We'll take two slop specials, a root beer, a coke, and an order of fried mushrooms," he rattles off. "To go."

The waitress skates away, and I stare at him in shock.

To go? Lord, where else is he taking me?

"You're gonna catch flies in there, if you leave that mouth of yours open too long," he teases. "Flies or not, I'll be putting it to use later."

My jaw snaps shut at his frankness, and I stow away the urge to text Titz.

She'd be proud.

A few older men stop by the truck, thanking Lachlan for his service and asking about his time overseas. He obliges them for a few minutes, happily talking about his tour of duty that I was more than familiar with now because of his letters. Just as the food arrives, the men disperse, leaving us alone with a bag of food between us. He backs out of the parking space without another word, heading out onto the road.

As confused as I was at first, I knew in an instant where he was taking me. *Catcher's Creek.* Our old make-out spot, during high school.

A few minutes later, I realize just how right I was, but the creek doesn't look anything like I remember it. Instead of the tall grass field edging it, there's a trail mowed down, leading back to our spot. *No doubt a part of his plan.* Lachlan hops out of the truck, food and drinks in tow, and opens up the door for me.

"Come on," he urges, before taking off down the lane. The freshly cut grass tickles my ankles, as we pass through it.

He pauses just before stepping off the path.

"My favorite childhood memories are being here with you, so it's only fitting that we start making our new ones here as well."

We settle down on a soft patch of grass next to the creek, and Lachlan divvies up the food between us.

I take a few bites, but the silence is deafening between us. Since the moment I read his letters, realizing just how much he still loved me, a question has been lingering in the back of my mind. One that never truly made sense in light of everything he had revealed on paper and in our talks.

"Why did you divorce me?" I blurt out.

Lachlan chokes on the bite of food in his mouth.

"Shit, I'm sorry." I apologize. "Maybe I should've led with something else."

"No," he answers. "It's fine. Just caught me off guard is all. I knew you'd ask, but I didn't expect you to lead off with that tonight."

I set the hot dog, covered in the best chili ever known to man, back down on the paper liner it came in on my lap.

"You don't have to answer. It just doesn't make any sense now with the letters and all."

"It's because I didn't file it. My parents did in my name. I was at basic training, when the papers were sent to my barracks with your signature on them. It wasn't until I came back that my dad fessed up about what he had done."

"That son of bitch," I growl. "I should've known." I pause, considering my words carefully. "But why didn't you come to me, before you signed them? You had to know something wasn't right."

"You were mourning your uncle, and it wasn't like I left with us on the best of terms," he says, taking my hand in his. "I'd planned to come back after basic to make things right, but I was immediately shipped off overseas. It's a part of the past now. Dad knows what he did was wrong."

"That's it? How can you just brush that aside?" I growl back. "He took the last string we had tying us together and just cut it, unbeknownst to the both of us."

"People make mistakes. His sins may be worse than mine, but he's an old man."

"He's your father, and he struck, while the iron was hot to get me out of your life, Lachlan. How can you stand to be in the same house with him?"

"It's not easy, but with Mom sick, I can't just walk away. The relationship between us will never be the same, but we have to move on from it. I can't change the past. I can only make up for it in the future."

If the roles were reversed, I would have hauled ass right out of their house and never looked back. That was the difference between us. He was raised with strong family bonds, while mine were tattered in the wind. Family is his number one priority. I just don't know if I can live with that tradition anymore.

"I don't expect you to be around them either. They're my burdens, and not yours," he adds, after my lack of an immediate response.

"Might not be a bad idea, since your mother nearly took me out earlier this week."

Lachlan's face is solemn. The pain and guilt are as clear as day on his face, as he opens himself up. It's eating him from the inside out. Just like the regrets of all the years we missed having together because of his parents. Their betrayal is something that I'll never forgive.

"My family was tearing us apart, and the worst part of it is that I let it happen. That's why I'm here, Dixie. To make it right again."

Lachlan leans forward, shoving the food off my lap, pulling my face towards his.

"The past doesn't matter anymore now that you're back."

"You're assuming an awful lot there. I may be here, but the question of what we are is still up for debate."

"My life doesn't make sense without you in it."

His blue eyes shine under the reflection of the moon. In them, I see desire and need. A need so strong that I can feel its intensity the longer we linger so closely together. Together, we make so much sense, but our past will always be there.

Do I want this? Do I want him? All too clearly, the answers form in my mind.

Yes. Despite everything, I want him back.

He smiles wide, and it's just like before. He knows what I'm thinking. His mouth descends on mine, sealing my answer with the best kiss of my life. He kisses me once, then twice, until our lips conjoin into a coil of heated passion, breaking through its chains. This kiss isn't just about reconnecting. He's reclaiming what he lost—his heart and mine.

His hands fall from my face to the hem of my shirt. He breaks our contact, only briefly, pulling the shirt over my head, before his lips crash back onto mine. His tongue slips inside, caressing my tongue in a delicate dance of desire and need. In one swift movement, his hands grip my waist, pulling me onto his lap, making me straddle his hips with my legs. He hisses, when I rub his hard cock between my spread thighs, which lights my core on fire.

My hands fall to his shirt. Ripping it off of him, I press our naked skin together, as the cool night air rolls off the creek near us. A moan escapes my lips, and he breaks contact.

"Here or the truck," he growls. "We're not gonna make it back to your place."

In all my wildest dreams, I never thought I would ever be back in his arms again. Let alone out, in the middle of nowhere in the same spot, where he claimed my virginity all those years ago. This may not have been in his plan, when he brought me here, but there isn't any other place I would rather be, while we find ourselves again.

"Here," I order, shoving him on his back. I jump from his hips and tug at my jeans, like the feel of them is burning away my skin. My panties go with them, falling in a heap to the ground. My bra goes next, and Lachlan looks up at me, taking it all in.

"The world has never known beauty like I do right now, seeing you standing there like that."

"Lord have mercy. Where did you get that line?"

He cocks a smile. "That's all me, Rogue. My rugged good looks can't be the only thing that I bring to the table."

"As much as I appreciate those sweet nothings you're whisperin', it doesn't seem to be gettin' those jeans off of you any faster."

His eyes go wide.

"You heard me. Get'em off."

In seconds, he's off the ground, and his hands go right for his fly.

"Still bossy as ever, I see."

"You ain't seen bossy yet, if you don't get going on those jeans."

As much as I would love to drag this out, my body is on fire. I can almost feel the burn of the invisible flames flickering up and down my skin, as I watch him kick off his boots. He shimmies out of his jeans, taking his boxer briefs with them, and I can't help but to stare. The years have been very, *very* good to Lachlan. I wonder if I wrote a letter to the head of his platoon, thanking him for this, would be too much? Nah. I'm *so* going to be thanking him for whipping Lachlan's ass into shape.

"This isn't a hurry-up-and-wait thing is it, Rogue?"

Hell no. It's been far too long with too many damn people getting in our way. Tonight is all about finding *us* again.

"Come and get me," I tease, spinning and taking off for the grassy path, like I had done so many times during our youth, and Lachlan is hot on my heels. It doesn't take long for him to catch me in my adult game of cat and mouse. His hands circle around my waist, and he spins me around to face him.

"I love you, Rogue. Never stopped, and never gonna stop, until the day I die."

"I love you," I reply. "Now take me to bed. Well, the grass."

"Never thought you'd ask," he growls.

His mouth crashes against mine again, and he holds my waist and pushes, until I trip over a large pile of cut grass, sending him spiraling down above me. We laugh as we land, but he cuts me off, when his mouth descends down my neck, kissing me from the bottom of my ear to the top of my shoulder, causing me to shiver. His tongue sucks and bites at my delicate skin, while my hand falls between us to wrap around his long, thick shaft. Lachlan moans at my touch.

"You have no idea how good that feels," he growls against my shoulder. "Been too long."

I tilt my head slightly, allowing him to target my most sensitive spot at the crease of my neck and shoulder, and I giggle, as his tongue licks circles around it. As he licks, I stroke his cock. Up and down, adding a twist at the end, which is something that used to drive him crazy.

"Keep that up, and this ain't gonna last long. You know what that does to me," he warns.

"Who says that's not what I want?"

He eyes me confused by my statement.

"We have the rest of our lives for long and slow."

Lachlan takes the hint and slides to his knees. I watch, as his fingers trace up my inner thigh, before I feel one of his fingers slide inside, followed by another, and then a third. He pulls his fingers away that are glistening with my wetness, and brings them up to his lips. He licks each finger clean one by one all while smiling and savoring my taste.

"Since someone's in such a hurry, licking this sweet fucking pussy is gonna have to wait."

My head falls back in frustration, knowing he's playing my own words against me. *Asshole.* My frustration doesn't last long, as he slides his length inside of me, inch by painstakingly large inch. At first, the pain is noticeable, but Lachlan's easy with me. Just like he was our first night together. He notices me flinch, but I reach up and kiss him, distracting him from the fact that I don't want to admit that it has been awhile, since I've done this. And by awhile, I mean seven years. Something that I'm so glad Titz never found out about. She'd have put up billboards, and put me on one of those one-night stand websites she likes to read to us at the clubhouse.

Fucking pervert.

Lachlan's hips rest against my pubic bone with him fully seated inside of me.

"You okay?" He asks.

I nod, and he pulls out slowly, before pushing back inside. The sensation of him inside of me again sends electrical currents zapping and zinging all over my body. Each thrust builds in intensity, before I start seeing stars from the arousal warming my core. My release is just over the horizon, and he knows it. Even after so many years apart, he still knows my body. *What each sound means. How I like him to touch me. What it takes to send me over the edge.*

Grabbing my waist, he hoists us both backwards, and never breaks the connection. My ass rests on the top of his lap, as he holds all of our weight on his haunches.

"You're too beautiful to be on the bottom, Rogue. I want to feel you," he groans, thrusting inside again. "I want to see you come around my dick. I want to hear every moan and feel every single fucking tremble that courses through your body, when you do."

A moan slips from my lips, and my legs shift to wrap completely around his waist, drawing us even closer.

"I'm claiming you, Rogue. Inside and out, and no one will take this away from us. Not my family. Not yours. Say it."

"No one," I cry out, as I grind myself against him. For the first time in years, I let my mind and body take control. I move my body forward and backward slowly, until I find my sweet spot. Lachlan watches my every move, guiding my hips with his hands.

"Claim me, Rogue," he orders. "Make me yours."

He lets me take control, riding and grinding my pelvis roughly against his, until the sensation pushes me over the brink. My orgasm hits hard, paralyzing me on top of him. My body jerks and pulses. Lachlan finds his own release shortly after, and joins me in the throes of pleasure, until sheer will is the only thing keeping us upright. But even that fails us.

We fall in the pile of grass, where we started. Both of our chests are heaving with the flickers of lightning bugs, dancing in the skies above us. Lachlan's sweaty arm hooks around me, pulling me in against his side.

"What do we do now?" I ask.

"We love each other, Rogue, and we never let go."

I guess there is such a thing as a happily ever after.

You Give Love
A Bad Name

By Winter Travers
AKA Stiletto

One

"I don't think fifty dollars is too much to charge for an oil change, tire rotation, and checking your fluids."

"I didn't ask you to check my fluids."

Deep breath. "When you dropped the car off, I told you everything that was included and the price, Mr. Johns."

"No, you didn't. If you had, I wouldn't be standing here arguing with you." Mr. Johns slammed his hands down on the counter that separated us. "I'm not paying for you checking my fluids."

Fuck me running. Was this man serious? Every time someone came in, I had a standard spiel for each service we performed at Bane Repair. "Then I'm going to drain the coolant, washer fluid, and water from the radiator."

"You'll do no such thing," he spat. "I'll get the sheriff down here. You know he's going to side with me and not some female grease monkey that rides in some gang."

I leaned across the counter, my hands planted on the fake Formica. "It's a motorcycle club," I enunciated slowly. I couldn't count the number of times I'd said those same exact words to some asshole who didn't know what the hell he was talking about. "And I may have grease under my fingernails, Mr. Johns, but at least I have better manners than you." I grabbed the invoice I had written up five minutes earlier and ripped it in half.

"What are you doing?" he huffed.

I was doing the damn man a favor before I decided to plant my size eight and a half foot up his ass. "You're square. No charge."

"You... why you... this..." he sputtered. "I'll pay for everything but the fluids. I can do that myself. I don't want you thinking you need to do it for me."

I wadded up the invoice and tossed it in the trash. "Your money's no good here. Have a nice day." I walked around the counter and held open the front door.

Mr. Johns slapped his ball cap on his head and stormed out, but not before telling me what a piece of shit I was.

Would this shit ever change? "Yes, Mr. Johns, I'm a horrible person for doing two hours of work on your truck for free. Have a splendid day, and I'll see you in three months to do it all over again."

He stormed over to his truck as I pulled the door shut. Twisting the lock, I spun around to lean against the door.

Fuck, it was a long ass day with a shitty ending.

Like fucking clockwork, every three months, Mr. Johns would come in needing an oil change. I would explain everything that came with an oil change and he would agree. Then he would get the bill, read that I checked his fluids, and insist on not paying for it. As far as I could remember, he hadn't paid. Ever.

Yet I always ended up being the evil bitch who was in a gang that was trying to somehow screw him over.

"Another day, another asshole," I mumbled.

Thank God it was the end of the day, and an ice-cold beer was only a short motorcycle ride away.

Ten minutes later, I twisted the key in the lock and heard the crunch of tires rolling over the gravel. I didn't need to turn around to know who had just pulled into the parking lot.

He called out of his window, "Trying to make an escape, River? You should've known after Mr. Johns left I'd be here."

I dropped my head and closed my eyes. "I'd been praying that the crazy old man was bluffing."

"Every three months for the past two years. You really thought he was going to stop calling me to report you for highway robbery?"

Pryor Jones.

Sheriff of Magnolia Springs, Alabama.

"It's not highway robbery if I didn't charge him, again."

He whistled low. "Poor ol' Mr. Johns failed to mention that part, again."

I heard his feet hit the gravel before his door slammed shut.

Dammit. I'd hoped he wouldn't get out of his truck.

"So, you checked his fluids and didn't tell him you were going to?"

"Do you have to make it sound dirty?" I slowly turned around and opened my eyes, but kept on the ground. "Couldn't you have just called me?" I couldn't see his face, but I knew the damn man was smiling.

"What kind of sheriff would I be if I didn't investigate every complaint we received?"

"The kind that knows the difference between a legit complaint and horse shit."

"Aren't you gonna look at me, River?"

He was challenging me. He knew by doing it, I was going to look at him. "I don't think I need to look at you to have this conversation."

"River," he chided.

Motherfucker. I slowly raised my eyes. *Don't do it, River. Don't get hypnotized by this man's moss green eyes. Don't let your heart skip a beat from the smug look you know is going to be on his face.*

Pryor Jones was a handsome devil. Even with that damn tan sheriff's uniform and gold star on his chest, the man looked like he stepped off the cover of a fucking magazine. While the two other officers who were on the police force looked like they were drowning in their uniforms, Pryor's fit perfectly. It was like he had the damn thing tailored.

The man was supposed to uphold the law, but in my opinion, it should be illegal to look the way he did. Couldn't God have given him a crooked nose, or maybe some buck teeth?

Noooo. He had to look like a cross between Brad Pitt and Johnny Depp. That's right, Brad Pitt and Johnny Depp. Let that sink in. Cue women around the world sighing.

A smirk spread across his lips, and I was added to the gaggle of women sighing around the world. "Why do you keep checking his fluids when you know he doesn't want you to?"

I lightly shook my head, trying to fall out of the Pryor fog. "I guess I'm a glutton for Mr. Johns' rejection of me. I don't feel whole unless I get accused of highway robbery every three months."

"Maybe next time, you can skip checking his fluids. See how it feels."

"He'll find something to yell at me for. It's in his nature." I'd accepted the fact that I was forever going to be yelled at by Mr. Johns. "Is that all you came by for?"

"You tell me, River. There anything else going on you want to talk to me about?"

I closed one eye and squinted. "I think for now, I'm good. You know I tend to keep to myself."

"Ain't that the truth," he muttered. "Try to stay out of trouble and stop checking people's fluids when they don't want you to." The damn man winked at me, sending my hormones into overdrive.

As he waltzed over to his truck, my eyes were plastered to his tight ass, but I fought off groaning until he was in his truck. He gave me a flick of his hand in farewell, did a three-point turn in the parking lot and took off.

I kicked the gravel with my steel-toed boot.

Pryor Jones was nice.

So nice, that it made me wary of him.

I was used to being treated like a second-class citizen around here. I had The Dirty Bitches, who were like my family, and my sister Kit. That was all I needed. Pryor talked to me as if he cared about what I had to say and didn't judge me by the dirt under my nails or the bike I rode. Judgments I was used to, but kindness I was not.

If only I had to deal with Pryor every three months, then it wouldn't be so bad.

I had a problem though. One that was my own fault.

I couldn't stay away from the man, even when I knew I should.

Pryor Jones threatened every brick I had laid on the wall I'd built around me.

He was a bulldozer, and I was weary if I stood a chance once he shifted into drive.

Two

"Another?"

I shook my head. "I do need to be able to walk, you know."

Gretchen shrugged. "And you know I need a good tip. The drunker you get, the looser your wallet gets."

"Have I ever stiffed you on a tip, drunk or not?" I drawled. I was tipsy, but I would still be able to get home on my own.

Titz scoffed from across the table. "I think you need to work a little harder for that tip, Gretchen. My last beer was warm."

Gretchen, our usual waitress, raised her middle finger to Titz. "It was warm because you let it sit there for fifteen minutes before you even took a drink."

"You watching me?" Titz questioned. She wiggled her eyebrows and raised her empty glass. "Bring me another beer, and I promise to drink it right away."

Gretchen snatched the glass from Titz and flounced over to the bar.

"You really need to give her shit like that?" Rogue rested her elbows on the table and stared Titz down.

"Do you really need to rain all over my fun with that disapproving look?" Titz retorted. She crossed her tattooed-covered arms over her chest and sat back. "It was a long damn week, and if I wanna give good ol' Gretchen a hard time, I'm going to."

"Doodling all over people must be really exhausting," Links muttered.

Titz pointed a finger at her. "Shouldn't you be out playing in your garden right now?"

"You get belligerent when you drink. You know that, right?" Links looked at me. "I'm a sweet drunk, you're a funny drunk, Rogue gets serious, and Titz just gets ridiculous."

"I am a funny drunk." That was the only thing I was going to agree with about her statement out loud. She was right, but if I agreed with her, Titz would get really belligerent. It was a snarky belligerent that was funny most of the time, but I'd also been watching how much she'd been drinking, and she was walking that dangerous line of snarky and just plain mean.

"I speak the truth, and the truth is that you spend too much time diddling in your garden when you should be looking for a man to diddle it *for* you." Titz raised her glass to Links. "I'm a truthful drunk. Stick that in your pipe and smoke it."

"She's right." I hated to admit it, but Titz was right.

Links scoffed and slammed her glass down. "I do not diddle in my garden too much."

Rogue leaned forward. "Can we clarify what Links' garden is? Is it an actual garden, or are we talking *garden?*" Rogue's eyes bounced up and down from Links to the table. "Because if we're talking about her *garden*, then I also need to know how Titz would know about that."

A grin spread across Titz's lips. "Have you been in her back yard?"

Rogue shook her head and raised her hands. "I give up. Your innuendos when you're drinking have no bounds."

Titz threw her head back and laughed. "I actually mean her back yard. It's like a well-groomed jungle back there. She doesn't have time to do anything but dig in the dirt and pull weeds."

"So you were talking about her actual garden?" Rogue clarified.

"No," Titz and I said in unison. I got Titz. She was hard to keep up with sometimes with her dry sense of humor, but most of the time I got it.

"Links can't diddle her own garden because she's always in her garden, so she needs to find a man to diddle *her* garden." It made sense to me.

"But she can't find a man to diddle her garden because she's always in her garden," Titz added.

Rogue opened her mouth and quickly shut it. She tapped a finger to her chin and pursed her lips. "How did we get here? Was it the last round that dropped us in the realm of talking about Links diddling her garden? If so, we need to drink more to boot us out of this conversation."

Gretchen walked over to the table and set a fresh beer in front of Titz.

"Allow me to do the honors." Titz lifted the glass to her lips and downed half the bottle's contents in four gulps.

I pulled a twenty out of my pocket and tossed it on the table. "I'm gonna head out, girls. It may be the end of the week for you all, but the garage is open for a few hours tomorrow."

Titz scoffed. "That's your own damn fault for opening. You're the boss, Stiletto."

I waved my hand at her. "And I need money, so I'm out."

I stood up and grabbed my helmet off the table.

"Your ass better not be driving," Rogue warned.

"Yes, Mother." I had no plans to drive, but Links always needed to put her two cents in. That was why she was the president of the Dirty Bitches. She kept us in line even though it annoyed us sometimes. "Not that you should drive in those contraptions you call shoes anyway."

They all moved to look down at my feet as if they didn't already know what I was wearing. Before I had come to the bar, I'd made a stop at home to change. "Is there ever going to be a time where you don't give me shit about my shoes?"

Rogue swung a leg up and slammed her boot onto the table. "This is a shoe. What you have on should be considered torture devices."

"Torture devices that you somehow manage to drive in," Links added.

I glared at her. "Really?"

She shrugged. "Don't mess with my garden, and I won't talk smack about your shoes."

"Trust me, I'll never mess with your garden, Links."

"Her garden or her *garden?*" Rogue wiggled her eyebrows.

"Oh hell, I'm out of here," I sighed. I didn't need to go into Links' garden again. "I'll touch base with you guys after work."

Titz downed the rest of her beer and slammed the empty bottle on the table. "I need another," she declared.

I made my way out of the bar at the sound of Rogue telling Titz the only way she could continue drinking is if she told her how she knew how often Links tilled her garden.

There was never a dull moment when we were all together.

I checked on my bike, making sure it was parked safely until I was able to pick it up in the morning, then started the two-mile trek to my house. A little bit more than halfway home was when my feet began to protest, and a blister began to form on my heel.

"Damn you, Louis. When will you make a hiking heel?" I muttered. With each step I took, the back strap dug into my heel, scraping away a layer of skin each time.

"River?"

Fuck.

I'd been so preoccupied with my aching feet that I hadn't taken my usual shortcut and was now standing in front of Pryor Jones's house. "Uh, no. It's not River." I double stepped, praying he would believe it wasn't me.

"Darlin', I'm looking right at you."

Of course he was. I halted in my tracks and turned to the right to see Pryor in all his glory, leaning against the railing of his porch. His chest and feet were bare, and a pair of ripped and faded jeans hung low on his hips. "Holy fuck," I whispered.

The man was a god—plain and simple. It was like he was chiseled from stone with how his abs were defined, and the glorious V that dipped into his jeans eluded to the heaven that was tucked inside of them. Not that I'd ever visited *that* heaven, but I had to assume the man was packing some heavy artillery down there.

Pryor Jones, god on earth. That was what his calling card should say.

I shook my head, trying not to think about…well, anything that had to do with Pryor and what was in his pants, god or not.

"You hear me?"

I blinked twice. "Um… yeah."

"Then answer my question."

Aw shit. He'd been talking to me while I'd been thinking about the bazooka he was packing. "The answer is no." I didn't have a damn clue as to what he'd asked, but I figured saying no to anything he had to ask was a safe bet.

He crossed his arms over his chest. "So, me asking you what you're doing is a yes or no question?"

Double fuck. "Erg…"

"What are you doing, River?"

"Why don't you call me Stiletto?" Everyone did, and I mean *everyone.* Everyone except for Pryor. Half the town didn't even know what my real name was, and that was how I liked it. "How did you even find out what my real name was?"

A sly smirk spread across his lips. "I'm the sheriff, darlin'. I know everything there is to know about Magnolia Springs."

Hmph. I didn't like that answer. I preferred no one knowing anything about me unless the information came directly from me.

"And Mr. Johns always calls you that crazy River."

"So you didn't run my name through your fancy computer?"

He shook his head. "I admit nothing."

And that was why I didn't trust the man. I hitched my thumb over my shoulder toward my house four blocks away. "I'm gonna keep on walking."

"You mind me asking why you're walking?"

I sagged my shoulders and sighed. I did mind him knowing because then I was going to have to hang around and talk to him some more. "Too many Harvey Wallbangers." There, that should explain it. He was the sheriff, so he should respect the fact that I hadn't driven after drinking one too many.

"And you're going to walk all the way home in those?" He nodded at my feet.

Did I want to walk all the way home in them? No.

Was I going to walk all the way home in them? Hell yes.

"That's the plan."

"Your feet are going to be bloody and raw by the time you step foot on your front porch."

"I've done it before." I had. Not in these exact shoes, but I couldn't even count the number of times I'd drank too much while hanging out with The Dirty Bitches. I shuffled my feet and grimaced at the increasing pain on my right heel.

"Let me put a shirt and shoes on, and I'll give you a ride home."

I shook my head. "It's late, and you really don't need to do that." Like, *really*, he didn't. I was ten feet away from the man, and it was impossible to deny the pull he had. Sitting barely two feet away from him in his truck wasn't something I wanted to experience.

"It's late, and besides, what kind of a guy would I be if I let you walk to your house in the middle of the night?"

Like all the other guys who had come into my life? Assholes. "I'm fine, Pryor."

He pushed off the railing of the porch. "You know, that's the first time I've heard you say my name."

"That's ridiculous. Of course I've said your name before."

He shook his head and stepped toward his front door. "I'd remember you saying my name, darlin'. Come inside while I get dressed." He pulled open the door and looked at me.

"I'll just stay out here." While he was inside, I could hobble my cookies down the road before he came back out. I didn't want to be trapped inside a truck with Pryor. At. All.

With the door wide open, he continued to stare at me.

I shooed him with my hand, but he didn't budge. "I don't need to come in, Pryor."

"I want you to come in, River."

Want in one hand, shit in the other. "Not what I want. I want to stay here."

"You really gonna have the whole mosquito population of Magnolia Springs fly into my house while I wait for you to stop being so stubborn?"

"I'm not stubborn," I insisted. I knew what I wanted, and I wasn't going to be bullied or talked into something I didn't want to do.

"Then come in if you're not stubborn."

I rolled my eyes. "I don't understand why I need to come in. I can wait for you out here."

"Because I know as soon as this door shuts behind me, you'll disappear."

"Me disappearing isn't a bad thing for you."

"I'll be the judge of that," he responded. "Get in the house, River." He wasn't leaving any room for argument.

"Fine," I huffed. "Although, I want it to be known that I'm coming inside because I want to, not because you're making me." I brushed past him, careful not to touch him.

"It's been noted, darlin'. Although, it doesn't matter."

I crossed my arms over my chest and moved into the living room, wanting to put more space between us.

"Get comfortable. I'll only be a couple minutes." He disappeared down a hallway next to the kitchen, leaving me to my own entertainment.

Entertainment that was going to be me snooping around his living room, trying to figure out who Pryor was from the pile of magazines on the coffee table, and the fact his living room was immaculate.

It was clean.

Like, *clean.*

Not that I had expected the man to live like a slob, but I had at least expected one empty pizza box, and maybe a few empty beer cans on the table.

There was nothing there besides four issues of *Sports Illustrated* and three remotes. An L-shaped sectional was on the opposite side of the room, and an overstuffed recliner was tucked in the corner. The furniture was all black leather. "Typical man." I walked over to the recliner and plopped down.

My feet were killing me, and since he wanted me to come inside, then I was going to sit down and take my shoes off. "Do you have a cleaning lady?"

"What?" Pryor yelled from down the hallway.

I slid the strap off the back of my heel and dropped the gorgeous, but offending shoe on the floor. "I said, do you have a cleaning lady?"

"No. Why the hell would you ask that?"

"Your house is clean," I said accusingly.

"No."

Interesting.

I rubbed my heel, taking in the fact that Pryor Jones was a neat freak. From what I could see of his kitchen, there was nothing on his countertops, except for a coffee maker and three bananas. The thing that totally blew me away was the fact that there didn't appear to be one single dirty dish in the sink.

That meant only one thing.

Pryor was an alien.

A sexy alien, but an alien nonetheless.

Pryor moved down the hallway toward the living room, tugging a shirt over his head. "Is there a reason why you want to know if I have a cleaning lady?"

I spread my arms out in front of me. "Do you even live here?"

"Name's on the deed, darlin'."

"Then why does it look like a showroom in here?"

"I don't even know what that means, River." He grabbed a set of keys off the coffee table. "You able to walk?" His eyes dropped to my bare foot.

"Are you going to carry me if I say no?"

Instead of answering, he took a determined step toward me.

Oh hell. I fumbled to grab my shoe off the floor and managed to slip it on. "I'm good, I'm good," I repeated. "I'm no damsel in distress you need to come rescue."

"Never said you were." He held up his hands and took a step back. "Was just gonna help you with your shoe."

I shot up from the chair and stood shakily on my aching foot. "Can we go?"

"Don't get why you wear those things if they hurt your feet."

"Foot. Just one foot hurts, and normally when I wear them, the only walking I plan on doing is from the parking lot to the bar," I clarified, like it actually mattered. "And besides, they're my thing." Now that was the truth. The shoes I loved to wear had been the driving force behind my club name.

"I get that they're your thing, darlin', but I would think if your thing was making you hurt, you would take the damn things off."

Under normal circumstances, I would've done just that, but walking down Burgess Street with one or no shoes on was not something I was going to do. "Do we have to stand here talking about my shoes? I know you're a neat freak, obviously, but I'm afraid this conversation might lead to you asking if you can try them on."

Pryor shook his head. "Just... no." He stalked to the door and threw it open. "Let's go."

"Did I touch a nerve, Officer?"

I moved to walk out the door, but he gently grabbed my arm, halting me in my tracks. "It's Sheriff, darlin'."

I tilted my head back to look him in the eyes. "You're off the clock, though."

"For a couple hours. Although, with Clint on shift, I expect at least ten phone calls from him."

My nose wrinkled, and I tried to tug my arm from his hold. "Perhaps you need to find a better deputy so you can get some time off."

"Clint will get it eventually."

I cleared my throat and looked down at his hand. "Is there a reason why you're touching me?"

"You don't like it?"

"I'm just unsure of why it's happening." That was the damn truth. Pryor had never touched me before. I didn't know why he suddenly was.

He leaned closer and pulled my arm to his chest. "Because you and I both knew this was eventually going to happen. I'm just sick of waiting for you to give me a sign that you want me closer than five feet away."

I gulped and tipped my head back. "Sign?" I squeaked.

"I'll wait a little bit longer."

For what? My mind raced, trying to catch up with what was going on. "I just… if you…"

He slid his hand down my arm and threaded his fingers through mine. "Let's go." He tugged me out the door and onto the porch. Reaching back to shut the door, he then marched us down the stairs.

"I don't know what just happened," I wondered out loud.

We made it to the passenger door of his Jeep before he spoke. "You'll figure it out, darlin'." He opened the door to the truck and motioned for me to get in. "Hop up."

Hop up? I was amazed I was still standing. Hopping up anywhere didn't seem to be possible. Officer Fine Ass had just told me he was waiting for some type of sign from me.

Being speechless wasn't something that happened to me often. One-liners, and being a smart-ass were my thing. along with the heels.

"Are you from a different planet?" Yeah, that was the only thought I had in my head. Being a neat freak and showing interest in me screamed being from another planet apparently.

"No," he said plainly.

"Well, I'm gonna have to see your birth certificate to believe that."

He looked from the Jeep to me. "You gonna get in, or am I gonna have to *put* you in?"

"You mean your spaceship?" Christ, maybe I was a bit tipsier than I thought.

"River."

I rolled my eyes. "Fine, fine. You can abduct me and take me home." I managed to teeter on one foot and hoist my ass up into the truck. "You may shut the door to the spacecraft."

Pryor rolled his eyes, but he had a smug smirk on his face.

He had gotten his way. I was in his truck. *Grr.*

He slid into the driver's seat, and I turned to look at him. "Do you know where I live?"

He turned his head to look at me while he stuck the key in the ignition. "I'm the sheriff."

"That doesn't answer my question."

Turning the key, the Jeep roared to life. He needed a tuning. "It's my business to know where everyone lives."

"No, that sounds more like a stalker thing." I sat back in my seat and crossed my arms over my chest. "Side note, your Jeep needs some work done. The timing sounds off."

"Gonna have to take your word for that one, darlin', because you know a hell of a lot more about that than I do."

"I hope you're talking about cars and not the stalking."

He shifted into reverse, splayed his arm across the back of my seat and backed out of the driveway. "I'm not a stalker, River," he muttered.

He had yet to prove it to me. "I'm sure all stalkers say that."

"How many drinks did you have tonight?"

"Three," I huffed.

He side-eyed me.

"Possibly four. I stopped when Titz started talking about Links' garden. Probably should have kept drinking to make it through that conversation."

"Gardening?" he questioned.

"It may seem innocent, but with Titz, nothing is ever innocent."

"She was in the drunk tank two weekends ago. I can testify to the fact."

That was a surprise to me. "Titz failed to mention the drunk tank to us."

"Rogue knew. She's the one who bailed her out."

That's why I didn't know. Rogue probably chewed her ass out and that was that. Not like it was going to stop Titz from being Titz, but normally, after Rogue laid into her, she'd settle down for a bit. Not like I could blame her for getting rowdy when we went out. She had four kids at home, so she had to let loose every now and then. "I hate to ask what she did."

"Let's just say that the name you guys gave her is completely fitting."

I should've known it had to do with her tits. I don't think I've ever gone a full week without her flashing them with me in her presence. "Lord."

"Yeah. She scared Clint."

That was also normal with Titz. "She's definitely not for the faint of heart."

"I'm afraid Clint will never be the same."

That made me laugh. "Most aren't after meeting Titz."

Pryor pulled into the driveway to my house and shifted into park.

I quickly unbuckled my seat belt and reached for the door handle. "No need to get out. Thanks for the ride. See you in three months."

"It'll be sooner than that, darlin'."

I glanced over my shoulder at him. "You keep saying that like you have some control over what I do."

"Don't wanna control you, darlin'. Just wanna be more than the sheriff to you."

I yanked on the handle to the door and pushed it open. "That's a tall order, Pryor. You might be waiting a long time." I slid out of the Jeep and slammed the door shut behind me.

I was determined to make it into the house without looking back at him.

"You can't keep running from me, River."

Don't turn around, don't turn around. "I don't run from anything, Pryor." I pulled my keys out of my pocket and jabbed the key into the lock.

"If you're not running from me, then I'll see you at my house tomorrow."

"And why the hell would I do that?" I called back. Damn fucker was challenging me again.

"See you tomorrow, River."

His headlights bobbed over the garage as he backed out of the driveway, and I slipped into the house. I spun around, trying to slam the door, but my eyes connected with his for a split second. He had a smug smile on his face, like he knew I would be there tomorrow, even though I didn't want to be.

I slammed the door, breaking the connection. "Motherfucker!" I screamed.

"Well, that's a weird way to say hello."

I dropped my head and closed my eyes. "What are you doing here, Sneaks?"

Three

"Who drove you home?"

I toed off my offending heels, kicking them in the direction of my bedroom. "What are you doing here?"

"It's Friday night."

"Is that supposed to mean something to me?" I pushed off the door and padded into the kitchen.

"I had a date tonight with Michael."

I pulled open the fridge and pulled out a bottle of water. "And?"

"I broke up with him."

This really wasn't surprising to me. "Why were we breaking up with this one?"

"His feet were too small, and..."

I scoffed and twisted off the cap. "So I'm assuming that means the myth that small feet equal small penis is true then?" I chugged half the bottle and turned to see Kit pulling out a stool from under the island. She was sitting down. Lord, this wasn't going to be a quick conversation. "I need to work in the morning."

She flitted her hand at me. "You can take a nap when you get home. I haven't seen you in a week."

That wasn't true. She'd stopped by the shop on Wednesday to rant and complain about her boss. She also demanded to know when she was going to become a full member of The Dirty Bitches. For the tenth time, I'd told her it wasn't up to just me, and Rogue had final say since she was the president of the club.

"Back to Michael."

I grabbed the stool next to her and plopped down on it. I was exhausted, and I knew that listening to Kit talk a mile a minute was going to tire me out even more. "So what happened with the sleazeball?"

She shook her head. "He's not a sleazeball."

"Kit."

"He's not."

"We're gonna have to get to the point soon here before I fall asleep."

She sighed and grabbed my bottle of water. She picked at the label, slowly peeling it off. "He's an ass, Riv. I was talking about the club and he completely cut me off, saying you guys are basically a bunch of hooligans on motorcycles."

I shrugged. Wasn't anything I hadn't heard before. "Am I supposed to be offended?"

She shook her head. "That's not all of it."

Hmm, this was interesting. "What else?"

"He said you had no idea what you were doing in the shop, and that you needed a man to come in and show you how to do everything."

I reared back. "Say what?" I hadn't even met this assclown before, and he somehow thought I didn't know a screwdriver from a broom?

"And if I thought I was going to join the club, he would only see me every now and then, just to hook up."

Sweet heavens above. "Where in the hell did you meet a piece of work like that, Kit?"

She finished peeling off the label from the bottle. "I was trying something different. He works at the bank two towns over."

"Well, good riddance, but I don't know why you thought dating a banker was a good idea."

She shrugged again. "I think it was a lapse in judgment."

"A huge one."

"Agreed."

I watched as she began to peel the label into small strips. She was like a cat with a roll of toilet paper, hell-bent on shredding it into the tiniest pieces she could. "What else is bothering you, Kit?"

She turned her head to look at me. "I don't know, Riv. Everything just feels off."

This took a turn I hadn't expected. "You're going to have to be more specific than that."

"That's just it, Riv. I can't be more specific because I don't have a clue why I feel the way I do."

"Would a beer help?" I really wasn't good at this sappy shit. I was always there for Kit come hell or high water, but that didn't mean I always knew what I should say. Life had been hard for Kit and I growing up.

When Mom died, I was seventeen, and everything fell onto me. I'd tried to find our dad to see if he could help us, but trying to find someone when all you knew was their first name and the kind of car they drove wasn't enough. "I think a new life is the only thing that's going to help, Riv."

I sighed and wrapped my arm around her shoulders. "Then start a new life, Kit. Right here, right now. Start new. List off everything you want to change and change it."

"It's not that easy. Nothing's that easy." She dropped her chin to her chest. "Don't you think if it were easy, I would've changed my life a long time ago by making Dad stick around?"

"That's where your problem is. You want people to change. I never said anything about that."

"You just said if I want a different life then change it."

Sweet Jesus. Kit and I may only be two years apart in age, but some days it felt like it was ten. "You can't change a person, Kit. I mean, if you want a new life, one where you'll be happy, then figure out what would make you happy."

She swiveled her head to look at me. "Being part of the Dirty Bitches."

That might be a tall order, but it was doable. "Then talk to Rogue, Links, and Titz. Get more involved with what we're doing. You know you're gonna have to go through some shit before you're able to put the patch on your back."

"I'm not afraid of hard work, River. You guys just never give me the chance to try."

I slammed my fist down on the counter. "All right. So that's the first thing you're going to change. What else do you want?"

"To get out of the hellhole I live in."

I hitched my thumb over my shoulder. "There's a two bedroom for rent over on Michelin. I know the guy who owns it. As long as you've got a deposit, I can get you in."

"River, always to the rescue." A sad smile graced her lips.

"Somehow, I don't think you mean that as I should be wearing a cape and saving the neighborhood."

"No, no. I don't mean it in a bad way. It's just… you have your shit together: the club, a house, the garage. Me? A shitty job at the foundry, a shithole apartment, and I can't keep a boyfriend to save my life."

"Three things." I held up a finger. "One, you don't need a man to save you. You save yourself, and then if some guy wants to come live in that life with you, fine." I added a second finger. "Two, making over twenty bucks an hour at the foundry is not a shitty job. There are a hundred people in this town who would kill to have your job." I added one final finger. "And three, I just fixed it. You'll be in the place in a week, tops."

She sighed heavily. "You make it seem so easy."

"Easy? Pfft, I think you're forgetting a lot of shit while having your pity party, Kit. I went to school for four years while working nights at the same foundry you hate. I dealt with every Tom, Dick, and Harry in school, telling me I wasn't going to make it because I was a chick. We lived in a one-bedroom apartment above the feed store till I was able to buy this place." Everything I had now didn't come easy to me. I worked hard for it. I sacrificed my time and social life to finally get ahead.

She dropped her forehead to the cool granite countertop. "And now I sound like an ungrateful little bitch."

"You do, but we're all allowed those moments every now and then."

"I'm such a shitty sister," she muttered. "You did everything for me to have a good life, and now I just told you it sucks."

"Man." I whistled low. "You're having one hell of a pity party tonight, aren't you?"

She groaned as she stood up and grabbed the label she had shredded. "I'm leaving. I've managed to annoy myself, and you have to work early in the morning."

"You don't need to leave, Kit. You can stay the night if you want." She was going through some shit and I didn't want her to be alone.

She shook her head and moved to the garbage can. She dropped the trash inside before grabbing her keys off the counter. "I can't. I need to get home to Mr. Nutter. He's dependent on me to feed him before bed."

I rolled my eyes. "You and that damn cat. You know he can go more than four hours without being fed, right?"

96

She moved to the back door. "You tell that to him. See ya later, Riv."

She slipped out the door and quickly shut it behind her.

Her bike roared to life, and I listened to her pull around the house, then head down the street.

I didn't know what to do with Kit. I knew she was struggling with figuring out who she was, but I could only do so much. Throwing money at her wasn't going to fix any of the problems she had, and that was about the only I could do.

Getting her out of that shithole apartment she lived in was going to be a place to start, though. When I bought my house, I'd offered Kit to come live with me, but she'd been insistent that she wasn't going to freeload off me anymore.

That had been five years ago, and she was still struggling to figure out what she wanted out of life.

I could stay awake all night worrying about Kit. Hell, some nights I actually did.

Except now I was going to have to split my night worrying between Kit and Pryor. I had no idea what the hell the man was doing. I wasn't dumb. I could tell he was attracted me, but from the way he talked, he was interested in more than a couple rolls in the hay.

Problem was, I didn't want anything more than to find out what the sheriff was packing in his pants. Forever wasn't in the cards for me.

Forever didn't exist.

Four

"Stiletto?"

"You got her." I squeezed my cell between my cheek and shoulder as I continued to wrench on the damn bolt that was refusing to budge.

"Uh, Clint here."

The wrench dropped from my hand and clattered to the floor. "Clint? Scaredy-Cat Clint?" What in the hell was Clint calling me for?

"Uh, yeah. I guess that's me. Although, I'd prefer you just call me Clint."

Well, the only way that was going to happen was when he stopped being terrified of Titz. "Can I help you?"

"I think I'm going to need you to come down to the station. There's been a situation with Titz."

I should have known. "I'm kind of in the middle of tearing apart a tranny right now, Clint. You sure you can't call Rogue or Links?"

Clint cleared his throat. "She's requested for you to be the only one notified. Seems she doesn't want Rogue to know what's going on."

"Don't you make me sound like a chicken, Clint!" Titz yelled in the background. "That better be Stiletto on the phone."

So she wasn't a chicken, but she didn't want Clint calling Rogue. *Damn, Titz.* "What did she do this time?"

"Well, it's more like what she didn't do. Seems she has some unpaid parking tickets."

I dropped my head. "Of course she does."

"Why in the hell do we have to have the damn fire hydrant right in front of where I park? Can't they move it?" Her voice carried over the phone, and I couldn't help but chuckle.

"She's claiming it's the fire department's fault, and that they should be the ones to pay the tickets, not her."

I glanced at the clock on the wall. "Is she drunk?" It was only ten thirty, but Titz didn't think there was ever a bad time to drink. There were always mimosas and Bloody Marys for the before noon drinkers.

"Uh, as far as I can tell, she isn't." He lowered his voice. "I'd ask her to do a breathalyzer, but I'm terrified she'll try to bite my finger."

Heaven above. Pryor was going to have to find a new deputy, or he was never going to be able to get any time off. "I gotta finish what I'm doing and then I'll be over. Tell her to keep her shirt on, and to keep her mouth shut."

Silence.

"Okay, don't tell her." Titz was likely to tell him to row, row, row his boat gently the fuck away from her. At least that's what I would have done. "Just try to keep her quiet for a bit and I'll be right over."

Thankfully, the Wright's were out of town until Tuesday, and I didn't need to have their tranny replaced before then. I shoved my phone into my pocket and worked on closing up the shop.

The four appointments I had that day had all been easy oil changes, and I was done with those before ten. Any plans I had of getting ahead for the upcoming week had just been blown out of the water by Titz and her parking tickets.

I hustled to close up the shop and took the two-block drive down to the police station. Yes, I was this close to Pryor Jones every day. Not that he was staying in the station all day, but he was there the majority of the time.

I grabbed the cold metal of the door handle and pulled it open. I silently said a prayer, hoping Pryor wasn't anywhere around since Clint had been the one to call me.

That hope dropped to the floor when the first person I met was Pryor, who was leaning a hip against the front desk, his arms crossed over his chest. "River."

Why could this man say my name and make me a speechless, spastic idiot who couldn't form a coherent thought to save her life? "What are you doing here?"

He looked around, then down at the gold star on his chest. "Last I checked, I was the sheriff."

"Yeah, kind of hard to miss, but why do you need to be here when I need to be here?"

A slow grin spread across his lips. "Just doing some sheriff stuff."

"Is that what it's officially called? Sheriff stuff?"

He shrugged. "Most would bore a nun." He hitched his thumb over his shoulder. "But then there are days where you manage to pull a familiar Pontiac over for speeding and fall into the mother of all late parking ticket offenders."

"Titz," I growled.

He tapped his nose. "Ding, ding, ding."

Titz was going to owe me big for this. Not like she knew I was trying to avoid Pryor, but her dumb shit with not paying her parking tickets had landed me right into the man's lap. "Mind showing me where she is so I can spring her?"

He nodded his head. "Sure thing. Just as soon as she pays all the fines."

"I'm not paying one cent to this place! I shouldn't have to pay to park on the street."

I nodded to the door halfway down a hallway. "I'm assuming I can find the ray of sunshine down there."

Pryor nodded his head. "That's where she is. Just have her write a check out for three hundred ninety-seven dollars and seventeen cents and she'll be free to go."

"Holy fuck. Almost four hundred dollars."

"That's what happens when you don't pay parking tickets for almost a year." Pryor pushed off the desk. "I'll let you see if you can talk some sense into her. Last I heard, she was saying she would just live here, turn the two other cells into bedrooms for the kids."

That was so Titz. She loved the hell out of her kids, and even being arrested for parking tickets wasn't going to keep her away from them. "I'll see what I can do to make sure that doesn't happen." Pryor didn't want Titz and her kids shacking up at the station.

He led me down the short hallway and opened the door where Titz could be heard yelling behind.

"It's about damn time your ass showed up. I mean, really. What did you have to do that was more important than springing me from the clink?" she demanded. She was sitting behind a long wooden table with her feet kicked up onto the chair next to her.

"Working. Trying to earn money to keep the lights on at the shop."

Titz turned to the corner, where I noticed Clint was cowering. "See? She was working. Same thing I was attempting to do before you so rudely pulled me over and dragged me into the station."

Pryor pulled out the chair across from Titz and motioned for me to sit down. "I'd hardly call it dragging you in. We let you drive your own car, and you're not even handcuffed."

I plopped down in the chair and glared across the table at Titz.

"I really don't think we need to hash out the details, do we?" Titz snapped at Pryor.

"I'd say we do if you can't seem to remember them," Pryor drawled.

Titz waved her hand at Pryor. "I don't really know if I like you much."

"Because you keep breaking the damn law and he's the sheriff?" I asked.

She pointed her finger at me. "Exactly."

"It's his job, Titz."

She sat back and crossed her legs. "He can go do his job elsewhere."

Titz was a piece of work. "Why don't you just write a check so we can go?"

Her eyes dodged to the left.

Clint piped up from the corner. "That's where we seem to be running into a problem. She says she can't."

Titz nailed him to the wall with a pissed off gaze, and he managed to shrink back even farther. "I don't remember anyone asking you."

He held his hands up, as if to ward her off. "Sorry, Miss Titz."

A smug look spread across her face. "Now that's what I'm talking about."

I scoffed and shook my head. "Pay them, Titz, and let's go."

"I can't."

I sat forward. "What do you mean you can't?"

"It means I can't pay them."

I turned to Pryor. "Do you think Titz and I can have a word alone?"

Pryor nodded his head. "You can, but you'll owe me, River." Pryor and Clint walked out and shut the door behind them.

"What does he mean you'll owe him?" she questioned immediately.

"It means nothing." I didn't need to get into whatever the hell it was that was going on with me and Pryor when Titz and I were sitting in the interrogation room of the police station.

She splayed her hands on the counter and dropped her foot to the floor. "You bumped uglies with the popo, didn't you?"

Just like Titz, straight to the point. "No."

She looked me up and down. "Maybe not, but you're going to. Soon."

"I'm not discussing this with you, Titz. Right now, we're talking about you and how you've been hauled into the police station one too many times."

"How did you… oh fuck. Popo Hot Ass told you." She threw her hands up in the air. "So much for client confidentiality."

"I'm not your lawyer, Titz, and it's public information that you were arrested," Pryor called out.

Titz's jaw dropped. "You're listening to us!" she screamed.

"You ain't a quiet talker, darlin'."

He was right about that. I snapped my fingers in her face. "Focus, Titz. We're trying to get you out of here, not get arrested for something else."

She glared at the door, as if she could see Pryor on the other side. "He's a dick," she hissed.

I rolled my eyes. "And you and I are both bitches. I don't see a difference."

Titz preened under my apparent praise of being bitches. She scooted closer and lowered her voice. "Are you really going to bump uglies with him?"

"If I answer your damn question, can we talk about you and your affinity for getting parking tickets?"

She nodded her head. "Totally."

"He likes me. Why? I don't fucking know. That's all I know right now."

She enunciated each word slowly. "Are. You. Going. To. Bang. Him?" She bumped her fists together and thrust her hips as she spoke.

"Yes, for God's sake, Titz. I plan on boinking the man's brains out!" I yelled. I slapped my hand over my mouth as Titz cackled like a mad woman. That's when I heard Pryor clear his throat on the other side of the door. "Oh, for fuck's sake," I muttered.

"Does that fall under client confidentiality?" Titz laughed.

"No," Pryor called out.

I closed my eyes and threw up a silent plea for the floor to open up and swallow me whole.

I didn't have such luck. Titz was still laughing, and I swear I could feel Pryor on the other side of the door. I opened my eyes and glared at Titz. "As soon as we get out of this police station, you're dead to me."

She waved her hand and wiped a tear streaking down her cheek from laughing so hard. "I just got you guys past the whole awkwardness you had going between the two of you. I'm sure you were throwing up all sorts of signs that you weren't interested when you were." She sat back and crossed her arms over her chest. "You'll thank me later."

"Doubtful." I leaned on the table, hoping to refocus Titz on the reason why we were in the police station to begin with. "Now we talk about paying these parking tickets."

She rolled her eyes. "I would if I could, Stiletto, but I don't have the money. At least not until the first of the month. I had to pay rent, Violet needed lunch money, Jasmin had two school field trips, and I had to pay for daycare for Dahlia and Rose. My check was gone before I could even cash the damn thing."

"Titz," I moaned. She was a single mom and was the only one there for her kids. I hated she had to work so hard for her paycheck, and it was never enough. "Why didn't you tell one of us you needed a little help?"

She shook her head. "I need a sugar daddy, not help. I wanna stay home with my girls every day, not work twelve hours a day. Sugar. Daddy."

I rolled my eyes. "Well, I don't have one of those in my back pocket, but I have enough to cover your tickets." I pointed my finger at her. "But you gotta promise you'll stop parking in front of the damn fire hydrant."

She huffed. "Do you know how far I'm going to have to walk? Legit, it's almost a mile from the shop to where I'll get a spot to park."

She was overexaggerating. "You're gonna have to deal with it because you can't afford to pay these damn tickets." I stood up and looked down at her. "I'll get the check written, and then you can get to work."

When I turned to the door, she said quietly, "I'm sorry about this."

This wasn't her fault. Well, it was her fault, but the reason behind why she was struggling to get by wasn't. "No need to be sorry, babe. You need to remember the club is there for you. You know between the three of us, we would have helped you out. We'll always help you out."

"Dirty Bitches for life," she whispered.

I nodded. Titz was going to be fine, once I sprung her from the clink.

First, I needed to face Pryor and try not to die from embarrassment from announcing to basically the whole station that I was going to boink his brains out.

"You figure out what's going on?"

I pulled the door shut behind me and looked him square in the eye. "Like you didn't hear everything we said."

He shrugged. "You guys got a little quiet at the end. It was hard to make out even with my ear pressed against the door."

"Are you always this honest?"

"Don't see a point in beating around the bush."

That was a trait I liked, but I didn't need to tell him that. He already knew too much. "I'm paying for the tickets. I just gotta grab my checkbook."

He grabbed my arm before I could turn away. "You don't need to do this, River."

I looked down at his hand on me. "You stop me from leaving a lot."

"Because it's the only way I seem to be able to talk to you."

"We were talking before you grabbed my arm."

"Why do you have to argue with every word that comes out of my mouth?" His voice was low, and it sent a shiver down my spine.

"I don't argue with you." *I did. I totally did.*

His sexy ass smirk spread across his lips. "You're lying to yourself, darlin'."

I was. But I was wanting to be blissfully ignorant, at least until I left the police station. "I'm paying you, and then we're leaving."

"I've got about five hours left of my shift. I can't leave with you."

Oh, for Christ's sake. Now he was a smart-ass. "Not you, Titz. I'm leaving with Titz."

"Don't you think that sounds weird coming out of your mouth? You know, saying you're going to do something with Titz?" He held his hands out in front of him and squeezed the air.

And now he was acting like an eleven-year-old smart-ass. The many sides of Pryor Jones I was seeing today were too much to keep up with. "I'm paying you and I'm leaving. I don't want to see you for at least a week."

The walkie-talkie on his belt went off. "Shots fired on Lawrence and Mickelson."

Clint came streaking down the hallway and skidded out the door, hollering to Pryor that he would meet him in the squad.

"I gotta go, darlin'. You and Titz are free to go. Tell her we'll square up on payment soon, and you and I will also square up real soon." He stalked out of the station without a backward glance.

I collapsed against the wall and sighed.

"Are they gone?" Titz hollered. She threw open the door with a huge smile on her face.

"Yeah. They had a call to get to."

She raised her arms over her head and a gave a weird battle cry. "Freedom!" She threaded her arm through mine and tugged me out the front door. "Let's go before they come back and change their minds."

"You know you still have to pay, right?"

She dragged me over to my bike. "Yeah, but he's gonna have to wait until the end of the month to get any money out of me. Besides, now you don't have to bail me out."

"You were never arrested, Titz." At least not officially. They just needed her to pay her damn tickets.

"I mean, you didn't have to financially bail my ass out, and now we don't have to tell Rogue about this little incident." She smiled brightly and slid her sunglasses over her eyes. "We all win."

I shook my head. "Oh, hell no, Titz. You're telling Rogue about this. I'm not going to get my ass in a sling with her about this."

"It can be our little secret, Stil."

That wasn't going to happen. Keeping a secret from Rogue wasn't a good idea. Ever. "You tell her or I will. Those are your two options."

She stomped her foot. "I thought you were supposed to be my girl. My ride or die."

I rolled my eyes and threw a leg over my bike. "I'm all of that, Titz, but you can't not tell Rogue. Like Pryor said, it's all public record that you got taken in today. Have Rogue hear it from your mouth instead of from someone else in town."

She flipped me off. "Links is now my girl. Even though she spends way too much time in that damn garden of hers."

I shrugged. "Cool. She can be the one you call to bail your ass out from now on." I cranked up the bike and kicked back the kickstand. Titz was pissed I wasn't going to cover for her. That was her own problem. We were part of a club because we were there for each other, not to do dumb shit and keep it from each other. "You have until church tonight to tell her or I will," I yelled over the roar of the engine.

I pulled away from the curb, headed back to the shop.

Titz was mad at me, and Pryor knew I wanted to have sex with him.

That was an eventful half hour I didn't want to repeat anytime soon.

Five

"You're five inches taller than me in those damn things."

I looked down at my feet that were encased in my electric blue Betsey Johnson pumps. "What's your point?"

Links shrugged. "Didn't really have one."

I plopped down in the chair to the right of Rogue. "Am I late?"

Rogue shook her head. "No. Titz called and said she was running behind. Some shit about a guy being a pussy, and she had to give him five breaks too many."

"She say anything else?"

Rogue turned to me. "No. Should she have?"

I held up my hand and shook my head. "Yeah, but I'll give her a little leeway since she was busy at work today."

"Maybe there's something you need to say, Stiletto." Links sat in the chair opposite me, a smug smile on her face.

"I'm here, I'm here," Titz sang out as she burst into the small room where we held our weekly meetings. She pulled the chair out next to Links and glared across the table at me.

She was apparently still mad at me for telling her she needed to tell Rogue what happened this morning. I also knew this because she normally sat next to me during the meetings.

Links turned, looking her up and down. "Are you lost?"

Titz huffed. "No, you're my breast friend."

Rogue snorted. "You mean best?"

Titz shook her head. "No, I'll stick with breast. Links has a rack I can appreciate." Titz winked, and ogled Links' chest. "Perky," she mumbled.

Links splayed her hand over her chest. "All right, this is too fucking weird. What the hell's going on?"

I leaned forward and rested my elbows on the table.

Titz pointed her finger at me. "Shut it, Stiletto. I'm still pissed at you."

A shit-eating grin spread across my lips. "I didn't say a word." I circled my finger above my head. "I'm an angel."

"Bullshit," Rogue scoffed. "You two were up to something, so one of you better spill."

I held up my hands and sat back. "I wasn't up to anything other than ba—"

Titz silenced me by slamming her hand down on the table. "I was pulled over today. Got pulled into the station because I owe four hundred dollars in parking tickets and fines."

Rogue laughed.

A reaction Titz and I hadn't expected.

"Tell me something I don't know."

My jaw dropped, and Titz squawked, "You knew?"

Rogue cracked her knuckles, and one word fell from her lips I didn't see coming. "Clint."

I threw my head back and laughed.

"Why that little rat!" Titz stood up and paced the short space behind her chair. "Here I was, worried as hell about telling you, and all along, you freakin' knew."

"Clint may be terrified of you, Titz, but he and I have an understanding. He takes in any Dirty Bitch, he calls to let me know."

"And this is why she's the president," Links smirked.

Rogue pointed at the chair next to me. "Sit your ass next to Stiletto. You being over there next to Links is throwing me off."

Titz stopped pacing. "I'm trying to adjust to the idea that not only is Stiletto nailing the sheriff, but now you're in bed with Clint."

Rogue shook her head. "The only person I'm in bed with is Lachlan."

Titz wrinkled her nose. "Ew."

Rogue looked at me. "You wanna tell me exactly why that's ew?"

I shrugged. "Not a damn clue. I think she's grasping at straws right now."

"The only thing I'm interested in grasping right now is a damn drink," Titz stated. She strolled around the table and sat down next to me. "You can be my main bitch, but only because you're shacking up with Sheriff Hot Pants, and you can get me out of those tickets."

Yeah, like that was going to happen. "That was a quick change of heart."

Titz shrugged. "I live with four girls. You have to know my hormones are crazy. It's like we all feed off each other. Lord help any man who tries to take us all on."

"I don't think there's a man born who can handle the five of you." Links flipped open her notebook and held her pen in her hand, ready to take notes.

"I can totally get down with being a cougar."

I looked at Titz out of the corner of my eye. "You lost me."

"My dream man isn't born yet. I've got a good eighteen years before I can properly rob him from the cradle. Cougar time."

"This is where her reasoning and thought process baffles me. I never in a million years would've thought so much into that." Rogue shook her head. "Have to give her credit on some level there."

"Can we get on with the meeting?" Links asked.

Titz stuck her tongue out at her. "Missing diddling in your garden?"

Links rolled her eyes, but decided not to engage with Titz in their normal banter over her garden.

Rogue grabbed her gavel from the table and slammed it down. "I love that," she said giddily. She cleared her throat and got down to business. "There isn't much to go over besides Titz having too many run-ins with the law. How's the garage doing, Stiletto?"

I shrugged. "Doing good." Technically, the club owned Bane Repair, but I was the only one who worked there. "Mr. Johns was in the other day. He called the sheriff on me about changing his fluids without asking."

"I heard," Rogue said, nodding her head.

"Man, Clint's really on the ball with reporting to you. We might have to make him an honorary Dirty Bitch," Links snorted, and I reached across the table to bump my fist with hers.

Titz growled and muttered Clint's name under her breath. There was definitely going to be some contention between her and Clint now that she knew Clint was reporting to Rogue about us.

"Other than that, all good. Sneaks mentioned to me that some douche she was dating had bad mouthed Bane Repair."

"What the fuck for?" Titz demanded.

I waved my hand. "The usual. I'm a chick and don't know what I'm doing was the gist of it."

Titz sat back. "I hear that shit every day. Don't know what having a dick hanging between your legs has to do with working on cars or holding a tattoo gun in your hand."

"Or being in an MC," Links added.

"Preach," Rogue mumbled. "What about the tattoo shop, Titz?"

"Slinging ink and trying to make money," Titz drawled.

"Business picking up?" It was like trying to get information from a rock when it came to Titz.

She shrugged. "I think. My closet of mystery is getting some good hits. I think it's all the stiff discounts I give."

Links groaned, and I couldn't help but snicker.

Rogue rolled her eyes. "I'll be over next week to see for myself."

Titz mimicked her in a high voice, but didn't tell her no. Telling Rogue no wasn't a good thing to do.

"Then that's it. We do have a run with Southern Lords coming up in a few week. Make sure you guys are there."

"Wait, wait. Why don't you tell us what's going on with the salon?" Titz had a smug look on her face. She was such a smart-ass. "I think it's only fair you report on how that's doing. It's club business after all."

Rogue rolled her eyes. "It's good. Playing with scissors for the sheer fun of it." Rogue banged the gavel and tossed it on the table.

We all groaned at her ridiculously puny joke. "And that's where the meeting ends." I stood up and pushed my chair back. "Who wants a drink?"

Links, Titz, and Rogue all raised their hands. "And this is why we're a club." Titz laughed. "Fifteen-minute meetings and drinks all night."

"You got a babysitter tonight?" Links asked.

"Yeah. Fifteen-year-old next door is saving up for a car, so I offered to pay her ten bucks an hour to watch the hellions when I'm doing club shit."

"So eloquent," Rogue muttered. "Club shit."

"Hey," Titz protested. "That's what it is."

Rogue put her arm around Titz's shoulder, and they walked out of the small room arguing about the fact that club business was not shit.

"Hey," Links called.

I raised my arms over my head and stretched. "What's up?"

"Pryor finally made his move?"

What? "What do you mean by 'finally'?"

She rolled her eyes and stood up. "I figured you had no clue."

"Hold the hell up. What do you mean? You had a clue?" How did Links have a clue when I didn't? I'd always thought Pryor was hot as hell, but I didn't think it would mean he was interested in me.

"I just had a hunch."

"Well, the next time you have a hunch about some hot guy having the hots for me, maybe you should throw the information my way."

Links laughed and closed her notebook.

"You know, for you being all techy and shit, I'm surprised you don't use a laptop to take notes."

"Eh," she mumbled. "I spend all day putzing around with a computer. Sometimes it's nice to hold a pen and write on paper."

"I get that. When it's time to do maintenance on my bike, it's more of a chore than it should be. Working on everyone else's cars exhausts me, so it's hard to do my own shit."

We walked out to the main room of the clubhouse and bellied up to the bar Titz was behind mixing drinks. "What do you bitches want?" she asked.

"Usual," Links and I said in unison.

"Harvey Wallbanger and whiskey on the rocks coming up." Titz grabbed two glasses and dropped ice cubes into each of them.

"Where did Rogue go?" I asked as I looked around.

Titz looked up from the glass she was pouring whiskey into. "Good ol' Lachlan called. I think Rogue was on her way home to get laid."

"What do we think of Lachlan?" Links asked.

"As long as Rogue is happy, I'm good with the guy." Titz set down the bottle of whiskey.

Links elbowed me. "What about you?"

I shrugged. "Doesn't have much to do with me. If she's in love, good for her."

Titz set the whiskey on the rocks in front of Links. "How nice of you, Stiletto."

I held my hands up. "Look, from what I've seen in life, love doesn't mean a thing. I hope Rogue and Lachlan last, but I know something like that doesn't exist for everyone."

"What if something like that exists with Sheriff Hot Ass?" Titz asked as she wiggled her eyebrows.

"Crazy talk, Titz. Once he gets to know me he'll run for the hills, just like every other guy in my life." Marcus, Zander, Del, and Monk. Names of the guys who said they were going to stay but always left when they found the grass was greener on the side. "Pryor and I have a few rolls in hay to look forward to, and then he'll find some sweet girl to spend the rest of his life with. I'll just be some crazy chick he used to know."

Titz rolled her eyes. "Not only was that all bullshit, but now you got the damn song stuck in my head."

"Somebody I used to know," Links sang.

Titz held her fist out and bumped it against Links'. "Sing it, sista. I'm glad I'm not the only one who's going to have it stuck in their head all night."

Links got off her barstool, drink in hand, and wandered over to the jukebox. "You know what song we should have in our head in honor of Stiletto thinking love sucks?"

"I never said love sucks." It just wasn't in the cards for me. Gave up on that shit a long time ago.

"You Give Love a Bad Name" sounded over the speakers, and I dropped my chin to my chest.

"Oh, hell to the yes." Titz pumped her fist in the air and abandoned mixing my drink in exchange for climbing on top of the bar to dance. She pulled Links up with her, and in-between singing and dancing, they tried to pull me up with them. I managed to brush them off, not wanting to become a part of their impromptu dance party.

I moved behind the bar as another Bon Jovi song played and made my own drink since Titz and Links were grooving. "For the record," I called out during an instrumental break, "that song doesn't really fit Pryor. He's actually a good guy."

Titz crouched down and grabbed the bottle of vodka. "The song is about you, not Pryor. You give love a bad name because you don't believe in love."

"That's not what the song is about," Links chided. She was jamming out on her air guitar and arching her back.

"How the hell do you know that?" Titz asked.

"Because it's about a chick who gets guys to fall for her, and then she's gone before they know what hit them."

I tilted my head to the side. "Really?" I guess I'd never really paid attention to the lyrics closely before, or actually thought about what they meant.

"Yes, really. I like this song, but "Unbreakable" will always be my Bon Jovi jam." She hopped off the bar and danced over to the jukebox. "How the hell do we not have that song on here?"

"Probably because the damn jukebox is from the eighties and hasn't been updated since." I finished making my drink and sat back down on my stool.

"Then "Bed of Roses" is gonna to have to do then," she mumbled.

Titz jumped off the bar and filled a glass with vodka, then dropped a couple of cherries into it. "So what are you going to do about Sheriff Hot Ass?"

"Go in there with no expectations at all, and not be disappointed when he leaves me for June Cleaver in two weeks."

Titz clanked her glass against mine. "To hot monkey sex for at least two weeks."

Links picked up her glass and finished it in two swallows. "I'm not cheering to that because you and Pryor are going to last a hell of a lot longer than that."

I rolled my eyes and took a swig from my glass. "You're delusional, Links."

She shrugged and set her glass in front of Titz for her to refill. "Just you wait and see, Stiletto. I think Pryor's just the man to make you see love is in the cards for you."

Titz pointed a finger at me. "As long as she doesn't become the heartbreaker from "You Give Love a Bad Name."

"No worries about that with me." I wasn't going to break Pryor's heart, because there was no way in hell the man would ever love me.

Six

I ordered a shit ton of Chinese. Be here at seven.

I looked down at the message on my phone for the fifth time.

Two things ran through my mind.

How in the hell did he get my phone number, and just plain why?

It had been over a week since I'd sprung Titz for unpaid parking tickets, and I hadn't seen or heard from Pryor since. Well, since before he sent me this text message an hour ago.

There was one thing I liked about the message and one thing I hated.

Chinese was my weakness. Well, Pryor was more of a weakness, but now that he was offering me Chinese, it was a double weakness. But, and it was a big but, he was *telling* me to be there by seven. I didn't have a choice. He wasn't asking me to be there. He was telling me to be there.

That didn't sit well with me. So much so, that even though it involved Chinese and Pryor, I didn't want to go just out of sheer principle of having someone telling me what to do. Especially a man.

"Earth to River."

I shook my head at Kit's voice and shoved my phone in my pocket. "I didn't hear you come in."

The loud music I'd been blaring was turned down to a quiet roar. "That's because it sounds like you're at a Bon Jovi concert in here." Kit yanked on her ear and shook her head. "Lordy, woman. I'm gonna have to get my hearing checked."

I grabbed a towel from the bench and wiped my hands. "You come here just to turn my music down?"

She plopped her ass down on a stack of tires. "No. I came to tell you I move into my new place at the end of the month."

The phone call I had placed to Marvin had done the trick to get Kit into the duplex two streets over. "That's good news."

She shrugged. "Yeah, I guess it is. Now all I need to do is figure out what I want to do with the rest of my life."

"Easy peasy," I smirked.

"Right," she drawled. "So, what's been going on with you? Wanna come over and help me start packing tonight?"

"Just been working." I thought about the text message Pryor had sent me and found that helping Kit pack was just the excuse I needed for why I couldn't make it. "I can come over after work with a pizza if you provide the wine." Packing sucked, but if I had pizza and wine, it would be bearable.

"Deal," she agreed. "You can confirm all the gossip I've heard about Titz getting arrested by Sheriff Hot Pants."

I laughed and tossed the dirty rag into the garbage. "I'm really not surprised you heard about that." You would be amazed at the number of people who listened to police scanners or checked the daily police beat that was posted in the paper every morning.

"You can also tell me what's been going on with *you* and Sheriff Hot Pants."

"What?" I gasped. "You read about me and Pryor in the newspaper?" I really shouldn't be surprised if that were the case. We lived in a small town where the drive-in in town made the news when they changed the specials.

Kit laughed and shook her head. "Nope. I saw him dropping you off last week, remember?"

My heartbeat slowed, and I took a deep breath. Thank God I hadn't made the newspaper. "There isn't anything to tell." And at this moment, there really wasn't anything to tell. He'd demanded my presence tonight, but I knew I wasn't going to go, so it wasn't anything I needed to mention to Kit.

She hummed and tilted her head to the side. "That's not what Titz and Links have to say."

"Those bitches!" I hollered. "So much for keeping club business in the club."

"You and the sheriff bumping uglies isn't club business. Well, unless you're bumping uglies with him because you're trying to get the club out of trouble, then it might be considered club business," she pondered.

I wrinkled my nose. "I would do a lot for the club, but whoring myself out isn't one of those things I would do."

"Duly noted."

The fact it had to be noted worried me a bit. "I assume that since you talked to Links and Titz, you also asked them about becoming a patched member?"

She nodded. "Talked to Rogue too. She's all in for me prospecting for a bit and then getting my patch."

A smile spread across my lips. "See? What did I tell you, Kit? All you have to do is know what kind of life you want and take it."

"Again, it's really not easy, but I have to say, I wouldn't have anything if I didn't take a chance and go after it." She chewed on her bottom lip. "I do have one more thing I want to ask you."

I couldn't do much else for her, so I had no idea what she was about to ask for. "You think I could get a job here taking care of the front end while you get dirty and everything back here?"

Say what? I'd tried to get Kit to go into business with me a few years back, but she had insisted that she wanted to do everything for herself, and working at Bane Repair wasn't a way to do things alone. "Can I ask why you suddenly want a job here?" I got why she'd turned down the offer before, but it had stung a bit when I said we could do it together as a family, and she'd shot me down faster than Tom Cruise with a volleyball in *Top Gun.*

"I was a stubborn idiot for turning you down before. Can I just say that I'm dumb and stubborn and move on from this?" She jumped up from the stack of tires and held her hand out to me.

"What's this?"

"A handshake, River. If you don't know what one of these looks like, then I think we need to get you out of this garage more often."

I titled my head to the side. "What am I shaking your hand for?"

"For agreeing to give me a job. Totally on a trial basis, of course, if that'll make you happier. I get you don't want to be stuck with me if I blow major donkey balls."

I looked at her hand, which was clean, having no traces of dirt on it. "You'll be here on time and be here for however long I need you to stay?"

She nodded her head. "Totally. I'll be here every morning before you."

I hesitantly shook her hand, hoping I hadn't made a bad decision.

"Now, let's talk about Pryor."

I released her hand. I wasn't going to talk about Pryor anymore. At least not until I figured out what the hell, if anything, was going on between us.

And while he wanted me to go over there at seven tonight, I wasn't going to. If I was going to go over to his house, I was going to do it under my own conditions. If he wanted anything to do with me, he was going to learn how not to deal with me real quick.

I did things my own way, and if someone didn't like it, then it was their problem, not mine.

I was going to find out real soon if Pryor was okay with that.

Seven

"Ugh." Sesame chicken was my favorite. "So good," I whispered to the delicious tray of ooey gooey chicken. Even if it was cold, it was still the best.

The light from the fridge shone brightly, and I glanced behind me to make sure the handsome man was still snoring peacefully on the couch. I could see the pillow his head had been laying on before, but now his head wasn't there. "Fuck." I crept away from the fridge, keeping the door open, and looked over the edge of the couch, hoping he had maybe fallen off and was sleeping on the floor now.

"I'm not sure if I should arrest you for breaking and entering, or just be thankful you finally came over on your own."

"Holy fuck!" My heart stopped, and I jumped up. The container of delicious food in my hand went flying, landing upside down on the rug.

Pryor chuckled from the dark hallway. "Pretty sure I'm supposed to be the one who's scared, not you, darlin'."

"Well I'm not standing in a dark hallway, am I? I was in the light of the damn fridge."

"Eating my food."

I pointed down at the container. "*Was.* I was eating your food until you woke up and rudely decided to scare me."

"I don't know how it happened, but somehow, I'm in the wrong in this, aren't I?"

"Yes," I hissed. "You can't scare people like that, Pryor. What would you have done if I came in here and stood two inches away from you until you woke up?"

"That wouldn't have happened because I heard you before you even came in the door."

I looked over at him. "Bullshit." I'd been quiet. *So* quiet. I didn't even have to pick the lock. "You should really lock your door at night."

He stepped into the kitchen and stood in front of the fridge. "It was. I unlocked it when I heard your bike."

I looked at the door, then back at him. "What do you mean you unlocked it?" I repeat, I'd been quiet. There was no way in hell he would've been able to hear me.

"Your bike, Stiletto. It ain't fucking quiet, even when you shut it off a block away and walk it."

My jaw dropped. "Bullshit."

He reached into the fridge and pulled out another container of Chinese food. "I'm the sheriff, darlin'. If you would've been able to break into my house without me knowing, I think I would have to hand in my shiny star and go work at the local fast food joint."

That was pretty true. As a citizen of Magnolia Springs, I should be happy he was good at his job, but as the woman who had tried to sneak into his house, I was mad. "Well, the fact that you're so good at your job is the reason I wasted a whole container of sesame chicken." I crouched down and flipped over the container. Yes, I was going to blame this whole thing on him.

"Good thing I bought two."

I glanced over at him. "Could you stop being a good guy for like, two minutes? Just let me be a bitch without feeling guilty about it, yeah?"

He shrugged and snapped the lid off the container. "You want this warmed up, or do you need to eat it by the light of the fridge for it to be good?"

"You ruined the thrill of eating it by the light of the fridge."

He stuck it in the microwave, and I finished cleaning up my mess. I dumped it in the garbage can, and Pryor grabbed the small rug I'd dumped it on and disappeared down the hallway.

"I can clean that for you!" I called out.

When I heard the sound of his washer starting up, I sagged against the counter. Why was I always making a fool of myself when Pryor was around?

He walked back into the kitchen, just as the microwave pinged. "Can I eat some of this or no?" He opened a drawer and pulled out two forks.

"It's your house and your chicken."

"You broke in just to eat it." He held the fork out to me. "You want me to open the fridge for the light?"

I snatched the fork out of his hand. "No, smart-ass. I told you the mood has been ruined."

He picked up the steaming container of food and nodded toward the living room. "Let's see if we can get another kind of mood going."

I opened the fridge and grabbed two beers. "The mood is awkward as fuck, Pryor. At least for me it is."

He chuckled and waited for me to move into the living room. Plopping myself down in the middle of the couch, I held my hands up for him to give me the food, but he shook his head and sat down next to me. "I'm controlling the chicken, woman. I know how you handle it from the fact that my washing machine is running at two o'clock in the morning."

I huffed and stabbed a piece of chicken out of the container. "Do I want to know why you have two big containers of sesame chicken in your fridge?"

"Links told me it was your favorite."

My jaw dropped with my fork in midair. "That traitor."

He shrugged. "She happened to be walking past the police station today and mentioned you were coming over tonight."

"*I* didn't even know I was coming over," I insisted. I'd talked to her earlier in the day, but I hadn't said anything about coming over. She'd asked me what I was doing about Pryor, and I hadn't answered. It was like the woman was inside my head and knew what I was going to do before I even did.

He shrugged and forked a big chunk of chicken into his mouth.

We ate in silence while I figured out what the heck I wanted to say.

"You done with this?" he asked.

I looked down at the half-empty container. I could probably eat the rest with no problem, but we needed to talk.

I grabbed my beer off the counter and watched Pryor strut into the kitchen and snap the lid back on the chicken. "Why do you like me, Pryor?"

He looked over his shoulder at me. "I feel like this might be a trick question."

"It's not." It really wasn't. I was honestly curious to know what it was about me he liked. I knew what I liked about myself, but I didn't think my tough as nails attitude and the fact I was a kick-ass mechanic were the reasons he shared his Chinese food with me.

He put the leftovers in the fridge and grabbed two more beers. "I like you, River."

I rolled my eyes. "I'm gonna need you to be a bit more specific than that."

He flipped the lights off in the kitchen and grabbed the remote to the TV on his way to the couch. "You're a Dirty Bitch."

He sat down next to me, and I turned sideways to face him. "I really didn't think that was going to be something you liked about me."

"I wasn't finished."

Oh. "Sorry."

He handed me a fresh beer, and I set it down on the coffee table.

"You're a Dirty Bitch, but I know you're so much more than that. While you walk around with a huge chip on your shoulder, the fact that you wear those tall ass shoes and take care of your sister, tells me there's a hell of a lot more to you than some club."

"What's wrong with my shoes?"

He shook his head. "Not a damn thing. I've never seen a woman with sexier legs than yours, and I know it's because of those shoes."

I looked down at the white canvas shoes I had on. "I chose stealthy over sexy tonight."

He chuckled. "Probably a good choice. I don't think pushing your bike a block in heels would've been easy."

"So you like me for my shoes?" Odd.

"No, River, I like you for you."

"But you really don't know me."

"But I want to get to know you. More than I already do."

I reached up and ran my fingertips along his jawline. "You want to know me, or you just want to fall into bed with me?"

He grabbed my hand and pulled it down to his lap. "If you think I want you here just to know what your body feels like under mine, then you don't know me at all, darlin'."

"That's the only thing I've ever been able to give, Pryor. No one's ever wanted more than that."

"I want that, but I also want a hell of a lot more from you." He grabbed me around the waist and pulled me onto his lap. "Though I have to admit, there's going to be at least one time where I fuck you with your heels on."

I rolled my eyes and rested my hands on his shoulders. "You were being all romantic, wooing my black heart, and then you had to throw that in there."

His hands rested on the curve of my ass and squeezed. "Don't act like you don't like that, darlin'."

"I don't know what the hell is happening with us, Pryor, so I can't say what I do and don't like because you've seriously fried my brain."

"I'm going to take that as a compliment."

I leaned forward and rested my forehead against his. "You're the sheriff, Pryor."

"Last I checked, that was true."

"The Dirty Bitches are my life."

"Also true."

I sighed. He didn't get what I was saying. "I'm not going to give them up to be with you."

"Last I also checked, I never said you had to do that. As long as I don't have to share my bed with Titz, Links, and Rogue, I'm fine with the Dirty Bitches."

"Do you really have to be so agreeable with everything?" Men like Pryor weren't a dime a dozen. I had somehow wound up in his lap, and I'm sure I was going to fuck it up at least once or twice.

"I try to see both sides to everything, darlin'. So while I have to detain Titz for showing her tits and unpaid parking tickets, I know that doesn't have anything to do with you or the club."

"Can I just say with Titz, you never really know what she's going to do. The fact that you try to see both sides is good, but you might have to *really* look to see her side."

He chuckled low. "I've come to find that out."

"So this is it then?" I asked.

"This is far from it, River. This is just the beginning of you and me."

I gulped and bit my lip. "I'm absolutely terrified and turned on all at the same time. It's a rather odd sensation."

"Stop being terrified, darlin', and just feel." He pressed his lips to mine before I could tell him that was easier said than done. He kissed me hard and deep, then his mouth went from mine, down my cheek to my ear, and I pressed into him. My fingers flexed into his shoulders as I ground my core onto him.

"I want you, River. God dammit, I want all of you," he growled into my ear.

My head turned so I could touch the tip of my tongue to his earlobe. "I want you too, Pryor."

His hand trailed around from my ass and cupped my breast through my shirt. "I've waited too long to hear you say those words." His voice was thick with need, and I flexed my hips around him. A growl slipped from his lips, and his hand squeezed my breast. His other hand moved across my waist to cup my sex.

"That escalated quickly," I gasped. I drew in a breath of needy anticipation as he turned his head and pressed his lips against mine again.

My fingers delved into his hair while my other arm wrapped around his shoulders to hold on.

I liked this. Yeah, I *really* liked this. This wasn't a gentle kiss. It was charged, greedy, and a little bit desperate. He took from me, but I also took from him. If this was a glimpse into how explosive things were going to be between us, we were going to burn the house down.

He didn't break the connection of our mouths as he leaned deep into me, slid his hands over my ass and stood up from the couch. I wound my legs around his waist as he turned and walked down the dark hallway. Prowling to the bedroom, he slammed the door open and tossed me onto the bed.

Flipping on the light, he pulled his shirt over his head and was on me before I stopped bouncing on the bed. He pushed me back, settling his weight over me. I arched up, wrapping my arms around his shoulders, and pressed my lips against his.

His hands went to the fly of his jeans and tugged the zipper down as my hands roamed over his bare back. "Hurry," I pleaded against his lips.

"Patience, darlin'."

I didn't have patience when it came to anything. Especially when Pryor Jones's hands were on me. "Fuck patience."

He chuckled and lifted off the bed with one arm and managed to work his pants down with the other hand. "From where I am, you're the one with all her clothes on yet."

Grabbing the hem of my shirt, I yanked it over my head and threw it across the room. I reached for the waistband of my stretchy yoga pants to tug them down, but Pryor knocked my hands out of the way and did it for me. "I'm not even surprised you don't have underwear on," he laughed.

I looked down at his rock-hard dick laying against my leg between us. "I see no point in underwear, and I see you share that same sentiment."

He shrugged and lowered his body over mine again. I ran my hands over his strong, muscled back and sighed. "Like what you feel, darlin'?"

"Feel *and* see." I could only imagine the hours Pryor spent working out to get his body into the immaculate shape it was in. The only working out I did was running my mouth.

His gaze connected with mine, and he pressed a quick kiss to my lips.

My hand swiftly trailed down his rock-hard chest, beelining straight to his dick. I wrapped my fingers around him and bit my lip.

He moaned as I moved my hand up and down, pumping his dick. "River," he growled.

He was ready for me. Close to the brink of exploding all over my hand.

He jackknifed off the bed, rummaged in his nightstand, and pulled out a silver little package.

I held my hand out. "Gimme."

He slapped it in my hand and stood at the edge of the bed. I rolled over, and his dick bobbed in front of my face. "I've never seen someone so excited to put a condom on," he laughed.

I tilted my head back and winked. "Safety first."

Wrapping my hand around the base of his cock, I licked the velvety tip. I had an ulterior motive to wanting to put the condom on. It gave me the chance to get my mouth on him and find out what he tasted like.

"Fucking shit," Pryor hissed.

My hand pumped his dick while I wrapped my lips around his shaft and sucked. He threaded his fingers through my hair, gently tugging me closer.

"You keep doing that and we're not gonna need the condom." His voice was strained, and I glanced up to see his eyes were closed as he breathed heavily through his mouth.

My mouth gave one last suck before I pulled back and sat up on my knees. My hand continued to pump his dick as he pulled me in for a kiss. "You're gonna be the death of me, River," he mumbled against my lips.

"No dying on me, Sheriff. I'm pretty sure we're gonna have to do this at least a couple more times." I ripped open the condom, rolled it onto his dick, and enjoyed his intake of breath when I gave him a slight squeeze. "All suited up. Time to show me what you've got."

"Isn't that what I've been doing the whole time?" he asked. He pressed a hand to my shoulder and pushed me back onto the bed. I laid back with my hands over my head and my legs fell open. Pryor fell between them and slowly kissed his way up my body. "You ready for me?" His hand cupped my pussy as he pressed a kiss to my neck.

"I was ready the second you took your shirt off. Apparently, I'm easy." At least when it came to Pryor Jones. The man got my engine running with a couple of steamy looks and removing one piece of clothing.

His fingers swiped through my drenched pussy and flicked my clit. "Not easy, darlin'. At least not for anyone but me." He sucked my nipple into his mouth, and I delved my fingers into his hair.

My hips moved with his hand as he pumped his finger inside me while his tongue swirled around my nipple. "Pryor, please." I needed to feel him inside me. I just needed him.

"You want me?"

Want was the wrong word. "Need. I need you," I gasped.

His hand moved from my pussy as I thrust my hips up, pleading for more.

He pinned me down on the bed with his body and pressed a long, demanding kiss to my lips. "Tell me what you need," he whispered.

"You. I just need you." I was beyond the point of caring. If I looked like a needy bitch, I didn't care. There was a fire raging inside of me, and Pryor was the only person who could put the flames out.

He thrust deep, his cock stretching and filling me. "Waited too fucking long for this, River. Too. Long," he said with each thrust.

This wasn't sweet.

It wasn't slow.

That wasn't what either of us wanted.

God, he felt good. So good. His face was buried in my neck, and I felt his teeth nip at my skin. The slight pang of pain mixed with the pleasure had me slamming my eyes shut.

My hips moved with his thrusts as my heels dug into the mattress.

My body jolted as his hips pounded into me harder and faster, driving me closer and closer to the brink of ecstasy. "River," he growled.

I flexed the inner walls of my pussy at the sound of my name on his lips. "Yes," I gasped. I lifted my hips higher to meet his thrusts.

He drove deep, giving me everything he could, yet I still wanted more.

Rough.

Hard.

Greedy.

"Come for me, River. Come for me," he demanded against my lips. His hand snaked down my body to flick my clit, causing me to explode around him. He thrust deep, his breathing labored, with his eyes locked on mine.

He fucked me hard while I rode out my orgasm. "Fuck yeah, River. Fuck," he groaned.

His eyes slammed shut as he thrust one last time, slamming into me. I wrapped my arms around his shoulders and pulled him close.

"Shit, River," he gasped. "Shit." He shifted his weight to his forearm and looked down at me.

"Um, hi?"

"Fuck her like my life depended on it and all she has to say is hi," he muttered.

So I guess I wasn't good at the whole talking thing. "Uh, that was awesome?" I gave a lame thumbs up, trying to rack my brain for something better to say. My problem was that I had no idea what to say. Pryor had fucked me into a stupor that was going to take me time to surface from.

He collapsed onto the pillow next to me. "We'll have to work on that."

"Does that mean we're going to do it again? Soon?"

He lifted his head. "Give me fifteen minutes. Ten if you help me along."

A grin spread across my lips. "I think I can help with that."

He dropped his head to the pillow and closed his eyes. "You really are going to be the death of me, River, but it's gonna be one explosive death."

Eight

"All available officers, please report to West Highland. Shots fired."

Pryor rolled out of bed as I cracked my eyes open. "Stay here, darlin'. I shouldn't be gone too long."

He pulled the blanket over me, and I rolled over on my side to watch him move about the room. Grabbing a pair of pants and a shirt from the closet, he put them on and grabbed a pair of socks from the drawer before sitting down on the edge of the bed.

"What are you doing?" I asked sleepily.

"Putting my boots on. Go back to sleep." He finished tying his boots before moving into the closet. I heard the familiar sounds of checking a gun for bullets. I sat up, wide awake, and pulled the blanket up to cover my bare chest.

"Pryor," I called out.

He walked out of the closet, a gun strapped to his hip. "Go back to sleep."

"Sleep?" I cried. "You're walking out of the house with a gun strapped to your hip, headed to where there's some maniac with a gun."

"It's my job, River. I need to go. We can talk about this when I get back."

He was out of the room before I could even form a cohesive sentence. The front door slammed shut, and I heard him lock it.

I looked around the dark room.

What in the hell?

Pryor was the sheriff.

This is what he did.

He ran in when everyone else ran out.

These were all things I knew, but now I was sitting in an empty bedroom all alone with Pryor's pillow still warm next to me, and I didn't know what to do.

"I started filing all the past invoices. You really had no filing system in place. It's a good thing you hired me."

I dropped my wrench on the workbench and grabbed my phone to see if there was a missed call or message from Pryor.

"River?"

I looked up from my phone, let down by the fact that there wasn't any word from Pryor, and looked at Kit. "Yeah?"

"Did you hear anything I just said?"

Honestly? Not one single word. I'd been in a fog all morning from my lack of sleep and worrying about Pryor. "No." I didn't even have it in me to try.

"What in the hell is wrong with you? Are you drunk or something?"

God, I wish I had a drink right now. Getting drunk might help kill all the craziness in my head.

After Pryor had left, I padded out into the living room to see it was only four thirty in the morning, which meant we'd only slept for maybe forty-five minutes before the call had gone out.

Pryor had said he would be back soon, but he wasn't. I'd curled up on the couch with the blanket he'd draped across the back of the couch and stared at the front door.

I sat there for three hours. He never came back. I tried calling him, but it only rang. I didn't want to seem like some psycho by calling and texting him, but I was worried. He went into a situation where there were shots fired, and I didn't know if more shots were fired after he got there.

When I couldn't sit there waiting any longer, I gathered all my clothes, took a shower, then headed back home to change. Now I was at the garage and it was half-past eleven with no word from Pryor. To say I was freaking out would be an understatement.

"Uh, nothing's wrong. I just didn't get a lot of sleep last night." I tossed my phone in my toolbox and sighed.

Kit skipped over to the workbench and hoisted herself to sit on the only clear space. "A certain sheriff wouldn't have something to do with that, would he?"

Was there really a point in denying it? I decided to go with silence. Didn't deny it, but also didn't confirm it.

"I happened to take a drive past good ol' Pryor's house and saw a familiar bike parked out front."

Oh, for Christ's sake. "Are you kidding me? Now you're checking up on me?"

She shrugged. "I was worried. I came by and you weren't anywhere to be found. I called Titz, Links, and Rogue to see if you were with them, but Links said you had plans with Pryor."

"How?" I demanded. How could Links have possibly known? "Links is physic. I swear to God she is."

"Nah. She just caught on that Pryor likes you." Kit cracked her gum. "So, how did last night go?" She wiggled her eyebrows.

"You looked way too much like Titz when you did that."

"You're avoiding the question. I don't need in-depth details, but I need something here."

"I went over there. We had a good time. Then he had a call about shots fired, and then he had to leave."

"Oh my God," she gasped. "Is he okay?"

I closed my eyes and dropped my chin to my chest. "I have no freakin' clue because I haven't seen him since he walked out early this morning."

"Did you call him?"

I nodded my head. "Four times."

"Text? Maybe he can't talk?"

I held up six fingers. Yes, I had texted him six times. Each text more desperate than the last.

"I'm sure he's okay," she said reassuringly. "He's doing his job, Riv."

"I let him in, Kit. Like, *really* let him in." Every wall I had built up around my heart had crumbled. Pryor Jones was one of the good guys and he wanted me.

Me, River Bane, who never really did anything good in her life except vow to take care of her sister and club, was who Pryor wanted. I'd fought it for as long as I could, but no one could resist a man like him for too long.

"That's good, River. You need to do that. You can't be alone for the rest of your life."

"I'm not alone," I insisted. "I have you and the club."

"Yeah, but the club and I aren't going to keep your bed warm at night."

I wrinkled my nose. "Well, of course not. You know what I meant."

"I do, River, but you need more in your life than me and the club."

"This is a change of pace. Normally, I'm the one spewing life wisdom on you, not the other way around." I opened my eyes and smiled. "I'm not really sure I like this at all."

The bell dinged out front, thankfully interrupting this weird heart-to-heart moment Kit and I were having.

"I'll get that. You try calling Pryor again." Kit skipped to the front office, humming under her breath.

She seemed happier. Working at the garage might not be her dream job, but it was better than working at the foundry for her.

I grabbed my phone from the toolbox and tried calling Pryor one more time. If he didn't answer, it was going to be a sign that I needed to stop. I held the phone to my ear, listening to the ringer.

One ring… two rings… three rings… "Kit, your phone's ringing!" I hollered. She must have dropped it when she was back here.

Four rings.

"Not my phone!" she called out.

I spun around in the direction the ringing phone was coming from, and saw Pryor standing there, his ringing phone in his hand.

"I saw you called me. Five times."

"Six text messages," I whispered.

"I was going to call you when I got out of the station, but I really wanted to see you."

I dropped my phone, sprinted the distance between us and launched myself into his arms. Thankfully, Pryor had good reflexes and managed not to drop me on the floor. I buried my face in his neck and inhaled.

"This mean you really wanted to see me too?" he chuckled.

"Shut up," I mumbled. Tears threatened to fall, so I wrapped my arms and legs tight around him and squeezed. "I hate you," I hiccupped.

"That why you're not letting me go right now because you hate me so much?"

"Hooray!" Kit squealed. I peeked over Pryor's shoulder to see her standing in the doorway to the office, clapping her hands together.

"Go home," I ordered.

She gave me a thumbs up. "Can do, boss woman." She shut the door to the office, and I resumed smelling Pryor.

His hands were plastered to my ass, and he moved farther into the garage. "What are we doing?" I mumbled. My butt bumped the workbench, and he set me down. He stayed between my legs, and I didn't unplaster myself from him.

"Darlin', let go of me for a sec."

I shook my whole body. "Nah."

"I go from not being able to get close to you, to now being unable to get your hands off of me."

"You scared me."

He held me close and pressed a kiss to my head. "Sit back, River. I promise, I'm not leaving."

I growled and sat back, but kept my legs wrapped around his waist. "You worried me."

"I was fine, River."

"But how was I supposed to know that?"

"Because I'm good at my job."

I rolled my eyes. "You deal with people who break the law, and if they break the law, then I'm sure they wouldn't think twice about hurting you."

"Titz breaks the law."

I waved my hand. "You know what I mean."

"There wasn't any danger. At least not to Clint and me. I can't say the same for Mr. Johns and his mistress."

My jaw dropped. "Mr. Johns has a mistress?"

Pryor nodded his head. "Well, he did."

"Shut. Up. Tell me what happened."

He tucked my hair behind my ear. "Normally, I can't say anything, but since it's about to hit the news, I can tell you."

I slapped him on the chest. "What are you waiting for? Spill."

"Mr. Johns is married, but also has a little side piece who decided she didn't want to be on the side anymore."

"Oh Lord."

He nodded his head. "So after Mr. Johns got his jollies off last night, he went home, but she followed him. One thing led to another, and Mrs. Johns got her gun she kept in the hall closet and shot at Mr. Johns and his mistress who were arguing on the front lawn. She thought they were trying to break into the house."

I wrinkled my nose. "Do we believe her?"

Pryor shrugged. "Still investigating."

"That's all you can tell, isn't it?"

"Yeah."

I sighed. "Well, that's exciting, and I'm glad to know you weren't in any danger."

"I left my phone in the cruiser and didn't see that you'd called me until we had the scene cleared."

"Guess that's acceptable. Although, I don't think I'm going to be able to handle this all the time. I might have to ride along with you."

He shook his head. "That's a negative, darlin'."

My smile dropped. "Come on, it'll be fun."

"No. Because if you start doing that, then you know Titz is going to catch wind of it, and then she's gonna want to come along too."

He had a very valid point. "Well, that sucks."

"Calls like that don't happen very often around here."

"You had one a week ago that was just like that."

"And I was back in the station thirty minutes later. It was Richard Melton shooting a crow, and his neighbor called it in not knowing."

"Oh, well." I guess that kind of changed everything. "Now I feel dumb for being so worried."

He pressed a kiss to my forehead. "You can be worried about me, darlin', but just know there isn't anything on this earth that will keep me from coming back to you."

"Dammit, Pryor. Do you really need to be such a good guy? I'm much more used to the "You give Love a Bad Name" guys."

Her furrowed his brow. "What?"

"The Bon Jovi song."

"Babe, the song's about a chick."

I waved my hand. "I know, I know. It's about a chick who breaks hearts and runs away. I had that in the man form in the past."

"You've lost me."

Shit. Now I was back to being the idiotic River. "I was talking with Titz and Links the other day. It made sense when I was talking to them. Although, they said I was going to be the chick to you."

"I think I follow you a bit, but I can tell you right now that if you try to run away, I won't let you, River."

"But what if I break your heart?"

He shook his head. "Not gonna happen, because then you would break your own heart."

I sat back. "That's assuming I love you."

"You may not just yet, but I have to say, from the way you threw yourself into my arms, you're pretty damn close."

I scoffed. "I was just thankful you weren't dead. I would've done the same thing if you were Titz or Clint."

"Oh really?" he laughed. "I guess I'm not special after all." He tried to pull away from me, but I didn't unwrap my legs from around him.

"Where are you going?" I asked.

"To get Clint. I'm sure you wanna hug him since he's not dead either."

I rolled my eyes. "I'll let him know the next time I see him."

"You sure?" He hitched his thumb over his shoulder. "He's just down the street."

I wrapped my arms around his neck and pulled him close. "So maybe you're a little bit more important than Clint."

"Just a little bit?" he whispered.

"Maybe a lot?"

"What's it gonna take to make you change that maybe into a definitely?"

I pressed a quick kiss to his lips. "Take me home and you'll find out."

He threw his head back and laughed. Wrapping his arms around me, he tossed me over his shoulder and slapped me on the ass. "You're going to be a handful, aren't you, River?"

"But I'm your handful."

The End

UNBREAKABLE

By Geri Glenn
AKA Links

Prologue

Shuffling the stack of boxes and packing tape in my arms, I turn the key to the front door and push it wide open. My lungs feel heavy as I stand on the threshold and stare into the house I once thought I'd live in forever.

I haven't even stepped inside yet, and already I can see the remnants of the night that changed my life forever. The night that changed me. Broken glass lays scattered across the entry hall, no longer remotely resembling the crystal vase my grams had given us as a wedding gift.

A bloody handprint on the wall draws my eyes to it, and for a second, I almost turn around. *I can't do this. I can't go inside this house. Not alone.* But I don't have a choice. Everything I've ever owned is in there, and I don't have a single soul to help me. I'm on my own.

Come on, Bernie. Just one more time. Taking a deep breath, I step inside and close the door behind me. The silence of the empty house thrums in my ears, echoing with every rapid heartbeat. As I take another step, it takes all my concentration to pull in one regular breath, then force it back out again. The lump in my throat grows as I turn the corner and look into the disaster of what's left of my living room.

My trembling hand flutters up to cover my mouth, but the sob escapes me before I can stop it. A large bloodstain lies in the center of the room, forever destroying the plush carpet we'd put in when we bought this place. I stare at it, absently noting the strange shape it's taken. It looks kind of like a giant mushroom.

My free hand instinctively goes to my belly and the tears fall. That blood is the only visible proof left that I'd once had a tiny baby growing inside of me. A tiny girl, or maybe a tiny boy, that I already loved so god damn much. Now that baby is gone, and the only thing left is that mushroom shaped bloodstain on my pretty carpet and a destroyed living room. End tables are knocked over and my lamps are smashed to pieces. The evidence of Blake's rage is embodied in this room, and I know the kitchen didn't fare much better.

Forcing my eyes closed, I take a deep breath and swipe away the tears that have slipped down my cheeks. *Just get what you need and go.*

Turning, I wait until I'm back in the hallway before allowing my eyes to open. I walk up the stairs, my heart squeezing painfully as I pass the room we'd started to decorate for our baby. I don't dare look inside. I hurry past the open door, my mission to get my things and get out. It's the only thing I allow myself to focus on.

Once I'm in the bedroom, I get down to business. I pull out suitcases and throw them on the bed, filling them with my clothes and shoes, and anything else I find that I can't bring myself to part with. My books and trinkets go into the boxes, and when I'm done, I look down to the pile at my feet.

Two suitcases, three boxes, and a broken heart. That's what I'm taking out of this marriage. Slowly, I lift my left hand in front of my face and gaze at my wedding rings. They're as beautiful today as they were when Blake had given them to me. The day he'd asked me to marry him at the restaurant where we'd had our first date. And the day we'd said "I do", promising each other love for eternity.

As angry as I am with Blake, I'm also angry at myself. This wasn't the first time Blake had hurt me. It wasn't even the second. I'd lost track of the number of times I'd accepted his tear-filled apologies and allowed him to patch up the wounds he'd left on my heart, only to allow him to rip it open again and again. But I was pregnant this time. I should have known. I should have gotten out of there. I should have left him the minute I found out a baby was on the way.

And maybe I would have…but I loved him. I find it so strange that when something like this happens, you're supposed to instantly switch from loving a person to hating them. Hearts don't work that way. At least mine doesn't, or didn't. The instant he killed my baby, I could feel my hate for him like a white-hot iron to the gut. But by then, it was too late.

Slowly, I twist off the rings and hold them in my fisted hand. Never again. Never again will I let another man do this to me. Never again will I fall victim to my own stupid heart and my own hormones.

I place the rings on the nightstand and step back. *Never.*

Turning, I grab my suitcases and carry them down the stairs. After loading them into my car and making another couple trips for the boxes, I find myself standing at the entrance to my house once more. This time, for the last time.

The moving company is scheduled to come by later today, and they'll take care of everything still inside. It will be sold and auctioned off, and I won't have to see any of it ever again. As for Blake, he's in jail, and though he hasn't been sentenced yet, he won't be out for a very long time.

I, on the other hand, am leaving. I don't know where I'm going or what the hell I'm going to do with myself. I've been with Blake since I was sixteen years old. He's been my everything for so long. I guess I lost myself along the way, but now it's time to find me. I don't know where or how, but even with the cloud of grief hanging over my head, for the first time in a very long time, I'm looking forward to what the next day may bring.

One

Eight Years Later

I crouch low on my motorcycle, eyeballing the gap in traffic between the slow-moving pickup truck and the semi If I hurry, I can make it. If I don't at least try, I'm going to be late *again* and Rogue will have my head.

Knowing it's now or never, I zip through the space between the two hulking vehicles, narrowly missing the front bumper of the pickup. Once clear, I open it wide and zoom down the road, intent on making our weekly church meeting before Rogue bangs down that gavel.

I don't know why I do this to myself. I'm always fucking late. *Every damn time*. And not even for a good reason. I'm usually just working at home and don't drag myself away from the computer until the last possible second.

Turning the corner, the road before me is clear, but for yet another pickup truck, loaded down precariously with boxes and furniture. I gun it around the curve, intending to get closer to speed around it, when the box at the top of the pile begins to wobble and sway.

I don't even have time to react. Before I know it, the box is falling off the back of the truck and crashes to the ground directly in front of me. I have no choice but to hit it. Its contents are crushed beneath the weight of my motorcycle.

The motorcycle shakes beneath me, and I try desperately to regain control, but it's too late. Luckily, neither myself or the truck were up to speed after turning the corner, because the next thing I know, I'm skidding across the pavement, gravel and cement gouging into my skin.

I come to a stop with my back against the curb, my motorcycle laying on its side just ten feet in front of me, along with the remains of the box jammed inside the wheel well. I lay there for a moment, still trying to wrap my mind around what the hell had just happened when he crouches before me.

He being a man in a dress shirt and tie, complete with a cardigan of all things. "Blimey, Miss. Are you okay? The ambulance is on its way." His hand comes up toward my helmet. "I'm so bloody sorry."

My daze dissipates when his fingertips are just a few millimeters away from me. Reaching up, I clamp my fingers around his wrist and yank it away. "What the fuck were you thinking, carrying that load like that? Those boxes weren't even strapped down."

His brows lift from behind his glasses and his mouth drops open. "I know. Again, I'm so sorry. This is all my bloody fault."

His British accent is thick, and would normally draw me to him, but at this moment, the only thing I want to do is claw this bastard's eyeballs out. "You're god damn right it's your fault." I glance over to my bike, and even from here, I can see the scratches in the paint. "Look at my bike!" The palms of my hands scream in pain as I use them to push myself up off the road. "It's mangled!"

Just as I get myself into some semblance of a full stand, everything starts spinning. The trees blur, and his sexy, yet annoying accent is murmuring something at me, but the sound is muffled.

"I said sit. Down." Forceful hands grab at my waist and I'm lowered to the ground, my head swimming and my eyes unable to focus. With shaking fingers, I fumble with the strap on my helmet. "Leave it on," he says, grasping my hands and pulling them away. "Wait until the ambulance arrives."

"Get off of me," I tell him. Or at least I *think* I tell him. My own voice sounds garbled and strange inside my head.

I can hear the wailing of sirens in the distance, getting louder with every measured breath I take. There's no denying it now. I'm going to be late for that fucking meeting and Rogue is gonna go ape-shit all over me.

"She's over here!" nerd boy shouts. His hands press down on my shoulders, and as much as it pisses me off, I'm thankful, because without them I'd fall over. "She was on a motorcycle and hit a box that fell off of my truck. She took a tumble, and I think she hit her head."

"I'll hit *your* head, Prince Harry," I slur, glaring at him through narrowed eyes, except I don't know which one of him to glare at, because suddenly, there seem to be three handsome, nerdy, annoying as hell British men in front of me.

I may be out of it, but I don't miss it when he grins, shaking his head as he moves aside for the medics to do their job. The next five minutes confuse the hell out of me. The world is still spinning and the medics have their hands all over me, dabbing at places that hurt like a bitch and asking me the stupidest questions imaginable. *Like I don't know my own fucking name.*

"Bernadette, we're going to take you to the hospital to be checked over. Is there someone you'd like us to call?"

I glare back at the medic and push at his hands where they're holding a cloth against the top of my head. "No," I snap. "No hospital." I push him back and place my hands on the ground again, pushing myself to get to my feet. As soon as I get my legs underneath me, my knees buckle.

Strong arms wrap around me, and again, I'm lowered to the ground. "You're going," Prince Farquaad snaps. "So just sit still and keep yourself settled, or I'll sit on you my damn self, you infuriating woman."

"Excuse me?" This man isn't just annoying, *he's* infuriating. Using every ounce of strength I have, I shove at him, pushing him away from me, but his arms remain around my waist.

"Sit still. I'm not going to tell you again." He tightens his grip on me, holding me in place. "Stop being a crazy woman and let these nice men do their jobs."

Oh, no he didn't. I'm about to rip this dickhead a whole new series of assholes, but for some reason, I just can't keep my eyes open. "Fuck you, Friar Tuck," is all I manage to get out before the darkness closes in on me.

"Why are you still here?" I growl at the Brit currently sitting in the chair next to this very unnecessary hospital bed I'm lying in.

"Bernadette," he says, disapproval heavy in his voice. "You can't honestly expect me to just leave you here alone, can you?"

"Yes, you Hugh Grant wannabe, I do. I don't know you. You tried to kill me with your fucking boxes. I want you to go away. Far away if possible. Back to England, maybe."

He just rolls his eyes and settles back into the chair. "You are the most insane American woman I have ever met, I'll give you that. But I'm not going anywhere. And you can take the piss out of me all you want with whatever cute little names you can dream up, but it's not going to change my mind."

"Knock, knock."

Harry Potter and I both glance over toward the door. Stiletto and Titz fill the doorframe, both of them clearly curious about my annoying new British babysitter. Stiletto's gaze moves to me and she raises a brow in question, but I just glare back at her. I don't feel like taking any shit from these two assholes. I just want them to get me the hell out of this fucking hospital bed.

Titz is the first to approach, her movements slow and calculated, like a lion about to take down its prey. "Well hello, handsome. I don't believe we've met."

I watch as Benedict Cumberbatch's eyes grow round, taking in all that is Titz. Her beautiful face, her curvy body covered in tattoos, and her tits, which are, as usual, only barely covered by her tiny T-shirt. He stands, his hand shooting out to take hers. "Roman. Roman Williams. And you are?"

Her grin is wolfish as she takes a step closer, her body invading his personal space. "Oh, a Brit. Accents turn me on, sugar. And you can call me Titz."

Redness rushes across his cheeks, right to the tips of his ears as he sputters, "Uh…yes. Um…it's lovely to meet you, Miss…"

"Titz," she says again, and I can't help but grin. She's making him uncomfortable on purpose. I'd bet money that this uptight dickwad has never met a woman quite like any of us, but especially never one like my girl Titz.

"Right." He turns to Stiletto and holds his hand out toward her, clearly wary of what she may say. "And you are?"

"Most people just call me Stiletto." She gives his hand a firm shake.

"You never told us you had a new man, Links," Titz says, her eyes raking over…*what did he say his name was again?*

I bark out a laugh. "He's no new man of mine. This dumbass nearly killed me and now he won't fucking leave."

Professor Snape holds up his hands and shakes his head. "My apologies once again, Bernadette. The police have my information, and I have put my card with your things. Now that your friends are here, I will take my leave."

"Bye, sugar," Titz calls after him, following him out into the hallway. "Be sure to stop by my shop. I've got a little room in there that I think you might enjoy." She laughs, her eyes likely glued to his ass as she watches him until he disappears from sight, then she turns and comes back into the room. "Take my *leave*? Who the fuck talks that way?"

"Seriously," Stiletto laughs. "That guy completely confused my vagina. He was both hot and a total fucking nerd. How is that possible?"

Done with this whole day, I heave out a sigh and swing my feet over the side of the bed. "Forget it. He's gone. Can we just focus on getting me the hell out of here?"

Three

"Can you fix her?" I grip the phone in my hand so tight, I swear it may shatter.

"Oh, I can fix her," Stiletto says. "It's just gonna take a little time. The damage is mostly cosmetic, though, and I can paint her up so she looks good as new. I can even add some pink flames on the side if you want."

"Not a chance in hell. You get her back exactly the way she was. No pink, no glitter, and no fucking cutesy bumper stickers, you hear me?" No way in hell is she taking my shiny Black Betty and girling her up on me. She's beautiful just as she is...or was.

"Jesus Christ," she says, chuckling. "Touchy today, are we?"

I huff and flop back in my porch swing. "Just frustrated," I admit. "This road rash stings like a bitch. I've got no work coming in at the moment, and my ride is currently sitting in your shop and not in my driveway where she should be."

My dog, Grimm, lifts his giant head from his paws and stares at me from his place on the porch as I twirl my hair around my pointer finger; something I've always done when I'm feeling anxious.

"One week, Links, and she'll be good as new. Better, even. Why don't you try relaxing for once in your damn life? Go hang out in your garden or some shit."

I don't know what it is with these bitches and my garden. They never shut up about the damn thing. So what? I like to have a place where I can work in peace. I like the tranquility of my water feature and the singing birds. Not everything has to be the rumbling roar of a motorcycle.

Just then, Grimm jumps to his feet. Like the good boy he is, he doesn't bark, but I know his alert pose when I see it. Following the direction of his gaze, my body locks solid when I see what he's staring at.

"I gotta go. Talk soon." I don't give her a chance to reply before pressing the button to end the call.

What the actual fuck? He's carrying a bag of garbage to the end of the driveway one house over, and he's not looking this way, but there isn't a doubt in my mind that man over there is my annoying Brit that doesn't know how to strap down a load.

"Hey, Austin Powers," I call out, and sure enough, he turns. It is him. *Of course it is. Who else in their right mind wears a cardigan in Alabama in the middle of July?*

The shock on his face mirrors my own. "Bernadette?" He starts walking toward the house, but stops before stepping foot on my lawn, his gaze on Grimm, who rumbles deep in his chest. "Don't tell me this is your house."

"Okay," I say with a shrug. "I won't tell you, but do you wanna tell me what you're doing next door? 'Cause I gotta say, Brit Boy, this stalker thing doesn't look good on you."

A crease appears between his brows and he moves again, walking closer to my porch. "I'm not stalking you. And please, feel free to give it a rest with the names. My name is Roman, and I'd appreciate if you would kindly use it."

Grimm's body grows tight as he approaches, and I reach out, placing a hand on his back to calm him. "All right, *Roman*, why are you next door taking out a bag of trash?"

"I live there. I moved in yesterday after leaving you at the hospital. This is where I was heading."

"There?" I clarify, pointing at the house next door. "In that house?"

He's made it to the bottom step of my porch, but doesn't try to come up. I'm not sure if it's manners holding him back or the Great Dane that could easily rip his throat out if he tries. "Yes. I didn't really look on the paperwork the police gave me to see where you lived. I hope this won't be awkward for you."

I stare back at him, trying to figure out the odds of this same man moving in next door to me just hours after almost killing me with one of his flying boxes. *And God, why does he have to be so damn polite all the time? Doesn't he know how hard it is to not like someone when they're so genuinely nice?*

"Whatever," I finally tell him. "I mean, it's weird, yes, but it's no big deal I guess. Better you than the last asshole who lived there. Dude was a slob. Keep your yard clean and I couldn't care less if you live next door."

His eyes travel along the flower beds fronting my porch. "You do have a lovely yard," he admits.

I shrug. "It's kinda my thing."

He nods, likely wondering what kind of sick joke this is, having to live next door to the woman who has done nothing but insult him since the moment we met. Grimm stretches his neck out, his nose twitching as he tries to catch Roman's scent.

Grimm is my baby. I've had him since he was just eight weeks old, and we're nearly inseparable. He's affectionate, loyal, and best of all, he's a woman's dog. He loves me, and he loves the ladies of the Dirty Bitches. He even loves Titz's kids. But he does *not* like men.

Just last month, Titz had invited some guy she met at the tattoo shop over to the clubhouse for a drink. Grimm had wasted no time in giving him a nip and chasing the guy out, his hands covering his ass as he screamed bloody murder. That was the last we'd ever seen of him.

Just then, Roman places a foot on the first step and slowly starts to climb the stairs, his hand stretched out for Grimm to sniff. "I wouldn't if I were you."

"Hello, old chap," he says softly, totally ignoring my warning. "Aren't you a big boy."

"Seriously, Roman. He's not a big fan of strange men."

Roman pauses, his intense blue eyes flashing to me. My breath catches. "That's the first time you've said my name."

My body hums with a new awareness as I stare back at him, his gaze doing strange things to my insides. My chest aches with the need to draw in a full breath, but as long as he's staring at me the way that he is, there's no way that's going to happen. Roman takes another step, and then another, and I'm shocked as

Grimm steps back to allow him onto the porch. Roman looks down at the giant dog, breaking the spell he'd bewitched me with.

For the first time, I look at Roman. Like, really look at him. His hair is neatly cut, but messy, in a carefree kind of way that suits him. His face is handsome and rugged, sprinkled with a scruff that comes from not shaving for a couple days. His glasses suit him as well, making him look intelligent and poised. His dress pants and cardigan are a far cry from my own ripped jeans and Harley T-shirt, but I can see the definition of muscle beneath the material that makes me wonder what he's got going on under there.

Grimm's giant tale wags as he presses himself against Roman's legs, nearly knocking him over in his effort to get closer to the petting Roman is dishing out. "He seems all right to me," Roman says with a chuckle. "Who is this magnificent creature?"

"His name is Grimm," I say, watching in horror as my dog licks and pants happily, lapping up every ounce of affection he can get from the same man that nearly killed me yesterday. *The traitor.*

I don't like that Grimm takes to Roman. Not one bit. They say dogs can sense if someone is a good person or not, just by meeting them, and I've used Grimm's dislike of all men as a shield to keep them as far away from me as possible. It's made me unattainable, and has kept me from having to endure the drama that comes with a relationship. Roman, though…I don't know what to make of Grimm rubbing himself all over him like that.

Finally, Roman looks up and flashes me a smile. "How's your hip?"

The truth is, my hip hurts like hell. I was lucky, really, that the damage to my body wasn't worse. Thank God for leathers. I'd walked away with a bit of a headache and a nasty case of road rash on my hip where my jacket had pulled away from my pants.

"It's fine," I tell him, suddenly feeling uncomfortable. I stand and start collecting my phone and laptop.

"Um, I actually have some work to do, so I'm gonna get inside now."

Roman presses his lips together and watches me for a moment before he finally nods. "Have a good day, Bernadette."

I make my way inside before he even gets a chance to step off my porch.

Four

"Ya gotta admit," Stiletto says, "it is kinda creepy that he lives right next door."

Titz looks up from the floor where she sits, rubbing Grimm's belly. "I don't see why you're making such a big deal about this. He's hot. Just fuck him and get it over with."

I roll my eyes as Stiletto says, "That's your answer for everything."

"And since when are you even into the preppy look?" I ask, an eyebrow arched in her direction.

Titz grins. "Since they started looking like that. I'd put a schoolgirl outfit on for him in a heartbeat. In fact..." She draws her lower lip between her teeth. "If you don't want him, I may take a crack at that myself."

Before I can tell her that there's no way in hell she's gonna be fucking my new neighbor, the door to the room we hold our weekly church meetings in swings open, and Rogue comes rushing in. "Sorry I'm late, ladies. I got held up."

Rogue's cheeks are flushed a healthy shade of pink, and her short-cropped hair is a matted mess on the back of her head.

"Got laid is more like it," Titz says with a smirk, and Stiletto and I try like hell to hold our laughter in, but fail when Rogue's mouth opens to respond, and then closes again.

"Titz," she snaps. "Shut up." She takes her seat at the head of the table, and the rest of us fall into position in our own places. She picks up her gavel and brings it down with a thud. "I officially call this meeting to order. It's gonna be a

158

quick one today, gals. I got shit to do down at DB's, and I can't afford to go wasting the afternoon here flappin' my gums with you ladies."

"Links," she calls. "Where's your clipboard of power?" With a smirk, I hold my dollar store clipboard up in the air. How I got dubbed the note taker, I'll never know. It's been my duty since the day I earned my patch, and will likely stay that way until my fingers curl up with arthritis.

"So," she says, motioning for me to get a move on. "Where we at?"

I scan the numbered items on my list. "We need to finalize the route for the rally. Figure out a budget for advertising and refreshments, and make sure we've ordered enough shirts to go around."

The annual Dirty Bitches Ride for Cancer is a cause near and dear to all of us for various reasons. It started out as a way for us to do something good for the community of Magnolia Springs. They weren't exactly welcoming to us in the beginning, but the rally has gone a long way toward earning us a modicum of acceptance.

Female MCs from all over the country come down, and we ride a fifty-mile course around the town and outlying areas. Afterward, riders and the entire town get together for a live band and dancing, topping it off with pulled pork sandwiches and peach cobbler.

"Oh," Titz exclaims, digging into her pocket. "That reminds me. I had five hundred of these babies delivered to my house yesterday." She tosses a compact purse hook onto the table.

Rogue leans forward and grabs it. "These look great." She passes it to Stiletto.

"I like," she says with a grin. "We're getting all classy and shit."

When she passes it to me, I hold the tiny purse hook in my hand. It's cute. A black rectangle with the Dirty Bitches MC logo printed on the front, and our website neatly centered underneath it. Except...

"Um, Titz?" I look up from the hook and try to keep from screaming. "These are great and everything, but this isn't our website."

"Fuck off," she says, leaning forward to snatch it out of my hand to take another look. "Yes, it is. Dirtybitches dot com."

"You've gotta be shittin' me," Rogue groans, her head falling back on her chair.

"No," I tell her. "Our website is dirtybitches*mc* dot com." I pull out my phone and plug in the website she'd had printed on all five hundred of these very expensive purse hooks. Sure enough, my screen is suddenly flooded with gyrating thumbnail images of tits and pussies, and all the cocks any woman would ever want to see. "Dude, you just ordered five hundred hooks advertising a fucking porn company."

Stiletto's hysterical laughter rings throughout the room. "Please tell me you can fix this," Rogue says, her eyes pinned on Titz.

Titz spins and points a finger at me. "I used the fucking graphic *you* sent, *Links*."

My eyes grow wide. I close out the site and flip to my photos, searching out the graphics she means. And sure enough, there it is in actual black and white. Dirtybitches dot com. *Fuck.*

Rogue runs a hand down her face. "Whatever. You two assholes figure that shit out on your own time. And it better not cost this club anymore fucking money. What's next?"

Stiletto's shoulders are still shaking with laughter across the table from me, and I flip her the bird as I look back down at my list. "Route."

"Titz," Rogue prompts, spinning her finger in a 'move it along' type motion.

"On it," she replies. "We're doing the same route as last year. I got the approval from the township and will finalize shit with the sheriff later this week."

"Good." Rogue looks to me again. "Next." *Geez. She really is in a hurry.* Ever since her and Lachlan got back together, Rogue hasn't been around nearly as much. I don't begrudge her that, though. She walks around with permanent sex hair and a smile I haven't seen on her in all the time I've known her.

"Just the refreshments and the band," I tell her. "I've made a list of the things we need for refreshments. The prospects have put together a team of volunteers to run that, and Cutz is working on the band."

"Good enough. That it?" I barely finish my nod before her gavel comes crashing down onto the table. "Meeting adjourned."

Rogue is up and gone before the rest of us even get a chance to stand up from our seats. "Somebody's getting laid, and good," Titz says with a waggle of her eyebrows.

"Is that all you think about?" Stiletto asks.

Titz shrugs. "It's not my fault if I have a healthy sex drive. Besides, the rest of you are just prudes." She turns to me. "Now what the fuck do we do with these damn purse hooks?"

Our eyes meet each other's, and our grins both grow as we say in unison, "Prospects."

What's the use in having prospects if you can't use them to do the dirty work?

Five

"What the hell am I supposed to do with these?" Cutz asks through the phone.

"No idea," I tell her. "All I know is that you need to do something or Rogue will have all of our heads on a stick."

Cutz sighs. "I'll see what I can do."

"Talk soon," I tell her, and disconnect the call.

I feel kind of bad, putting the task of doctoring up all those purse hooks on Cutz, but at the same time, she is a prospect. What's the good in having prospects around if you can't use them for the shit jobs you don't want to do yourself?

Cutz was one of the first people I met when I'd first moved here to Magnolia Springs. She was a hellcat with an amazing sense of humor, and an impeccable talent with a pair of scissors. I'd met her when I walked into her salon looking to reinvent myself. She's been one of my best friends ever since. I just hope she's as creative at fixing up those porn site purse hooks as she is with people's hair, or we're all in some serious shit with Rogue.

I toss the phone on the wicker table beside me and grab my laptop. Since it was my image that contained that disgusting error, it seems I would need to go online and fix every one of my images and advertisements I'd made to draw a larger crowd. Nobody's going to show if they think they're coming for a casting call for a porn company.

For the next two hours, I sit in my garden, surrounded by sunshine and the singing birds, working on the design of the Dirty Bitches website and correcting my botched graphics. This is by far my favorite place to spend a day. It's peaceful and quiet, especially since I banned Titz and Stiletto from stepping foot on even a single blade of grass back here. Bitches don't appreciate the quality of solitude a nice garden can bring.

So lost in my task, I'm startled when the roar of a lawnmower breaks the silence of the afternoon. Glancing over the fence, I watch as none other than Roman Williams steps around the corner, pushing the lawnmower, his body naked from the waist up.

Damn. Roman is ripped. I watch as his muscles flex, his skin developing a sheen of sweat as he works. Roman might look like a nerd, but he's all man. Right down to the sexy V shape that disappears inside the waistband of his shorts.

It takes him about five minutes before he looks up and notices me, one hand coming up in a flick of the wrist type of wave. *Shit. He totally just saw me watching him.* I raise a hand and wave back before ducking my head to my laptop once again. *He's not for you, Bernie.*

I can't help it, though. The harder I try to stay focused on my website, the harder it is to fight the urge to look over at the private show going on right next door. Finally, I just give up. It doesn't hurt to look, right?

The second time Roman catches me watching him, I could swear I see him smirk, but he only nods, continuing with his lawn. The third time, he shuts it down and walks away. *Fuck.*

"Bernadette." I turn toward the voice and see Roman walking around the side of my house. Grimm jumps up from his place at my feet, lets out one loud bark, and barrels toward him, all happy tail wags and gangly limbs. "Hey, boy," he greets him, scratching him on the back. He looks to me. "I just thought I'd come and see how you're doing today."

He's still not wearing a shirt, and his abs look even better up close. His chest shines in the sun.

"Bernadette?"

I rip my gaze away from his glistening muscles. "Yeah?"

Roman grins. "I asked how you were feeling today."

I'm feeling like I haven't had sex in over a year, and that I'd like to stop that bead of sweat traveling down your pec with my tongue. "Good," I tell him. "I'm feeling good."

He nods his head and scrubs a hand over the back of his neck. "Look, you and me got off to a bloody bad start."

I bark out a very unladylike laugh. "That's putting it mildly."

Roman steps forward and takes a seat in the chair directly across from me. *Don't look at his abs. Don't look at his abs.* I force my gaze to stay focused on his eyes, but if I'm being honest, that's not any better. His eyes are beautiful. Clear blue and intelligent, and right now, the way he's looking at me, I feel exposed. Vulnerable.

"What do you say we start over?" He thrusts a hand out toward me and my eyes drop to it. His hands are flawless. Without a single callus or grease stain.

I glace over at Grimm who sits between us, his tongue hanging out, his mouth wide with one of his handsome doggy grins. *Still a traitor.* But if Grimm likes him, maybe I should give him a chance. What's the worst that could happen? I make a new friend?

Finally, I reach out and place my hand in his. His palm envelopes mine in warmth, and the smile on his face reaches all the way to his eyes. "Hi," he says. "I'm Roman."

"Bernie," I tell him, unable to hide my own smile. "Nice to meet you."

Our eyes are locked, and my heart races as he holds my hand in his. "Likewise."

The shrill ringing of my phone breaks the spell surrounding us. Roman releases my hand and I reach for my cell. Stiletto's number is lit up on the touch screen.

"Hello?" I answer, not sure where to look now. I can feel Roman's eyes on me, but I don't dare look.

"Bitch," she says in greeting. "Black Betty is ready to go and itching for a ride."

I grin. "Be right there."

Six

I run a finger across the sleek black tank of my girl. "Babe, she looks incredible."

Stiletto grins. "Of course she does. I knew you were missing her, so I put in a little extra time to get her done early."

I swing my leg over the seat and settle in. "Thank you."

"What about you, handsome?" Stiletto asks, looking to Roman, who stands off to the side. "You gonna go for a spin?"

When she'd called for me to come pick up Black Betty, Roman had offered me a ride. He'd ran over and grabbed a shirt, much to my sadness, and we came straight here.

Roman looks to me. "I've never been on a motorcycle before."

Stiletto claps her hands together. "Never too late to try new things. Let me grab you a helmet."

As she disappears around the corner, I pull back the jiffy stand. "You don't have to come if you don't want to."

Roman eyes Black Betty a moment. "You won't kill me?"

I smirk and lift my shoulders in a carefree shrug. "No promises."

Roman chuckles. "Very reassuring."

"Here ya go," Stiletto sings, coming around the corner. "One shiny black brain bucket for the Brit."

She hands the helmet to Roman, who glances at me one last time before placing it on his head. He fumbles with the straps a little, but after a moment, he's ready to go, helmet in place, eyes possibly showing at least a tiny bit of the terror I'm sure he's feeling.

Stiletto and I glance at each other and grin. This is going to be fun.

Using my feet, I walk Black Betty the few feet out of the garage and start her up. Her engine roars to life, the sound like music to my ears. Being on my girl again brings me peace. "Hop on if you're coming," I call out over the noise.

I've never had a man on the back of my bike before. Most of the men we associate with wouldn't be caught dead riding bitch for a woman, and even if they did, I mostly stay as far away from men as possible.

Maybe that's why when Roman gingerly settles in behind me, my belly does a couple back flips. Maybe that explains why when he places his hands on my hips, every ounce of air in my lungs suddenly weighs five hundred pounds.

Stiletto is still grinning as she waves. "Have fun, kids! Don't do anything I wouldn't do."

Seeing as there's not much Stiletto wouldn't do, I guess that leaves it pretty open for us. With a grin back at her, I gun the engine and peel out of the lot. Roman's arms wrap tightly around my waist as we drive off, and I feel his swift intake of breath against my back. *Poor bastard didn't know what he signed up for.*

Five days without my Black Betty has been hard. Sure, I have a pickup truck I can drive if necessary. I have no choice if I want to take Grimm anywhere, but my motorcycle is my freedom. It's my alone time. My escape.

As I drive out of Magnolia Springs and hit the open road, I feel Roman's body relax behind me. His arms remain around my waist, but they're no longer holding me in a death grip. Several times, he points at different things over my shoulder. The lake in the distance, an elk running into the trees, and an old man riding a bicycle along the side of the road.

When I'd first set off, I really had no plan in mind, but now that I'm out here, there's only one place I want to go. As the highway stretches on as far as the eye can see, we come across a gravel road on the left-hand side. It's one I've traveled down many times, but I wonder now what Roman will think of this place.

It's far off the beaten path. We travel almost a full mile up the road, through trees and brush, until finally we come to a clearing. The lake before us is crystal clear, the water as blue as the sky above it. A waterfall roars off to the left, and my favorite place on earth sits just in front of us.

I turn off Black Betty and wait as Roman swings his leg over. "Where are we?"

I grin and climb off, slipping my helmet off of my head and shaking my hair out. "Lund's Falls," I tell him. "Pretty, right?"

He places his helmet on the seat and steps over to the rock where I've spent countless hours just thinking. Existing. Finding myself. "It's stunning."

"I come here sometimes when I need to think." I lower myself down and sit on the rock, my feet hanging over the side, dangling several feet above the swirling water below.

Roman takes a seat beside me. "I can see why. I've never seen anything like it."

I turn and focus on him. "How long have you been here? In America, I mean."

"Barely a year," he admits. "I got a job at the university as a professor of mathematics. I was living in a room I rented from another member of the faculty until I found the house next to yours." He gives me a sheepish grin. "To be honest, before then, I'd barely left the campus."

I'm still stuck on that first part. "You're a math professor at the university?" He nods, and I let out a low whistle. "Wow. You must really be dumbing yourself down to hang out with me."

A crease forms between his brows. "Don't talk that way. And no, actually, I quite enjoy your company. Even if you are yelling at me and calling me names of fictional British characters."

I force myself to keep a straight face. "It's a gift. I'm irresistible."

Roman chuckles. "Ah, that is turning out to be very true." He nudges my leg with his. "What about you? You don't have the same Southern accent as your friends. You're not from around here either, are you?"

Okay, this may be treading on dangerous ground. Keep it simple. "I'm actually Canadian."

"Which explains why you know the names of every British man alive. So, why Alabama?"

I nibble on the inside of my lip, unsure of exactly what to tell him. I've been faced with these questions before, but this time feels different somehow. I don't want to lie to Roman, but I'm not ready to tell him the truth either. "Long story," I finally tell him. "Let's just say I needed a change, and Magnolia Springs is the first town that actually felt like it could be home."

Roman's eyes search mine before turning to look out over the water. "Fair enough. Maybe someday you may want to tell me the rest of that story?"

"Maybe. But that's not going to be today."

We sit in silence for a while after that, our legs pressed together, the only sound that of the waterfall and birds. As the sun starts to set, I stand and dust off the seat of my pants. "Ready to get home?"

"Absolutely," he says, making his way to his feet. "But this time, maybe we could go a little slower?"

I grin. "Not in my vocabulary, Professor."

Seven

"Where are you off to?"

I spin at the sound of his voice, and my heart leaps as his smiling face comes into view. It's been a busy couple days, and I haven't seen Roman at all since our ride three days ago. "I'm heading down to DB's Saloon for a bit. I need to unwind and hang out with my girls."

He nods, his eyes boldly raking over me, causing my belly to do a little flip. "You look..." He smirks and gives his head a little shake. "Fucking ravishing."

I can feel my eyes grow round and my face heat. The truth is, I feel fucking ravishing. I'd spent forty minutes smoothing my wild curls into perfect winding tendrils, and I'd used the new eye shadow trick Cutz had taught me. But for Roman to just lay it out there like that takes me by surprise. So far, from what little I know of him, he's always so polite and proper.

"Thank you," I say so softly, it's almost a whisper.

Roman moves closer, his tall frame standing on the opposite side of Black Betty, but still close enough that I could reach out and touch him. "I had a lot of fun with you the other day."

I stare up at him, my heart thumping wildly at this new bold approach he's taking. "Me too."

"I'd like to do it again sometime. Soon."

I swallow loudly as he places his hands on Black Betty's seat and leans closer. "I'd like that too." *What? Why did I just say that?*

Roman's eyes bore into mine, and I feel exposed. Vulnerable. "Would you have dinner with me tomorrow night, Bernie?"

Fuck. Shit. Fuck. "Yes." *Fuck.*

His full lips tip up in a smile and he leans forward, one hand pressed to the seat, the other coming up and wrapping around the back of my neck. I'm positive he can likely feel my racing pulse as I stare up into his eyes, searching them, begging him not to do this to me. But at the same time, wanting it more than I've ever wanted anything in my life.

He pulls me closer, his head bending low until his lips just brush over mine. Electricity shoots through my body as he stays that way a moment, until finally, I can't take it anymore. Standing up on the tips of my toes, I lean into him, pressing my lips against his. Our kiss is slow. We explore each other, taste each other. We just feel.

When he pulls away, he tips his head, pressing his forehead to mine. "I'll pick you up at six. Have fun tonight, Bernie."

Stepping back, he smiles and watches as I put on my helmet and swing my leg over the seat. My body trembles with the unexpected rush that kiss had just given me, and it takes effort to maintain my cool and act unaffected. "Night, Professor."

His smile widens. "Good night, Bernadette."

I pull out of the driveway and head toward DB's Saloon, my mind racing. *Since when is Roman so forward? What had I just agreed to? And why do I want to turn around and go back there and kiss him again?*

The truth is, after everything I went through with Blake, I'd sworn to myself that was it. Never again was I going to allow someone that kind of power over me. The kind of power to destroy me. Blake did destroy me. At least, the old me.

It had taken two years before I found Magnolia Springs and Dixie. It had taken a lot longer than that to get to a place where I felt complete. But I do now, and the idea of starting something with a man again scares the hell out of me. I love my life. I don't want to lose the good thing I have going. *But Roman isn't Blake.*

I pull up to DB's Saloon without any answers to my own questions. I need a beer and a good chat with my bitches to sort this shit out.

Eight

"Let me get this straight," Titz says, her elbow propped on the table, her drink clutched in her perfectly manicured hand. "Professor Peabody not only lives next door to you, but he's now won over your dog and is wanting to take you to dinner?"

"Yes."

"And he kissed you," she clarifies.

"Yes."

"You gonna fuck him?"

"Oh, lawd. Not every single thing is about sex, Titz," Rogue drawls in her thick Southern accent. She shakes her head and looks to me. "Girl, you've been alone a damn long time now. You ain't the same girl I met all those years ago, and you definitely ain't the same girl your husband beat to a pulp way back when either. This time, you have your head on straight, and you have a man that seems to be a gentleman in every way."

"I bet he's a freak in the sheets, though," Titz interjects, elbowing a snickering Stiletto.

I bite back a grin of my own as Rogue rolls her head back and looks to the ceiling. "Sweet merciful Lord, give me strength."

"Links," Stiletto says, hopefully attempting to be the voice of reason. "I say go for it. What do you have to lose? You're too careful all the damn time. Rogue's right. You're not the same girl that motherfucker beat down back then.

You're fucking Links, the Enforcer for the Dirty Bitches MC. You're one bad bitch." She shrugs. "I'm just sayin', don't let your past dictate your future."

I take a swig of my beer and mull that over. They're right. The woman I am now would have kicked Blake's ass or died trying. And again, Roman isn't Blake. Blake was an alpha male with an asshole complex. Roman is a gentleman that, besides the little box incident, has treated me with nothing but kindness.

"All right, I'll go," I tell them.

"Links is gettin' lucky," Titz sings. "Oh, I know! Do him in your garden!"

I roll my eyes and pin her with a glare. "You fuck off about my garden. Even your thoughts are banned from it."

"You can't ban my thoughts."

I take another pull from my beer and set the empty down on the table with a thunk. "Just did."

Titz just shrugs and leans toward Stiletto, stage whispering, "I hope they get their junk tangled in the rose bushes."

Nine

"I hope you don't mind," Roman says with a shy smile, "but I decided to cook dinner for us at my place instead of going out."

His confession is like music to my ears. I'd been stressed as hell not knowing where we were going or what I should wear. There aren't many choices of restaurants here in Magnolia Springs, and I doubted he'd want to drive into the city on a weeknight, so I just went ahead with my usual jeans and dressed it up a bit with a low-cut blouse. The jeans are dark and hug every curve, making my ass look incredible. The blouse is white and off-the-shoulder, looking bright and sexy against my tanned skin.

"Your house is good," I say, pulling the door closed behind me with one final wave to Grimm.

I follow him in silence down my walkway, along the sidewalk and up his drive. Butterflies spin circles in my belly, and I suddenly don't know what to do with my hands.

"I hope you like steak," Roman says, pushing open the door and motioning for me to step inside.

His house is cute. It's exactly the same model as mine, but the interior decorating is completely different. Where my house is all modern rocker girl, his is completely masculine and minimalist. There's no clutter or knickknacks. Everything is black, gray, and white. It's attractive, but obviously a man's home.

I follow him down the hall and into the kitchen. "I've got beer or wine. Which would you prefer?"

"Beer."

Roman moves toward the fridge and pulls out two beers, twisting off the caps and tossing them into the garbage before handing me a bottle. "I've got everything mostly ready. I just have to start up the barbecue." He turns and moves toward the patio door. "Follow me."

Like his house, his yard has no frills, though since he just moved in, that's not entirely up to him. From where I stand on his deck, I can see my own yard, lush with flowers and greenery. His own holds a single willow tree.

Roman sets about lighting the barbeque, while I take a seat in one of his lawn chairs. "Your place is laid out exactly like mine."

He glances at me over his shoulder while he works. "Yeah? How long have you lived there anyway?"

"About four years now. I'd been living with Titz before that, and decided it was time to get out on my own."

He chuckles. "Yeah, that woman is something else."

I grin. "She's great. She just talks big. Her and her kids are the first family I've ever really had."

His eyes grow wide as he takes a seat across from me. "That woman is a mother?"

I can't help but laugh at that. "The best kind. She's a great mother. Once you get to know her, you'll understand."

He leans closer. "Does that mean you'd like me to have a chance to get to know your friends, Bernie?"

Shit. "I don't know. Maybe?"

Roman's eyes are doing that whole looking right into the very depths of me again when my cell phone rings. I reach into my purse and pull it out, breaking our connection. "It's Rogue. I have to take this." Rogue is a texter, not a chatter. If she's calling, something's up.

"What's wrong?" I say as a greeting.

The sounds of men and women yelling blast through the other end. "There's a fucking brawl goin' down, that's what's wrong. I can't contain this shit on my own. Need you to get your ass down here before they tear up the joint." Her declaration is accentuated with the sound of something breaking.

"Be right there." I disconnect the call as I'm standing, then look to Roman. "I'm sorry. I have to go."

His brows knit together. "What's wrong?"

"Brawl down at DB's Saloon," I tell him, making my way to the patio door.

He follows me, but he still seems confused. "And why is that your problem?"

I really don't have time to explain this to him. "It's the club's bar. I'm the club's enforcer."

He gapes at me. "Are you taking the piss?"

Luckily, I read enough to know what the hell he's trying to say, but I also still don't have time for this. "I gotta go. We'll have to do this another time."

Turning, I rush through the house and dig my key out of my purse. I stuff that into my saddlebag and flick on my helmet, then hop onto Black Betty.

The weight of a body climbing on behind me startles the crap out of me. "What the hell are you doing?"

Roman's arms wrap around me tightly. "Coming with you."

Time is ticking, and arguing with him will just eat up more of it. I pull out of the drive and zip through town, making the seven-minute drive to DB's in under four. Several men are outside, bare knuckle fighting right there in the parking lot.

I sidestep them and hurry toward the door where Titz stands, a baseball bat at the ready. "It's bad, Links. These are the ones we managed to get outside. There's still plenty inside. We saved some for ya."

I shove through the door and step directly into chaos. Broken barstools lay scattered on the floor. Bodies are everywhere, fists flying and blood flowing. Members of our brother club, the Southern Lords, are going head-to-head with a group of bikers I've never seen before, which isn't going to end well. Rogue, Stiletto, and the prospects are right in the thick of it, attempting to break up separate pairs of men.

Rogue's shotgun is nowhere to be seen, but if she hasn't used it, there's a reason. Walking straight into the middle of the room, I approach the biggest biker from behind and tap him on the shoulder. He swings as he turns, but I'm shorter, easily ducking the punch.

When his eyes land on me, he grins. "Well hello, pretty lady."

"I'm gonna have to ask you to take your crew and get the fuck out of here."

The grin slips from his face, his eyes narrowing on me. "Fuck you." He spins, throwing a punch at Leeds, the road captain for the Southern Lords. I tap him again. This time when he turns back to me, he earns himself a fist to the nose, followed by a quick kick to the balls. He drops like a stone, unsure of which injury he should be holding with his hands.

I stand behind him and place my fingers in my mouth, letting out a shrill whistle. Every eye in the room turns to me. "Gentleman, I'm going to kindly suggest you get your shit and get the fuck out of here before each and every one of you end up like your pal here."

The giant on the ground groans, apparently having chosen his ballsack as the worst of the two. He cups it with both hands, his groan ringing out through the now silent room.

"Fuck you, cunt," one of them says.

I smirk and glance toward the man who'd said it. "I wouldn't fuck you with *his* dick," I say, pointing to his buddy on the ground. "Now, I've already asked you nicely. The next time, I won't."

Leeds puts his hands up. He knows better than to mess with me and my girls. We may be smaller than them, but we don't fuck around. As women in the MC world, we've had to prove ourselves many times over, and the Southern Lords know what we're capable of. "Sorry, Links." He looks to Rogue. "Sorry, doll. We'll take this elsewhere."

As the Lords move toward the door, the mouthy one, who is obviously not from around here, laughs. "You fucking pussies. You're afraid of a woman?" He turns to me. "Bitch, you don't know who you're dealing with here."

I smile. "Why don't you show me then?"

His eyes narrow and his face turns an interesting shade of red. He's not the first asshole I've had to stand up to and he won't be the last. He reaches me in five giant steps, and nobody moves as he stares me down. "You need to learn not to play with the big boys, bitch."

I tilt my head to the side. "I am the big boys, bitch."

His red face grows impossibly darker, and I'm ready for it when he pulls his fist back. I easily duck, and am just about to land the punch to end all punches when the sound of fist on flesh breaks the shocked silence and the asshole drops like a stone.

Roman stands beside me, fists clenched, his eyes hard and angry. I'd forgotten he was even here. I look from him to the man out cold on the floor, and back to Roman. "Holy shit. Are you okay?"

Roman just nods, his narrowed eyes still on the form on the floor. I turn to the others. "Anyone else?"

With an angry grumble, the Lords file out, and the rest of us stand by and watch as the visiting club collects their wounded and carries them out of the bar. When they're gone, it's just the girls, me, and Roman.

Rogue rushes behind the bar and fills a towel with ice, then hands it to Roman with a grin. "You knocked that boy so hard, he saw tomorrow today. You must be Links' new Brit boyfriend."

He gingerly places his swelling hand into the towel and grins. "I'm working on it."

I hand Roman a beer and sit down on the couch beside him. "I can't believe you hit him."

He glowers at me. "I can't believe you dared him to hit you!"

After helping Rogue and Shotz clean up the mess, Roman and I had bid our goodbyes and came back here to my house. Roman's hand was swollen and turning blue. "He never would've gotten one in," I tell him, picking up his mangled hand to inspect it. "And even if he did, I can take a hit, and he'd only ever get one."

Roman studies me, and I want to ask what he's thinking, but part of me knows he's wondering how I know how to take a hit, and that's not something I'm ready to share. "You need to learn to punch," I huff.

Roman scoffs. "I think by knocking that wanker out cold, I know how to punch just fine."

I'll admit, that part was sexy as hell. "You need to learn how to do it without breaking your hand."

"Fuck my hand," he grumbles. "Does that happen often? You, barging into a brawl of raging bikers?"

I shrug. "No, but when it does, I'm pretty good at breaking it up."

Roman pulls his hand from mine and turns, his body facing me. He reaches out with his good hand and places a finger under my chin, tilting it until our eyes have no choice but to meet. "Love, it's dangerous and reckless. You could be hurt, or even killed."

Love. He called me love. "Roman, I'm fine."

"You scared the hell out of me, Bernadette." His gaze burns into mine, and my eyes fall closed as his thumb brushes across my lower lip.

I don't mean to kiss it. Well, I do. I just mean that it wasn't a conscious decision. As his thumb whispers across the center of my lip, I place the softest kiss to it, and suddenly, everything changes. My eyes are still closed when I hear his quiet groan, and then his lips are on mine.

This time is different than the last. Before, when he'd kissed me, he'd been showing his interest. This time, he's claiming me. And for the first time in eight years, I want to be claimed. I want to be consumed by this man.

Pressing forward, I immerse myself in him, drowning in the sudden passion that threatens to consume us both. As my lips part, his tongue slips inside and grazes mine. Every nerve in my body is electrified, my pulse racing out of control.

Roman leans toward me, lowering me to my back on the couch. My hands grasp at his T-shirt as he braces himself above me. With every sweep of his tongue, I melt a little more, quickly becoming addicted to his touch.

Lifting up on his forearm, he pulls his lips from mine. I reach forward to yank him back down and he chuckles, pulling off his glasses and placing them on the coffee table. "Patience, love. I'm not going anywhere."

His eyes hold mine as his hand comes down to press against my hip. His gaze doesn't waver as he pushes it under my shirt and over my belly, then up until he's cupping my breast in his hand. I moan as he squeezes, my teeth sinking into my lower lip.

"Touch me," I whisper, not even recognizing the raw need in my own voice.

His nostrils flare, and then he's on me again, his lips nipping and biting and feasting on mine. I yank his shirt out from the waistband of his pants and tug it up and over his head. I scrape my fingernails gently down his back, and revel in the groan he gives me in return.

My own shirt joins his on the floor, and he yanks down the cups of my bra, propping my breasts up like a feast. And boy, does he feast. His tongue laves at first one nipple, and then the other. He sucks one deep into his mouth, his flicking tongue sending jolts of pleasure directly to my core.

Roman's hand slides down between us to the waist of my jeans. He fumbles with my button, and then smoothly undoes my zipper. His mouth breaks away from mine as his fingers slip inside. His eyes search my face, taking in every expression as his hand steals inside of my panties.

When his fingertip brushes my clit, my breath comes out on a stutter, but I don't allow my eyes to close. I don't want to miss a single second of the way he's looking at me right now. He dips his finger down farther, into the pool of need at my core, then drags it back up, circling my sensitive nub. I gasp and pant as pleasure rockets through me.

With both hands, I grip his muscled forearm and roll my hips, riding his finger. Roman's lips part and his breaths quicken as I do, writhing with pleasure beneath him. His touch goes from languorous and slow to fast and fierce, his stormy eyes still burning into mine.

"Fuck, Bernie. You are magnificent."

My orgasm erupts like a volcano—hot and wet, and all-consuming. As my body trembles and my cries grow louder, Roman watches, his finger still rolling my clit with a caress that curls my toes. As I come down, he slows his hand, and then slowly pulls it out, his lips coming down to press against mine.

"Take off your pants, love," he says, his accent thicker than usual. He stands, unbuckling his own jeans and slowly lowering them.

With shaking hands, I do as he says, never taking my eyes off of him. When we're both naked, we stand there, just staring at each other, taking it all in. He's perfect. His body is incredible, his cock long and thick.

He leans down and snags a condom from his wallet, then tears the wrapper open with his teeth. He grasps his dick in his hand, about to roll it on, but I spring up, turning my body so I'm sitting directly between his legs.

"Let me," I whisper, taking the condom from his hand. Slowly, I roll it over his length and look up at him from beneath my lashes. His flesh is heated beneath my touch, and his eyes are completely primal as he watches what I'm doing.

Condom in place, I take his hand and give it a gentle tug. "Sit."

With narrowed eyes, he takes a seat on the couch beside me, and as I swing one leg over him, my knees positioned on either side of his hips, his hands come up to squeeze my ass. Our mouths are meshed together, devouring each other as I take hold of him and position him at my entrance.

A soft whimper escapes my lips as I lower myself onto him, connecting us until we move as one. Slowly, I rock my hips, my lips meeting his in a hungry kiss. Pleasure courses through me as my moans come out in fits and gasps. Roman's hands grip my ass, lifting me up and thrusting me back down, burying himself inside of me.

I pull back and stare down at him as we move, taking in the ruddy hue of his cheeks and his flushed chest. His mouth is parted, his brows low as I brace my hands on the couch and take him faster, harder, deeper.

Heat builds low in my belly as my release hovers just out of my grasp. I reach for it, slamming into him with unguarded abandon, desperate for the carnal pleasure he's giving me. It's his own hoarse cry that sends me over the edge.

"Fuck. Bernie, Jesus." His lips clamp onto my nipple as together, we come undone, our bodies quaking in tandem.

As my hips slow, I lean forward, pressing my forehead down on his. "Not bad for a professor," I gasp, attempting to catch my breath.

Roman grins and brings a palm down to smack my ass. "You haven't seen nothing yet, love." My giggle turns to a squeal as he flips me to my back, burying his face in my neck.

It's been three days since Roman and I went on our date, and things have been amazing. He's not clingy or needy. He doesn't demand to know where I am or what I'm doing. He doesn't attempt to take up all my time either.

What he does do is cook me dinner. One night, he brought over his laptop and sat on my back deck with me, working on his own stuff, while I spent some much-needed time catching up on work. He's also given me more orgasms in the last three days than I can count. That boy knows how to work his tongue.

As I head from the clubhouse after a long day of finalizing plans for the rally, I can barely contain my grin. I'd made a little stop by Titz's tattoo shop this afternoon and picked out something I think Roman is going to like very much.

I pull into my driveway and shut down Black Betty. I climb off and slide my helmet off of my head, just in time to see Roman walking toward me. I beam at him, feeling like a teenager for the giddy feeling just the sight of him gives me, but the smile quickly fades from my face as he gets closer.

Something's not right. Roman's not smiling. In fact, he looks upset. Angry, even.

"You had a visitor just a little while ago," he says, stopping in front of me, but just out of reach.

I just stare back at him, confused about what could possibly be making him this upset. "Okay?"

"Big guy. Good looking. Blond hair. Tattoos. Sound familiar?"

My blood turns to ice in my veins. *Blake.* But it couldn't be, could it? He was sentenced to ten years in prison. It's only been eight.

"He said he's your husband, Bernadette. Is that true? Are you married?"

I stare up at him, unable to move. "No. Not anymore."

"Not anymore?" Roman throws his arms in the air. "That's not what this guy thinks. And were you planning on telling me about this?"

The sudden feeling of being watched nearly overwhelms me. Blake could be here. He could be anywhere. Watching. Waiting. Planning to finish what he'd started.

"Roman, I need to get inside."

"Are you serious right now? We need to talk about this, Bernadette."

"I'm sorry, Roman. I have to go in." I push past him, forgetting all about the slinky outfit I'd bought just for him. I need to get off this street and into my house where I can lock the door and figure this out.

I knew the day would come when Blake got out of prison, but I'd gone to great pains to escape. I thought I was safe here. I didn't think he'd ever find me. I changed my name back to my maiden name. I'd moved to another country for fuck's sake.

Roman doesn't follow me, and when I turn to close the door, he's staring after me, anger clear on his face and heartbreak in his eyes. I hurt him. I know that, but I can't deal with his pain and my fear at the same time. It's just too much.

After locking the door, I rush to my computer and turn it on. I quickly type in the name Blake Pearson in the search bar, and am provided with several links to his rap sheet. Most of the articles involve the one incident where he'd nearly killed me and had murdered our unborn child.

But it's the third link that catches my attention. The one listed as from just three weeks ago. 'Blake Pearson out on parole for good behavior.' *Fuck.*

Twelve

"That boy best be givin' his heart to Jesus right about now, because if I lay eyes on him, his ass is mine."

"Get in line, Rogue," Stiletto's man, Pryor, growls. There are times when it feels strange having one of the girls attached to the town's sheriff, but this particular time isn't one of them. Pryor's outrage comforts me.

"Thanks, Pryor." I sigh and lean back in my chair, exhausted, and just ready for this nightmare to finally end. "Back when shit went down with Blake, the cops back home weren't really much help. Most of them were his buddies. It wasn't until I ended up in the hospital that they finally took notice, and by then it was too late."

Pryor rounds the table and leans down, putting his face at eye level with mine. "Not this time, Links. Not in my town. Not on my watch. You see even a glimpse of that motherfucker you call me, you hear?"

I attempt to force a smile. "Yeah."

Looking around at my crew, both the club members and their partners, along with our three prospects, my fear subsides, even if just only a little. Back when Blake and I had been married, he'd been my entire world. I didn't have a family. I'd been in foster care my entire life, and Blake was the first person to ever show me any kind of love. His love had come with repercussions, though.

But now, this room full of people–my sisters–were mine. They were here for me. Supporting me. Loving me. And Blake had nobody.

"What are you gonna do?" Titz asks, her usual smart-ass comments long gone, her face more serious than I've ever seen it.

I lift my shoulders in a half-hearted shrug. "Slumber party?"

Thirteen

Our little slumber party lasts three days. At first, I just didn't want to go home because I didn't want to be alone if Blake showed up again. But after the first night, I didn't go home for an entirely different reason.

I was avoiding Roman. He'd been calling my cell phone several times a day, but I didn't answer. He left no voicemails, but I know he's worried. I hate how I'd left things with him, but at the same time, I never should have gotten involved with him in the first place.

Each night I spend here, cements that realization deeper into my mind. Roman is kind and caring, gentle and smart. I run with bikers. A crew full of rough, tough, crude men and women. I also have an ex-husband on the loose that would kill Roman if he knew who he was to me. I can't put him in that position.

That's why, when I finally go home to get a change of clothes and more food for Grimm, I do it in the afternoon when I know Roman will be at work. It's a sneaky move, I know. Cowardly, even. But I can't face him right now. Not before I get my head on straight about where I want to take this with him, and definitely not until Pryor finds Blake and deals with him.

I slip inside and lock the door behind me, intending to do just a quick grab and dash. In and out, and back to the clubhouse before Blake or Roman, or anyone else, ever knows I'm here. It doesn't work out that way.

I've barely made it up three steps before there's a knock on the door. I freeze, my heart relocating itself firmly in my throat as I listen, my ears straining for any sound outside. The knocking comes again, this time, turning into a pounding.

"Bernadette, I know you're in there!"

Who knew it was possible to be both relieved and terrified at the same time? Dread washes over me. It's Roman. *What am I supposed to tell him?* I stare at the door as if it holds all the answers. *The truth, Bernie. Just tell him the truth.*

I move to the door and place my hand on the knob, fear holding me in place. This fear is different than any fear I may have of Blake. This is a fear of a broken heart. Of losing the relationship Roman and I had been building.

Finally, I pull open the door and come face-to-face with a man that no longer looks angry. He looks a mess. His hair is disheveled, his shirt untucked. It looks like he hasn't shaved in days. I open my mouth to say something, but the words are knocked out of me when he steps inside and crushes my body to his, his nose pressing into my neck.

"Fuck, Bernie. I've been so god damn worried about you."

I'm an asshole. In my freak-out over Blake, I never once considered how things looked to Roman. Sure, he didn't have all the details, but I was there one minute and gone the next. That would have terrified me too. "I'm okay," I tell him, my hands rubbing up and down his muscular back.

Using his body, he walks me backward, far enough so that he can close the door behind us. His hands come up, gripping my face on either side. "Don't you ever disappear on me like that again."

"I'm sorry," I whisper, hating the stupid hot tears pricking at my eyes.

Roman's lips crash down onto mine, his kiss desperate and hot. I reach up and curl my fingers into the hair at the nape of his neck, pulling him to me as if I could mold us into one entity. Our kiss is frantic, starved, and single-minded.

When Roman's hands come down to the backs of my thighs, lifting me, I wrap my legs around his waist, keeping my lips fused to his. I'm vaguely aware that he's walking, but I don't pause long enough to see where we're going.

My shirt disappears in a flurry of hands and skin. My bra quickly joins it. My nipples scrape on the fabric of his T-shirt, the sensation erotic and sinful.

It's not until my back lands on my own bed that I realize where he's taken me. Roman stands above me, doing that sexy over the back of the head shirt removal thing before reaching down and yanking off first my boots, and then my jeans and panties, together.

I lay on the bed, naked and vulnerable, my need for him driven to the point of madness. I watch breathlessly as he drops his pants to the floor and rolls on a condom, eyeing me like a predator about to devour its prey, and I want nothing more than to be devoured.

Standing before me, his hands go to my knees. "Spread these for me, love. Let me see you."

My desire has me panting as I obey, allowing my knees to fall to the sides, watching him as he stares down at my pussy. His eyes flick to mine, then back to my sex. "Do you have any idea how fucking gorgeous you are, Bernadette?"

He reaches out a single finger and traces it along my clit. I whimper and jolt, but his finger keeps going, slowly moving lower. "This pussy was made for me." When he reaches my core, his finger slips inside, and the sensation is so great, and I need him so badly, I can't help but arch my back off the bed, my moan echoing throughout the room. "You were made for me. Do you understand that?"

"Yes." I gasp as a second finger joins the first, then he adds his thumb to my clit.

"You're mine, Bernadette." His fingers plunge in and out of me, deeper and faster, hitting the place that can undo me in seconds. "This pussy is mine, isn't that right?"

I can't speak. I've become a boneless, writhing mass of sensation.

"Is this pussy mine?" he asks again, but harsher this time.

"Yes!" I cry.

"Bloody right it is," he growls, and I lose his thumb. With wide eyes, I watch him drop to his knees. His head tips and his mouth attacks my already throbbing sex. His tongue is silky and soft, but the pressure he puts on it, coupled with his hungry growl, has fireworks exploding everywhere inside of me. My clit burns with pleasure as his teeth and lips join his tongue, nipping and suckling, tugging at my already sensitive nub.

When my release hits me, I shatter into a million tiny pieces. I scream and I sob. I say words I'm not even sure are in English, but Roman doesn't relent. His mouth continues its beautiful torture, leaving me no choice but to surrender myself to his mercy.

As my climax comes to an end, and my body is nothing but a boneless mass on the bed, Roman lifts his head and his eyes sear into mine. "I missed you."

Those words seal my fate. All the silly reasons I'd had to stay away from Roman are pointless and stupid. It may be just the beginning of our relationship, but already, I'm starting to believe that he's *it* for me. He's my person. My reason.

This time when he takes me, he does it soft and slow. His touches are gentle and reverent, his thrusts dragging two more releases from me before he finally gives me his. It's beautiful and sultry, and when it's over, he collapses on the bed beside me, taking my hand, and we just lay there, reveling in each other and in the love we'd just made. In the relationship we were building. In the unbidden trust we'd just promised each other.

It's one of the most memorable moments of my life. That's why, when he jumps from the bed, shock clear on his face, it catches me off guard. "What the fuck?"

Fourteen

Laughter takes me over as I look to where Roman is focusing. I laugh so hard I can't breathe. Tears form in the corner of my eyes, threatening to spill over. "Roman," I gasp through uncontrollable, shoulder shaking cackles, "meet Charlie."

Roman's brow furrows, his eyes filled with confusion as he stares down at me, and then back to Charlie standing in the corner. After a moment, he gives up on me explaining any further and moves toward the figure.

I have to admit, as sexy as Charlie is, a naked Roman standing in front of him is even sexier. The vision gives me a whole new kind of fantasy. Roman reaches out with a single finger and pokes Charlie in the cheek. His head swivels to frown over at me. "What the hell is this?"

I force myself to settle as I sit up on the bed. "It's Charlie Hunnam."

Roman rolls his eyes. "I see that, love, but what is our good friend Charlie doing in your bedroom?"

I shrug, desperate not to let the laughter escape. "This is where he lives."

Roman gives Charlie a little shove and my laughter fades. "Hey," I cry, jumping from the bed and standing between the two men in my life. "Be careful! He's delicate."

Roman looks at me like I've gone insane. "You've gone mad, love. Who in the world has a wax figure of Charlie Hunnam standing in the corner of their bedroom?"

I grin up at him and pop up on my toes until my lips brush against his. "Only the lucky ones."

Roman glances over my shoulder, his face still twisted in confusion. "Is he…" He motions to his own manliness. "Ya know…"

I wag my brows at him. "Anatomically correct?" I offer. "I wish."

That's when he loses his hold on his own laughter. "You're positively barmy, you know that?"

"Does barmy mean horny?" I grin up at him and press my naked body to his, feeling his cock twitch.

"No, you nutter, barmy does not mean horny." His shoulders shake with laughter as he holds me tighter. "Do I want to know why you have this in your bedroom?"

I pretend to consider the question. "Probably not."

Roman chuckles and leans down, brushing his lips against mine. "Barmy," he says again.

After a sweet and tender kiss, he reaches out and spins Charlie until his face is in the corner. "Stay," he orders, and then he turns to me. "You, bed."

I arch a brow and place my hands on my hips, but when he lifts me and throws me onto the bed, I collapse into a fit of laughter and pull him to me as he climbs on top. Roman falls to the side and takes my hand, pressing it to his lips. We lay in silence for several moments, and I can't help but wonder why I never knew things could be like this. Fun and light, sexy and hot.

"Bernie?" he asks, breaking me from my thoughts.

I turn and face him. The look he's giving me has my smile disappearing. "Yeah?"

He props up on an elbow and reaches out to caress my cheek with his thumb. "Who was that man?"

So I tell him. I tell him everything. I tell him about growing up in foster care and not knowing my parents. I tell him about meeting Blake as a teenager and falling hopelessly in love. I tell him about the beatings and the fear, the helplessness and defeat. It's not until I'm telling about my baby that my tears start to fall.

"He won't get to you again," Roman growls.

"He'll try," I tell him. "But I'm not that woman anymore. I've changed. I'm tougher now. I've taken self-defense classes and martial arts training. Beating me won't be so easy this time."

"I'll kill him if he tries." You'd think hearing a math professor state those words with so much conviction would be funny, but it's not. He's dead serious, and I have no doubt he means every word. I just hope we never have to find out if he'll follow through.

Fifteen

"You ever gonna get a bike of your own?" Lachlan asks Roman, a clear taunt in his tone.

Roman chuckles and settles in behind me. His arms wrap around my waist and he draws me back until I'm pressed against his chest. "Not a chance in hell," he says. "This whole riding bitch thing works out for me just fine."

Lachlan's head falls back and laughter rings through the air as we roar away from the crowd. It's rally day in Magnolia Springs. Motorcycles of all makes and models line every street, and female bikers fill the town, bringing much-needed business to our tiny community.

So far, everything has gone off without a hitch. We've raised a large amount of money for the cancer foundation. Our fifty-mile ride was publicized by a national news network. Even Cutz had pulled through with those damn purse hooks, managing to scrape the website off of each and every single one of them.

Doing the ride with Roman on the back of my bike had been a welcome change. I've always done these charity runs alone, and though it had never bothered me before, there's something to be said about riding my Black Betty alongside my favorite people in the world, with a pair of strong arms holding me close.

The clubhouse is the hub of activity this weekend, and as we pull into the parking lot, the smell of pulled pork fills the air. Most of us Dirty Bitches are lucky to cook for ourselves, let alone the masses, so we hired one of the local restaurants, The Slop Bucket, to do it for us. They always come through with a good feast.

As I turn from Black Betty, I see Pryor heading straight for us, his face grim. "Links, I need a word."

I pull off my helmet and shake out my hair. "Anything you have to say can be said in front of Roman. He needs to know too."

Pryor's good, I'll give him that. He manages to wipe the surprise from his face almost instantly. He knows I'm not one for relationships, so that means he also knows that this is me saying that Roman means something to me.

"One of my officers picked up a man just outside of town about an hour ago," he says. "Asshole was drunk as a skunk and shooting at the Welcome to Magnolia Springs sign. He won't tell us his name, and he had no ID on him, but we're pretty sure it's your ex."

"What makes you so sure?" Roman asks. He looks just as hopeful as I feel.

Pryor pulls out his phone and pulls up a picture of Blake on the screen. "All my officers have this photo. My guy says he's almost positive this is the same man sitting in the drunk tank down at the station right now."

Roman's arms wrap around me from behind, just as my eyes fall closed. They've got him. That fucker never even got a chance to get near me before they got him. This doesn't mean it's over, but this does mean that I can stop searching the crowds for his angry face, or avoiding the home I've been so proud of because I'm afraid he'll show up there and try to kill me.

"Thank you, Pryor. You don't know what a relief that is."

"I'm just glad that fucker's behind bars and you can rest easy. Go. Relax. Eat food, drink beer, and go home with your man."

I grin back at him. "Sounds like a plan to me."

Roman and Pryor do one of those weird man conversations that involve only head nods and a hand shake, but are somehow an understanding between the two of them, and then we move toward the smell of roasting pig and the blaring music of the live band.

"Roman!" Titz calls out, waving us over to a picnic table occupied by her, Stiletto, Rogue, Cutz, and Shotz. "I hear you met Links' other man, Charlie."

The ladies around the table roar with laughter as Roman and I take a seat. Roman sits sideways and pulls me toward him. "Telling stories of our bedroom antics, love?"

My face heats. "Just that one."

Roman gins and shakes his head before looking up at the others. "I did. Bernie won't tell me his story, though, but I'm sure I can count on you...*Titz*." None of us can help but snicker when he says her name. It's clear it makes him uncomfortable, but it's the only one he's been given, so he's left with no choice but to use her road name.

Titz looks to me. "You didn't tell him?"

I groan. "Am I ever going to live this one down?"

Titz cackles. "Not as long as I'm around, no."

Roman's hand comes up and covers my mouth. "Tell me."

"Okay," she says, settling in to tell her tale. Something she never gets tired of doing. "So Links and me are on a run to Birmingham to pick up some supplies for my shop, right? We take her truck because we know we're gonna have a shit ton to bring back."

She chugs back some of her beer and leans forward. "So we're on the highway, just coming into the city, and there's this truck that's all over the road. It cuts us off a bunch of times, and every time Links goes to pass it, the fuckers speed up. She gets pissed."

I groan and bury my face in my hands. This isn't something I'm proud of.

"The truck is still ahead of us when it pulls into the parking lot of the new wax museum that hadn't opened yet. Links parks across the street, and we watch as these assholes get out and start unloading these big wooden crates."

Roman turns to me. "You didn't."

Titz laughs. "She did! She waited till those bastards took a crate inside and raced over to the truck. She didn't even look to see what was inside, just told me to get my ass out and help her load it up. We got it into the back of the truck and kicked up dust, getting out of there before those fuckers came back out. It wasn't till we got home she realized we'd lucked out and stolen ourselves a very realistic Charlie Hunnam dressed as Jax Teller."

"You're insane," Roman tells me.

"She has road rage issues," Titz says.

Roman opens himself a beer. "Do you have any more stories about Bernadette I should know?"

Titz pretends to check her watch. "How much time you got?"

Sixteen

"Thank you, Sheriff," I singsong through the open door as I climb out of the back of Pryor's cruiser.

It had been a good night, one I'd desperately needed. There'd been tons of laughs, good music, and more whiskey than I've drank in a long time. Roman had fit right in with the girls. We'd danced, we'd mingled, and we'd enjoyed being there as an actual couple. We'd also drank far too much, which meant we'd had to leave Black Betty at the clubhouse and get a ride home with the town's sheriff.

"Be good, kids," Pryor calls out as he pulls away.

I take Roman's hand and start heading for the front door of my house. "I had fun with you tonight, Roman Williams."

He chuckles and gives my hand a squeeze. "I had fun with you too, love. Your girls are crazy, but I like them."

He's right. My girls are crazy, and that's why I love them. I poke my key into the lock and open up the front door. "Grimm," I call out. "Momma's home." Roman locks the door behind us as I kick off my boots. "Grimm?" I call out again.

Maybe it's the booze. Maybe it's the fact that everything seems to be going my way for once, but it takes a moment to understand that something isn't right. Grimm is always waiting for me at the door. I've never had to call him before.

"Call Pryor," I tell Roman, the drunken high I'd been floating on crashing to the ground.

"Bernie? What's wr–"

The sound of glass shattering behind me has me spinning on my heel. The first thing I notice is Roman, his body crumpling to the floor in a limp mass of flesh and blood. Blood currently seeping from a wound on his temple.

The second thing I notice is Blake. A very angry, narrow-eyed Blake, holding the shattered end of a beer bottle in his hand. "Hello, Bernadette."

My body is frozen in place. I can't move. I can't speak. I can't scream. I watch in horror as Blake steps over Roman's seemingly lifeless form and comes closer to me.

"Don't you have a kiss for the husband you haven't seen in more than eight years?"

"You need to leave, Blake," I whisper, wrapping my arms around my trembling body.

Blake's handsome face turns up in a hateful sneer. "Not on your life, bitch. You think you're pretty smart, don't ya? Contesting the divorce I refused to give you. Changing your name back. Changing your hair. Changing your fucking country?"

He takes a step, and his voice rises with every word spoken until he's screaming in my face. I still can't move. Fear has me paralyzed in place, and right now, I hate myself for being that weak woman I was all those years ago. I thought she was gone. I thought she was dead and buried. Turns out, she was right here all along, pretending to be someone she wasn't.

Blake's hand shoots out and wraps around the back of my head, tangling in my hair and yanking it back so fast, my neck screams in pain. "I told you what would happen if you ever tried to leave me. I fucking warned you time and time again, yet here you are, living in buttfuck Alabama with a Poindexter boyfriend and your fancy dog."

"Where's my dog, Blake?" Tears slide down my cheeks as I stare up into his wild eyes. I hate myself for crying. I hate that he can still make me feel so god damn helpless.

"Where's my dog, Blake?" he mimics, and then catching me completely off guard, he throws me to the ground. "Shut up!" His foot connects with my ribs, and I feel the distinct crack of bone. Something I'm all too familiar with thanks to him.

He doesn't even give me time to catch my breath before he grabs a handful of my hair and drags me to my feet. His hand wraps around my throat and he presses me against the wall. Everything I've ever learned about self-defense is gone. I forget all about raising my arms and twisting to the side to break his hold on me. I forget all about kneeing him in the nuts to incapacitate him. I forget to scream. I forget to do absolutely everything but what he himself had trained me to do, and that is be totally compliant as he beats me to a bloody mess.

"Your dog had an unfortunate encounter with a piece of steak covered in a drug that'll hopefully kill the big son of a bitch."

I look past him and into the living room. From this angle, I can only make out Grimm's giant feet, laying limp and unmoving. Anger begins to take hold of me then. "What are you going to do, Blake?"

He grins again, pulling a revolver from his back pocket. "I'm going to fucking end this marriage on my terms, Bernadette. You don't get to just walk away from me." He presses the barrel of the gun to my forehead. "Not after you sent me to fucking prison."

"You killed our baby," I tell him, silent tears still falling freely.

His evil grin slips then. "I know, babe, and I'm fucking sorry about that. You know how I get sometimes. You should've just stayed away from me that night." But he and I both know that staying away from him on that night, or any night, was impossible. He wouldn't have allowed it. He sought me out when he was in a mood like that. I was his release.

From the corner of my eye, I see Roman stir on the ground behind Blake. I flick my gaze back to Blake, praying he didn't notice, but he's so lost in his own crisis, he doesn't see anything but his end game, whatever the hell that is.

A soft groan comes from the living room, and when I glance that way, Grimm's feet are gone. That's when I realize they're waking up. Both of them are coming to, and this motherfucker is still here. He still has this damn gun with Lord knows how many bullets, and he'll not stop until he's killed each and every one of us. Maybe even himself.

"Tell me you love me one last time, Bernadette," he says, pulling back on the hammer.

I stare deep into his eyes, and I make a decision right then. Blake may succeed in killing me tonight, but I'm taking him with me. Grimm and Roman are not going to go down this way.

"Fuck you," I sneer, then using every ounce of force I can manage, I drive my knee up into his groin.

A shot rings out so loud my ears ring, and I can feel wetness dripping down the side of my head and onto my shoulder. I don't stop to think about it. Bending low, I wrap my hands around the barrel of the gun and pull, desperate to pull it from his grasp.

"You bitch," he gasps, one hand cupping his destroyed manhood, the other keeping a death grip on his gun.

I pull a fist back and aim a punch to his face, but he spins, knocking me off-balance, and I fall to the ground beside him. His blows land one after the other, and even though I fight back with everything I have in me, he's winning. I can feel myself slipping, the world around me slowly fading to black, my vision blurring to the point I can barely see more than fuzzy colors.

The mighty growl that rings out right then, both fuels me to keep fighting and scares the life out of me. Grimm. Knowing he's okay gives me what I need to stay conscious. But his very presence here puts him in danger of meeting the business end of Blake's gun.

I shake my head, attempting to clear the cobwebs, just as Blake starts to scream. Grimm's growls grow more ferocious and angry. As my vision clears, I see the revolver drop to the ground as Grimm's teeth dig farther into Blake's forearm, his head shaking violently from side to side.

And then in a flurry of fists, fur, and blood, Roman appears, tackling Blake, his fists slamming into the man I once promised my everything to, my dog ripping into whatever part of him he can sink his teeth into.

The gun lays forgotten on the ground at my side, just out of reach. Gingerly, I stretch out my arm, my fingers scrambling to pull it close enough to get my hand on the grip. That's when the front door is kicked in.

Pryor Jones, yet another hero in my life, rushes inside, his gun drawn, his face full of rage and determination.

"Grimm," he barks, his foot kicking the gun farther out of reach. "Stand down."

Grimm has never been formerly trained as an attack dog. Hell, he's never even really liked Pryor enough to listen to a command from him, but it's like he just knows. My beautiful, strong, loyal dog steps back, blood glistening on his muzzle, and he moves immediately to stand protectively over me.

Blake isn't even fighting anymore. His arms and face are unrecognizable as he lays sobbing on the floor like a baby. "Roman!" Pryor barks out. "I got this!"

Roman keeps hitting.

"Roman, don't make me fucking cuff you too."

He lands another punch.

"Roman, for fuck's sake, man. Your woman is bleeding on the fucking floor. I got this."

That gets his attention. Roman pulls back, gingerly coming to his feet, his eyes instantly moving to me. It's not until his strong arms wrap around my trembling frame that I lose the hold on my tears.

Seventeen

"I'd made it halfway to the station before my dispatcher told me they had an ID on our drunk," Pryor says. "It wasn't your ex at all. I went back to warn you, when I heard Grimm going crazy inside."

I sit on the edge of the gurney in the emergency room, my broken rib already bandaged and my head cleaned. It had been a flesh wound I'd taken to the side of the head. The bullet had grazed the hair right off in that area, but I didn't care. I was lucky.

Nobody had died tonight. We'd all come close, but aside from a couple of broken knuckles and a mild concussion, Roman is fine. Grimm was currently in the care of Titz and her children, who were washing him up, and I'm sure giving him lots of love.

Blake, on the other hand, is in jail, and according to Pryor, he'd be staying that way. He'd also be getting firsthand experience of the American prison system, who would be very interested to learn of his prior assault conviction. His new attempted murder charges would ensure he wouldn't be getting out again.

Roman's hand squeezes mine. He hasn't let me out of his sight any longer than he's had to. He hasn't stopped touching me since the moment Pryor slapped those cuffs on Blake.

Pryor accepts our thanks and makes his exit, leaving Roman and I alone to wait for the nurse to come with my discharge papers. They weren't admitting me, but they were prescribing me some heavy-duty pain killers and strict instructions to take it easy for a few weeks. That I could do.

"I'm sorry," I tell Roman, unable to meet his eyes.

"Love, don't you ever apologize for that dick again. I'm just glad I was there." He shakes his head. "I hate to think of all the things that could have happened if I wasn't." His lips press against mine, his arms carefully wrapping around my shoulders. "I'm just glad you're okay."

It's funny. All these years, I've avoided men. I've prided myself on not needing one in my life at all. I didn't need a man for validation or safety. I didn't need one for anything. But that was all wrong. I'd been all wrong.

That simple embrace, accompanied by those simple words from Roman, make me feel more loved and safer than I have ever felt in my life. "I think I could be falling in love with you, Roman Williams."

His forehead presses against mine. "I think I'm way ahead of you on that one, love."

Eighteen

My hands fist the sheets on each side of Roman as my hips roll, taking every inch of him deeper inside me. "Fuck yes, love," he moans. "Don't stop."

I have no intention of stopping. The electric buzz of my impending release builds stronger in my belly, and the bed frame slams against the wall as I fuck my man. I stare into his eyes as I start to tremble. "Roman," I sob, my hips faltering.

He doesn't let me slow. His hands come down to grip my hips and he lifts me up, then drives me back down onto his rock-hard cock, impaling me with every delicious inch of it, driving me wild with that incredible rumble he makes low in chest when he's getting ready to cum.

When his thumb hits my clit, I can't take it anymore. I shatter, my gasps for air coming out on a shriek as I fly over the edge, the only thing on my mind being Roman and me, and how fucking right this feels.

Roman's hips drive up into me, taking me even faster and harder, his eyes never leaving mine. When he finds his own release, his cheeks turn a sexy shade of red, his mouth open, his own scream silent.

His hips slow, and then stop moving altogether. I drop my chest to his, keeping him firmly planted inside of me as we try to catch our breath. Roman's fingers trace lazy lines up and down my spine as I revel in the aftermath of our lovemaking.

"Roman," I say softly.

"Hmm?"

"I think I fell in love with you the first time you kissed me."

He wraps his arms around me and hugs me close. "I fell in love with you the first time you told me to fuck off."

I grin and press my lips to his chest. Who knew that the man who almost killed me with his flying boxes would be the same man I'd find I couldn't live without?

Born To Be My Baby

By GM Scherbert
AKA Titz

One

I don't know why the fuck we gotta have church so god damn early in the morning. I mean, fuck. I know it's pushing ten, but I was up late working on somebody at the shop, and Momma needs her sleep. I would've been out of there earlier, but the guy wanted a whole back piece, and he thought giving it a go in one session was a good idea. I tried twice to explain to him that's not how this works, that it's not how any of this fucking shit works. He, however, dug out his macho shit, and when I say macho shit, I mean his cock was practically on the counter as he explained to me that he could take it. Ha! I showed that loser just how "manly" he really was. Idiot.

Walking into the kitchen, I can smell the coffee screaming my name. I wonder who was in here first, but I should be able to tell as soon as I taste what has drawn me here. Links' coffee tastes like it was brewed in a mulching bag from the grounds of all those fucking plants she tends to, using water from Grimm's dish. Please, tell me that Stiletto or Rogue were the ones that got in here to make it first.

Grabbing up the pot, I fill up my **Cunty McCunterstein** mug after throwing a splash of RumChata into the mix. Taking a sip, I'm happy to find that Links had nothing to do with brewing it, and head toward the office. Stopping short at the bar, I grab up a couple treats for Grimm from the stash I keep there. Pulling the door open, I shut and lock it behind me, seeing as everyone's already here.

All eyes are on me, and I can't help the snark in my tone when I ask, "What?"

Rogue shakes her head. "Never on fucking time, Titz. Not a single time when we've had church have you actually shown up when you were supposed to. You know how I feel about people being late all the time." Taking her eyes off me, she slowly rolls them to Links. "The one thing that the two of you agree on, and it has to be that deadlines and promptness aren't for y'all."

Being on time and promptness, as Prez so neatly puts it, just ain't a thing for me or Links. We're both different in that way. We're more free spirited, more worried about the path than the destination. I'm an artist, and that shit leads my mind all over the place. Taking another sip, I smile wide. "Time is an arbitrary thing. You know that, Prez. I can't speak for Links, but I'm on time for all the important shit."

Stiletto's chuckle has me smiling even wider. Me and her are tight as fuck, and I for one know exactly what it is she's thinking about right now. Links doesn't find our silent communication funny or as amusing as we do, though, feeling the need to throw her two cents in.

"The only time I've ever seen you on time for anything is when you got thrown in jail for flashing your tits."

Rogue can't stop herself from adding, "Nah, she was even late then because I'm the one she called to bail her out, and I waited at the station for close to three hours."

"Wait just a damn minute, Prez. I only called you 'cause I knew these other bitches were at work and you were playing hooky that day with your old man. You're just pissed because you had to get dressed and outta bed long enough to come get me out," I say, remembering that day like it was yesterday. "And it wasn't three hours, it was more like one and a half," I try to explain, and get a rise out of them as I do. "I mean, I was practically on a date with that guy, and he had his hands all over the girls." Gesturing to my tits, I make sure to give them a squeeze. "When I asked him to take me into a private room and help me take my jewelry out, that's when it got really interesting."

"The fuck, Titz? You better be talking about Clint because that's my old man that did your intake and put you in lockup. You best be misremembering that shit. He better not have had his hands all over your tits, and heaven help you if you were asking him to go into a private room with him."

"What can I say? That man's had his eyes on me since the day I got here."

"Yeah, because you've been arrested more times than I can count. Remember that time he threw you in the slammer because you had all those unpaid parking tickets? Who gets thrown in jail for that shit? You better stop all that talk about my old man because that shit doesn't fly with me and you know it." Taking a step toward me, the scowl that crosses Stiletto's face is fucking priceless.

"Those were trumped-up charges and you all know it. The fire department putting those fire hydrants right in front of where I wanna park? Oh, and calm your titties, Stiletto. Sheriff Jones didn't want to play with me any more than that fucking Prince William talking teacher of Links' or Rogues old man did. They only have eyes for you girls it seems." I can't let it go. I've got to poke the bear a little more. "Fuckers must be blind or some shit."

Sinking down into my chair, I pat my thigh under the table, getting Grimm's attention. Getting up and on his feet, he moves over to me quickly. This dog has been around us for a long fucking time, and is a better predictor of people than I am for sure. He hated that last panty waste I took up with. Grimm had him by the balls before we were three steps inside the clubhouse. Reaching a hand down, I stroke him behind the ears for a bit, before reaching into my pocket and digging out the treats I brought for him.

"Grimm, get over here," Links calls out, but Grimm doesn't move, his face still licking up the treats out of my hand. "Titz, stop feeding him that shit. He's gained weight, and the doctor says he needs to keep away from all those table scraps and treats you feed him."

"Fuck that. You know my Grimm boy likes his treats, and there's nothing wrong with him having a little extra weight to him. I like my men a little meaty." Seeing that Grimm has finished the treats, I pat him on the head once more before he trots back over to Links.

As soon as Grimm walks away, I grow bored with this shit immediately, and the meeting hasn't even gotten underway yet. Rogue calls the shit to order and starts checking things off her list. Dues. An upcoming charity event that I've got to put together a ride for with our brother club, Southern Lords MC. The charity that we've decided to donate to. And also, the stops we'll make during the poker run. She then goes over the totals coming in from not only the tattoo shop, but the bar, and the auto shop, as well as a few investments that we've made with the profits. I zone in and out as she speaks about the prospects that have recently began their servitude. No one's got time for that shit, leading someone around by the hand and teaching them about this life. The only people I'll be doing that for are my kids, and I'm not really looking forward to that happening either.

Speaking of, I have to get home as soon as this meeting is over and make sure that all four of my girls made it to school on time. Violet, the oldest, has really been trying to show her independence, and that shit ain't flying with me. Trying to skip school and do whatever it is she does. She's freaking eleven for fuck's sake. I guess my momma was right, that they were going to give it to me ten times worse than I gave it her. Hopefully, Dahlia, Jasmin, and Rose are a little less trying to my nerves as they hit puberty.

"Titz, you here with us?" Prez asks, drawing my thoughts back to church.

Raising my hand, I wave toward her. "Yeah, Prez, right here."

"Really? What were we just talking about then?" Links questions, trying to catch me not paying attention, picking on me for giving her grief all the time. I love her, don't get me wrong. It's just the way we are and will probably always be toward each other. That sappy shit just don't work for us.

"Prospects, *Links*," I say in a snarly tone. "I don't have one, though, and I can't really see myself ever wanting to try and help one out, so I guess I just kinda zoned out when Prez started talking about that shit. That okay with you, Links? Or is that something you need to head to your garden to think about?" Picking my mug up, I take another long swig before Prez cuts into my thoughts.

"Links, leave her alone. Titz, knock it the fuck off," Prez says, glancing between us. "Just because Titz and Stiletto are always talking shit about your garden, you've been a real hard-ass to her as of late. Anything going on that I need to know about? Well, more so than the shit that's always between the bunch of you bitches?"

"That garden is my place of Zen, and I need that shit when I have to deal with those two day in and day out! You know what happened at the beginning of the week for fuck's sake. He's my old man."

"Yeah, well, club rules are club rules, and she hasn't broken any them that I know of yet. Maybe when the three prospects get patched the vote will go differently, but as it stands, she'll have Stiletto voting with her so nothing's gonna change. When the prospects get patched in, maybe we'll have a chance, seeing as Titz hasn't gotten herself one yet and swears she won't."

Thinking through what Prez is saying, I'm quick to cut in. "Whoa, wait a minute. Maybe I'll find myself somebody then, 'cause we need to keep this shit fair by having an odd number. If it's not in my favor, it ain't gonna work for me."

Prez shakes her head, trying to keep her composure over talking about this shit again. "Jesus, it's like we can't get anywhere because we're always talking in circles. Links, we all know why Titz and Stiletto aren't allowed into your garden anymore. It's over and done with, so will all of you just stop bringing that shit up!"

With that, the gavel goes down and Prez calls the meeting. I stand and walk to the kitchen to wash my mug before heading to my bike. This mug holds a special place in my heart. One of my clients sent it to me when she moved away, and I still don't know if I should be offended or honored at the gesture. I don't know if she was calling me a cunt or just thought I would appreciate the humor in it. Either way, I love it just the same. I have a similar mug that was sent to me at the shop, from another satisfied customer that reads **I Have the Patience of a Saint. Saint Cunty McFuckoff.** God, some days I love my life, and any day I can get a little joy out of these mugs, and maybe even piss somebody off with them, is golden.

Checking my phone, I see I don't have much time, needing to check on the girls before heading into the shop for my one o'clock appointment. I'll be late, always am, but I still give it the old college try to be there on time. His name is Adrik, and he's a new client. By luck, I was the one assigned his ink. I'm sort of happy about it, though, because this ink will be something I haven't had much experience in doing. I'm usually doing more girlie shit, or some of the ink from the Southern Lords which is exactly the opposite of that. This new client hadn't given me much to go on when we exchanged emails about what he wanted. Only a few directions, such as size, detail, and a picture of Lady Justice with her scales.

After chasing off that guy last night after six hours on that back piece he wanted, I'm hoping todays victim—I mean client, isn't such a pansy. The tattoo I have drawn up meets all of Adrik's demands, save for one.

Two

Being just a few minutes before opening, I unlock the shop, wondering where the fuck Billie Jo is. She works the counter, doing the scheduling and shit. She's usually here, waiting for me by the time I come in with her red hair heaped onto the top her head, and those little loose ringlets falling out here and there.

Pulling my phone out of my purse, I text her, then call and leave a message with the lawyer's answering service about my court date in a month and a half. Fucking Sheriff Hot Ass starting shit again. Dropping the phone onto the counter, I walk around to open up the shop—throwing on the lights, turning on the radio, then flipping over the open sign. Hearing my phone buzz against the glass, I head over to it. Pulling it up, I see that it's Billie Jo. *On my way. Be there in 5. Sorry, boss lady.*

Billie Jo is young, probably twenty. Although, she's come over to the clubhouse (not that she has to be twenty-one there) and out drinking with us to Killjoys, so maybe she's twenty-one. Her curvy body reminds me of my own when I was that age, and I want nothing more than to get her out of her shell and more comfortable with herself. I'm not sure about much of her story, but the way she shies away from certain things has me thinking the life that led her to this place was a rough one. Maybe even one that reminds me way too much of my own time spent with that fucker

Doug. Don't get me wrong, not all the time we were together was bad. After our youngest was born, though, shit went south fast and right quick.

Heading back to my station, I pull out the drawings and get my iPad hooked up, getting a mix going low that almost everyone hates. It's my one weakness in life. Well, one of two dirty little pleasures that have to do with music at least.

Hearing the bells jingle above the shop door, I call out to Billie Jo, "Anything I can help with? I know how hard it can be sometimes to do it all alone."

The snort that I hear stops me dead in my tracks. My head swivels toward the security TV up in the corner of my station. Definitely *not* Billie Jo.

The man that stands just inside the door is big…like, fucking huge. He has Chucks on his feet, and dark blue jeans that are so fucking tight, I'm sure his dick is tucked to the right. A white long sleeve button-down shirt that hides a wide as fuck chest, a dark, full beard that I would love to run my hands through, and long dark hair, which is currently getting fingered by those big hands of his as he puts it into a messy man bun on top of his head. I can't see his eyes because the security feed is black and white, and shoddy at best, but if his complexion and hair can tell me anything, they'll be dark, just like the man I'm drooling over. Plus, those aviator shades are dark as fuck, and don't give me one hint about the eyes behind them.

"Fuck me!" is all I can think to say, and I must've said it a hell of a lot louder than I thought because his voice is the next thing I hear.

"Well, if you insist, I don't have a problem doing just that. But we'd have to rush it, and I think I could spend more time than that on your body. I mean, your voice is sexy as fuck, but I don't know what you look like, considering you're still in the back, but I'm guessing you're one of the folks that make up these photos and none of y'all are too bad looking. I think I could take one for the team no matter which one you are."

Glancing toward the camera, I see that he's walked over to the photos that adorn one of the walls in the waiting area. Most of the photos are of work I've done, or of the Dirty Bitches while on a ride. His hands linger on one of my favorite photos, of me all done up before a tattoo exhibition I did at a burlesque club last year. "Also, I'd hate for my artist to think that I'm backing out on my appointment. It took me forever to get in here, and I'd hate to lose that deposit. I'm guessing we'll need more than one session, and I'd hate to piss them off before we've even met, let alone gotten done with my ink." Running a hand through his beard, I'm not sure what must be going through his mind, but he glances at the damn burlesque photo again and adds, "We could set up something for after my sessions, though. I'd love to know more about you. Maybe about what your life is like, how free your evenings are, where you hang out. If you enjoy anal, being tied to a bed when you fuck. You know, basic type stuff."

Realization sinks in, and I know a couple things for sure. One, I definitely said that out loud and loud enough for him to hear me. Two, this has got to be my new fucking client, Lady Justice. And three, I think I just creamed my panties from that voice, especially it asking those dirty fucking questions of me.

"Adrik?" I squeak out as I make my way toward the front of the shop.

His head bobs before he speaks, but I barely notice it. "Yes" is all he says as my staring becomes real life, in the flesh perusal instead of using the shitty black and white TV. He's so much better in real life, and his broad chest is just so big. I'm not sure how that shirt isn't splitting in two, or how the fuck the buttons aren't screaming out from the strain.

The chime ringing out from above the door draws my attention away from him, as Billie Jo walks in. Her red hair is a mess. She pushes her shades up onto the top of her head, and I notice the heavy makeup around her eye. I know instantly what it is, remembering the times I had to do the exact same thing.

I finally make my way into the waiting area. "Sorry, big guy, but I'm gonna need a bit before our session can start. Pull up a seat and get comfortable, I'll come get you in a bit." I nod to Billie Jo, then turn to make my way back down the hallway toward the breakroom. "Come on," is all I say as I finish the short trip down the hall, holding the door open while waiting for Billie Jo to walk through it.

"Tell me what's going on." Looking at her, I can see the wheels turning, and decide to cut that shit off at the fucking pass. Using the 'momma voice' I've been perfecting for the last twelve years, I add, "Just tell me the fucking truth, Billie Jo. I ain't got time for whatever you might come up with. I've already got an appointment out there waiting."

"I was late 'cause I had to pack up my shit and try to find a place to live today. My ex fucking came home drunk last night, and when I pushed him away while he was coming on to me, this" she says, pointing up at her eye, "is what he did." She runs her hands over her arms. "He apologized and all that shit, but I don't fuck with that sorta behavior, so I left."

Nodding my head in understanding, the memories come flooding back from my days in a similar relationship, and I'm glad she was smarter than I was. I stayed in that situation for fucking years, and it wasn't until my girls were able to understand what was going on that I fucking woke up and got the hell out of there. I sure as shit haven't turned back since.

Dragging myself from the memories, I pull her in for a hug. Speaking from the heart, I tell her, "If you need anything, and I mean anything, don't hesitate to let me know." Pulling back, I add, "The apartment above the shop is opening up on the 15th, and if you'd like it, it's yours."

"Oh, wow. Really, boss lady? I would love that. One of my girlfriends said I could stay on her couch until I found a place."

"What are friends for, right? If you have any other problems, you know me and the Dirty Bitches will be there for you, no matter what you need." I move back toward the doorway. "Us girls gotta stick together. Stay back here and get your shit straight. Tittytat and Juggz aren't coming in till, like, two, so once I get started on this guy, we'll be good for a bit."

With that, I grab up the drawing out of my room and head back out to the front. Stopping at the counter, I lay the sketches out before speaking, raising my eyes toward the chairs. The man has still got those aviator sunglasses resting on his face, but when I address him, he pushes them up to the top his head, and his chocolate brown eyes meet mine, melting my lady bits to goo in seconds. "Hey, guy, you wanna come up here and let me know what you think about the sketches I did for your ink of Lady Liberty?"

"You'll be doing me today." His smile widens.

The slew of concern that surfaced when Billie Jo arrived, looking as she did, goes out the door and is instantly replaced by thoughts of the ten-year-old boy who lives somewhere inside me. I can't help but giggle at his words. "Huh? Yeah, I'm the one doing your ink today. Did you have a problem with that or something?" Taking a deep breath and collecting my thoughts, I add, "Do you have something against a woman doing your ink?" Placing a finger against my cheek, I tap it a few times while waiting for a reply that never comes. "Wait, you just said it like you knew I'd be the one working on your piece today. How's that?"

My shop, my rules. I never give names or details when doing ink. I don't know if it has something to do with that asshole ex of mine or what. But, unless it's a repeat client, or somebody that we know, it's just a rotation of who gets assigned. The two other artists in the shop are both great at what they do or they wouldn't work here. We might be in Magnolia Springs, Alabama, with less than one-thousand people here, but that doesn't mean folks don't come from far and wide to get one of us to stain them.

"Well, other than this being the only tattoo shop in town, or within two hundred miles, might I add, I did my research on the shop. You know, internet type shit, and thought it was weird as fuck how you work. Randomly assigning people to do your ink, not having bios or shit on the website, not having your own portfolios on there either." He moves a few steps closer to me. "I mean, I had to make this appointment weeks ago, and the deposit was no drop in the bucket. I just wasn't really sure what would come of it. When I saw the pictures up on the wall, the motorcycle gang and the other artists, I really hoped it would be you that worked me out."

"It's a club, not a gang, guy."

"Oh, a club. Right. Yeah, I've seen Sons of Anarchy." Looking toward the photos, his eyes stop on the burlesque photo again. "Well, that photo of you doing that show at the burlesque club is hot as fuck."

"Thanks."

"You dance while you were there? Show off more than those tattoos?" He meets my eyes. "I've been to a few shows in my time, and can only wish I would've been lucky enough to see you perform. Maybe in the future, we could arrange that. Did you let anyone take a turn with you while you were there?"

"Come the fuck on, man. You don't talk like this all the time, right?"

He just smiles, apparently enjoying this back and forth between us. Either way, this session needs to get started so that this ache I'm feeling looking at him, wanting him to put me in my fucking place, can be put out of my head. Far out of my head, because I swore a long time ago that I would put my girls before any and everything else.

Showing him the design, he seems pleased with what I've worked up, and doesn't mention the one thing that he'd asked for that I left out. Letting it slip from my mind, I head back to get the print made up and finish setting up my station. Billie Jo settles up with him for the six hours we'll hopefully get done today, and makes sure that she has him fill out the state required paperwork. As she's filing the shit away, I ask her if there was anything on the paperwork that I needed to know about. Shaking her head in answer, I holler out to Adrik to let him know it's the second door on the left, and that he can head back, take off his shirt and get comfy while I use the restroom and wash up.

Stepping through the doorway of my station, I gasp at the sight before me. The ink running up and down this man's arms is impressive. I hadn't seen a lick of ink poking out from under that button-down shirt he had on, which is now neatly hanging up. Taking another look over his arms, I can't help but stare at the ink, and fuck me, there's a lot. The more I stare, the more I see. Running my eyes over his body, I see that a few look like prison ink. Some give the impression that they were worked on overseas, some even give the feel that they have Russian ties. As I glance up, I catch his eyes staring not only at me, but almost through me.

"Like what you see there, цветок?"

"Ubetuke?" Why the hell did he call me that? I don't even know what the hell it means. Shaking my head out of the thoughts of the two of us getting nasty together between the sheets, against a wall, on a table—anywhere, really, I apply the stencil and have him get up to check the position in the long mirror.

"Perfect," is all he says before meeting my eyes in the mirror. As he walks over and lays back down, he places his arms to rest under his head. When I go over to turn the music back on, I hear him growl.

"I'm not listening to this girlie ass shit while you ink me for the next six fucking hours, Цветок. You might as well put something else on or turn it the fuck off so we can get to know each other better. You can tell me all about this motorcycle club you're a part of and how you spend your free time. You can answer any and all of those questions that I asked earlier as well. You know, all the typical first date shit, 'cause that shit," he points toward my speakers, "don't fly with me. This music is like a fucking cat in heat or some shit. I mean, to each their own, but how the fuck old are you?" Tucking his arm back under his head, he huffs, "I might give you a little leeway here or there as we spend more time together, but this shit…what the fuck is it?"

His voice sends shivers through my body, but nobody tells me what to do in my shop. "Are you kidding me? Where have you been the last fifteen years? It's fucking JT." Taking a deep breath, I hold back the next words that I would like to say, hoping to save myself a lawsuit. Which reminds me, I've got to call the lawyer again and actually speak to someone this time, to make sure he's available for my court date next month. I don't know why Sheriff Jones is always up my fucking ass, but that shit's getting tedious to say the least.

Getting back to the situation at hand, I say, "We seem to be at an impasse, because this here is my station, in a shop that I'm the CEO of, inside a building I'm on the fucking deed for, getting ready to put my ink on you." My mind is rolling with laughter. "So, I'm gonna have to disagree and say that we'll be listening to whatever the hell I want." Pausing briefly, I shake my head before laying a hand on the table, grazing his skin as I go to push myself up. The jolt that goes between us as our skin meets, draws my hand back from him quickly, like it's been burned.

He must feel it as well, because his head pops up from the table, and those brown eyes are on me in a minute. "Okay, цветок. Go ahead, listen to this or whatever you want for the next six hours, but know that when you are at my mercy, I will not forget this right here. It'll be the first thing tallied against you." Putting his head back down, he faces away from me. "Let's get this shit going. The sooner you start, the earlier we can get off, right?"

Trying my damnedest to ignore his last comment, I pull on a pair of gloves and get to work, not giving him any notice that I'm starting. Well, other than the buzz of the gun. My mind starts to wonder about his words, and I fall into a good rhythm with my work. The silence between us is comfortable, and I for one am shocked by it. Usually, people are chatty when getting ink done. I get it, I do, but fuck, I don't like that many folks, and I feel like a god damn hairdresser half the time with how people ramble on.

Glancing up to the clock, I see that about two hours have passed, and my hands on his flesh has fucking got me hot. I stop for a few moments, pulling off my gloves, then my sweatshirt. Taking a swig or two from my coffee, I pull on another pair of gloves and get back to it. Not seeing him move while I grabbed my drink, I'm guessing he fell asleep while I worked. My mind wanders as I start back up again, and fall right back into my zone. Finishing up the outline and some of the shading, I look over to the clock again, and find that I've been working for almost seven hours.

"Цветок, if you're gonna go back to it, you're gonna have to let me up to stretch and relieve myself. I don't think my cock can take much more of your hands running over my body without some kind of fucking relief." His words only get louder as he faces me. "And when I get a taste of you, Цветок, I won't be giving that up."

The shock must be evident on my face, because I can't speak at his words. I just sit there, glaring at him, as he swings his legs off the table. "Цветок, wipe that look off your face. I won't ever speak something that's untrue to you, and right now, I got one hell of a fucking hard-on from you putting that ink on me, having your hands all over my back, your breath on my skin, and shit needs to get worked out."

Glancing toward his crotch at the mention, I see the problem, and it's fucking huge. "Shit, let's just call it quits for the day then." Raising my eyes up to his, the smile on my face grows wide, but I can't help but poke the fucking bear with my next words. "You know, if you can't take anymore from me…" I trail off, shucking off one glove, then the next, and toss them into the trash can.

Taking in the meaning of my words, his hand shoots out quick, grabbing my wrist as the gloves hit the can. Tugging me toward him, he places my hands on his hips, pulling me into the space between his legs, snug up against his rock-hard cock. "цветок, don't start this shit with me if you're not ready to finish it. This fresh ink on me makes me think that I might not be able to take you the ways that I have been picturing these last seven hours, though."

His pupils are dilated, the irises so dark, his lust is practically jumping out of them. He's not the only one that'll be rubbing something out right quick. The tension between us is so fucking thick, it could be cut with a plastic knife. I try to push myself off his body.

"Okay. Well, again, we seem to be at a stalemate, so let's just call it a draw and move on from here. I'll head out while you get your cock on." The blush that creeps to my face at my mistake heats me from the inside out. "Shirt! Fuck, I meant shirt. Let me get off your cock—lap, so you can get dressed. After I put your wrap on, that is."

Trying again to step away from him, his arms only close tighter around me, before his breath brushes against my ear. "цветок, I'm so glad to see that I affect you the same way you do me. We'll need to go out soon and see what this thing between us is. I know when I get you beneath me, we will have one hell of a time." Lifting a finger to my chin, he raises my head so that our lips are mere inches apart. He licks his lips before speaking again. "When are you free?"

Trying without success, my eyes hit the floor, seeing the determination, desire, and domination in his. "No, that won't be happening, sir." The word slips out of my mouth, and the groan that falls from his overwhelms me.

"Sir is not what you will be calling me, цветок. By the time I get what I want from you, though, you will be calling me by a different name entirely." And with that, he releases my body and turns his back to me.

Taking only a few moments to right myself, I grab up the salve and apply a liberal coat before getting out the wrap and tape. Making sure that everything is wrapped up tight, I turn and walk for my office at the back of the shop, throwing over my shoulder, "All done, Adrik. Schedule your next session with Billie Jo on your way out. If you'd like me to finish it, that is."

The chuckle that comes from my room is close to a growl. "Run, run, run, little цветок. You'll come back just like the flowers in the spring, and I'll be waiting, making you beg when you do."

Locking the door up tight as I make it to the office, I slump back against it. That man back there has me feeling this way after just meeting him. I'm in trouble. The way he speaks to me, the things he says, the way my body feels when I'm around him, makes me want to do nothing except drop to my knees and worship his cock. Fuck, I need to stay the fuck away from that man because after the shitshow that went down with my ex-husband, I swore that I would never kneel down to a man again.

Grabbing up the keys for the closet, I head inside, getting the newest addition out. Knowing the hundred and fifty it costs will be a good use of money, considering the feels that Adrik gave me and the desires that he has forced out of me as well. Throwing myself down on the couch, I pull the new vibrator from its package. Knowing that pre-charging these things is the recommendation, I ain't got time for that, and pray to God that this baby has a little something in her.

Switching it on, I'm happy to see that I'm right, and the buzz I feel will get me there. That, and the thoughts of that man. Scooting my jeans under my ass a little, I dive right in, rubbing the Hitatchi along my pussy. As I continue, my mind drifts to him, the one I have only just met that has me twisted up in knots. Pushing the device harder into my swollen heat only serves to drive a moan from my mouth.

Moving it slowly up to my little pink pearl, I hit the button, forcing the speed to pick up, and am instantly rewarded with the tingles. As the tingles continue to build, I hope to hell nobody comes back to this end of the shop. Hearing me moan out like some whore in heat would really serve me well, trying to be the constant professional. Don't get me wrong, I like watching people fuck in public. Hell, *I* like fucking in public, but this is my place of work, something that I've busted my ass off for.

Just as my orgasm takes hold, I picture him taking his pleasure from me, using me as he would like, and bringing this fucking orgasm ripping from my body. My breathing, along with a few other noises, fill the room as I keep writhing around under my new best friend. Fuck Stiletto, her role as best friend has just been rewritten 'cause she ain't got nothing on this new Hitachi of mine. As his name spills from my lips, my legs start to tremble and I almost miss the deep voice speaking from the other side of the door.

"That won't be the name you're calling out when I finally get you kneeling underneath me, цветок. You won't be able to fight this thing between us forever. See you in two weeks for our next go 'round. If I don't catch you before, that is." With a chuckle, I hear his boots retreating down the hall, and wonder how I missed that noise coming closer to the office.

Fuck me, I need a fucking drink. Glancing at the clock, I see it's about an hour before the shop closes, and I clean myself up before heading to the kitchen and pulling the premade pitcher of punch from the fridge. As I get back to the office, I grab up some paperwork and get down to it. I fill up my cup, draining about half before refilling it and sitting down. Knowing he heard me does little for my focus, and I find myself with little work done an hour later, when Billie Jo knocks on the door.

"You hiding back here, boss lady?"

"Nah, just trying to get through some of this fucking shit before heading out for the night. You all ready to go? The other two got their sessions all sorted and shit?"

"Yeah, boss lady. They were done shortly after you finished up with that tall drink of water." Moving a few steps toward me, she places some bills on the desk. "He sure was something to look at. Even you had to notice that, Titz." With that, she turns to go back to the front. Looking down at the cash, I see five one hundred-dollar bills, and the smile that takes hold is big.

"We're going out tonight, no ifs, ands, or tits about it. Let Tittytat and Juggz know we're heading over to Killjoys."

Nodding her head, she turns with a smirk and makes her way toward their stations. This money is going to help me out a lot. Maybe I'll finally be able to pay those fucking parking tickets and fines Sheriff Hot Ass keeps giving me before he throws me in the slammer again. I swear he gets his rocks off feeling me up and throwing me into that little cell.

Four

It's been two weeks, and he's coming back in today to work on that Lady Justice again. I've bumped into him a time or three in town, once of which he was wearing an expensive tailored three-piece suit, with his beard and hair groomed to a T, looking like some sort of model for one of those erotic, mommy porns I like to read. My mind couldn't help the stories it tried to come up with, justifying his getup. A gangster here in Magnolia Springs starting up his own chapter or whatever they call it, for whatever bratva he belonged to? One of those billionaire CEO types with a heart of gold, looking for the perfect virgin to bow down to him after carving a path to his dark, dead heart? Maybe more of the businessman by day, filthy talking Dominant by night kind of guy, who needs a sweet little piece to serve him. The shit my mind comes up with. Okay, I might read too many of those trashy smut novels. And with each new story about him, my hormones rage, and my new Hitachi is put to use, day in and day out.

The way he would talk to me the times we'd met on the street did little to deter those thoughts and fantasies either. Each of us could, I don't know, sense the other person within fifty yards, and it was like the world stopped...at least for me. He would come into view, and whatever I was doing, whomever I was with, would drop away. My sole focus would go to him, and I would be drawn in.

"цветок" he would growl, causing my eyes to drop to his expensive shoes. "Raise those pretty little eyes up to mine, Precious." And the fight within me to not do just that would not last long enough, because his chocolate brown depths would be my sole focus within only a few moments. The first time "Good girl" spilled from his lips, I came on the spot with a little moan. And fuck my ass if he didn't chuckle with the knowledge of his hold on me.

"Oh цветок, you have just made me a very happy man." Reaching a hand up, he only brushed his fingers against my cheek before I turned and headed back to the shop. "Run, run, run цветок."

The last two weeks have been trying to say the least, other than the thoughts of him that seem to be at the forefront. Getting the ride organized with the Southern Lords has been a pain in my ass. They're always so put off by me calling to try to work out some of the details. Their road captain, Leeds, seems like a nice enough guy, but every time I try to pin down the ride route, he gives me the runaround. I haven't been able to pin him down about the stops for the poker run either, where and who they're raising money for or anything. It's gotten to the point that I'm just gonna let Billie Jo deal with his ass. She moved into the apartment above the shop last week, and she's been helping out more and more around the shop. Showing her appreciation for the niceties that not only I, but the other Dirty Bitches have shown. She has no bones about going toe-to-toe with him, which I have heard firsthand the few times he's actually returned my calls and she's acted as go-between.

Pulling up to the shop, I notice an old Harley Sportster out front and wonder who the fuck is at the shop this time of day. Billie Jo usually turns up about a half hour before the rest of us, and I can see her bike parked down the street a ways. Pulling on the front door, I find it hard to believe that I have to take out my keys to unlock it. Glancing down the street, I double check that it is indeed Billie Jo's bike, because I've never known her to lock the front door once she's inside.

Unlocking the door, the chime sounds as I step through, and I don't see any signs of life. Deciding against calling out, I move through the shop, stopping with a big smile on my face when I hear the noises coming from the kitchen area. Something's getting eaten, but fuck me if it's food. Creeping my way the last few steps, I lean into the doorway of the kitchen, and see Billie Jo splayed out over the table, skirt piled up over her waist, panties around her ankles, while someone feasts on her like it's their last supper. I'm guessing from the guy's cut, and the way they've been going at it the last two weeks, this is Leeds. Letting her have her fun, I pull up a chair into the doorway, quiet as a mouse, and plop my ass down for the show. The only things that would make this shit better was if I could get some of my punch and some popcorn to eat while watching this shit. Maybe I got time to run to my office and grab that Hitachi. That thing is just as fucking amazetits as everyone said it would be.

As the guy stands, unbuckling his belt, button, then zipper, he pulls his cock out, and I can see the metal gleaming off the lights. Leaning to the left, I try to size up which piercing he has, and hope it's the ladder for her pleasure. He stops short of driving home at my words. "Excuse me, boy, but don't you think you should be wrapping that shit up before sinking balls deep in my employee there? I could go grab you some wraps if you need them. Have no fear, I'm accommodating like that."

The screech the comes out of him at my voice has me laughing like a fucking hyena. Billie Jo doesn't seem to be all that concerned. She does, however, roll her eyes hard when she sees that I've pulled up a chair, and had been watching from the front row, so to say.

"Boss lady, are you fucking kidding me right now? You pulled up a fucking chair? Really?" is all she says as she tries unsuccessfully to get up, almost falling to the floor, which has this guy bending over quickly to help.

"Well, I was a little worried when I came into the shop and had to use my fucking key to unlock the front door." Never getting up, I nod toward the man who's righted himself, and is now tucking his cock back into his pants. "Now, though, I see what that was all about. You and this Southern Lord seem to have been too wrapped up in each other to think about protection, so I'm glad I was here to save the day."

A deep rumble comes from behind me. Turning my head at the noise, I'm greeted with a bulging cock covered in tight blue jeans, about six inches from my face. It's tucked away to the right side again today, and I wonder if men always keep their cocks on the same side.

The laughter that spills from his lips forces my head up. "Yeah, цветок, men tend to keep their cocks to the same side. It might just be a force of habit, but I think I'm flattered that you seem to remember that I like mine to the right. You'll know where to find him when I decide it's time."

Glancing into the kitchen area, Adrik is quick to take in the situation, and the laugh he had when I'd accidently asked about his cock is nothing compared to the belly laugh that is now coming out.

"Fuck, цветок, you running a live porn studio in the kitchen? That's weird, but kinda hot. I mean, I've had thoughts about taking you on every surface I've walked past these last two weeks. I read about the closet of kink that is in the shop somewhere, but this…this right here takes the cake."

Taking my eyes off of him is like taking candy from a baby, and I'm screaming on the inside with the loss. Pushing up out of the chair, I nudge him, trying to return it to Tittytat's station, with no luck getting him to move.

"Hey, big guy, could you move outta the way so I can drop this chair back in Tittytat's room before she realizes I snagged it? She hates people touching her shit, and I'm not gonna take one for the team if I don't have to."

"Tittytat?" comes out as a rumble. "Who the fuck names themselves that?"

"I gave her that name, big guy, so watch what you say." Walking past him, I place the chair back and exit the room, just as I hear the front door chime. "Thank fuck," comes out quietly as I turn to see Tittytat walking down the hall.

"Hey, Titz, what's goin' on? Why you standing around by my station? You looking for something?"

"Nah, girl, I was just walking him back out to my station after Billie Jo gave us a little show in the kitchen with one of the Southern Lords. If only you would've been here, like, five minutes earlier, you could've seen the show!" I laugh, walking toward my station, with Adrik following close on my heels.

Moving toward the inks, I turn on my tunes before starting to set shit up, feeling him behind me. I don't turn, but say over my shoulder, "It's gonna be a bit, so if you wanna go up front so you don't have to listen to this shitty girlie music, as you so nicely put it, I'll come grab you when everything's ready."

I know he steps closer, because I can feel his breath on my neck before his finger trails along the flesh of my bare shoulder. Fucking summer weather making me wear this off the shoulder dress. "I can smell you from here, цветок. Watching them like that, I bet your panties are fucking drenched." His voice drops lower, and I feel his lips against my skin as he says, "Your cunt is fucking calling to me."

The shiver that shoots through me at his words, only serves his purpose and gives my panties more moisture. He places his hands on my hips before squeezing tightly. "I have thought of little except you these past two weeks. Seeing you in the street those times has done little to quench my desires for you. Tell me, цветок, have you thought of me too?"

I shake my head, knowing that my voice will give me away with the deception.

"You lie."

Shaking my head again, I try to focus on the task at hand, setting up my station. Trying yet again to step free from him, I only make it a foot before his voice stops me dead in my tracks.

"You will have to stop running at some point, цветок. I know the effect that I have on that lithe body of yours." And with that, he moves out of my station and toward the front, letting me finish setting up and try like hell to get this ache to subside. Which doesn't work, even in the twenty minutes I give myself. Even with the little bit of Hitachi action I gave myself before heading out to collect him.

"I'm all setup. Come on back and let's finish your Lady Justice up." Putting his phone down, he glances over at me before giving a sharp nod of his head, shoving himself up and heading back toward my station.

I'm almost there when Tittytat pops her head out of her station. "Titz, you went digging in my fucking station. Why the fuck would you do that? You know how much that shit pisses me off. What did you fucking touch, 'cause now I'm gonna need to get a new one, and don't think I ain't putting that shit in to have you pay for it."

"Jesus Christ, Titttytat." I smack my hand against my forehead. I knew she'd fucking figure it out. She's got some fucking weird OCD shit or something 'cause I've never known someone so obsessed with their stuff before. "I borrowed your fucking chair to watch Billie Jo and that Southern Lord fuck in the kitchen 'cause I couldn't go in there and grab a chair without them noticing that shit."

"You and your fucking voyeuristic tendencies. You're gonna get in trouble one day for that shit, you know?"

"What are you talking about, Tittytat? You know the sheriff busted me a couple weeks back. My court date is all set."

She shakes her head. "No, that's not what I mean. Getting busted breaking into the garage and getting caught watching the sheriff fuck Stiletto isn't shocking, it's just stupid." I stick my tongue out at her. "I'll order a new chair today. Expect that bill to be on your desk no later than tomorrow, Titzhole!"

"Fuck," I growl out as I make my way into my room. Lost in the argument with Tittytat, I forgot who was waiting for me, but as soon as I step into the room, his scent fills my nose, and my eyes dart to the table. His bared back is on display for me, his tight jeans hugging that fucking ass of his nicely as he rests his head on his arms, facing me.

Seeing his shoulders jiggle, I know he's trying to hold back his laughter. "You did mention that she wasn't going to like you using her stuff. I guess I just thought that you might have been exaggerating." Dropping his voice low, he adds, "She got OCD or some shit like that?"

"Yeah, something like that." Grabbing up a pair of gloves, I pull them on.

"What about that court date she mentioned? What the fuck was that all about?" he asks with a smile on his face.

"Never mind about that shit. I'm your tattoo artist, not your friend, not your fuck buddy, not your servant, or God forbid old lady. And I'm most definitely not your sub."

The look he gives confuses the fuck out of me. I know that we share this fucking draw between us, but why would he be sad about me shutting him down on this?

Grabbing up my gun, I zone out once I find a rhythm to his ink. Again, this session passes by with nothing other than my "shitty girlie music" passing between us. This time, it's not JT, it's my 90s mix with more hair bands than should be allowed anywhere. Bon Jovi's "Born to Be My Baby" comes on, and I find it hard not to sing along with the words. The silence that would usually be filled with nothing but small talk is filled with a silence, something I would normally feel so uncomfortable with. With Adrik quiet on my table, though, I feel nothing but ease.

My hands on his flesh for the last three hours has done little for the desire he's caused. I spray him down, needing to take a good look at the piece before going on. Moving my head side to side to loosen some of the tension in my shoulders, I slowly take in the whole piece, and can picture where I need to work from.

Raising his head up, I see him turn toward me.

"Time for a break?"

"If you'd like? I could use a few minutes." Shrugging my shoulder, I try stretching the ache from them. "You know what? Let's take a few. You gonna head outside? If you are, I should probably wrap you up."

Reaching for the wrap and tape, he cuts me off quickly. "No need, Katarina. I don't smoke, so no, I won't be heading outside." My name on his lips sends another jolt of desire right through me. Like my hands all over his back wasn't enough, or his smell filling this little room.

"Oh, okay. Well, I just got a call to make, so I'll be right back. Two more hours on this piece and we should be golden."

"Then me and you are gonna have a talk, цветок," is all I hear before making my way out of the room as he's pushing himself up. Running away before he has the chance to catch me.

Locking the door behind me, I grab up the receiver and place the call, yet again, to the lawyer. At least this time, I actually talk to someone in his office, and she lets me know that Mr. Smirnov has taken a leave and his son has taken over all clients. She tells me that the younger Mr. Smirnov will be at the court date, and has been informed of the situation, as well as the previous times that I've had to appear and what they have been for.

Her voice is overly cheery as she adds, "He's been told of your case. Mr. Smirnov will get you off; no worries, dear." And with those words I hang up, thinking back to this last time that Sheriff Hot Ass pulled me in, booking me for "Peeping" on him and Stiletto. Got his panties all in a twist because I might've pulled up a chair and watched for a bit as they were going at it in the garage. Fuck, what did they want me to do when they were in public like that? Well, as Stiletto told me behind a locked door in her office, it wasn't a fucking public display meant for me. Ugh. I have a key to that door in case I ever need to get in there to get something. How the fuck was I to know what they were in there doing?

Making my way out of the office, I head back to my room and find him again, laid out flat on my table. Hearing me come in, his head barely pops up from the table as he asks, "We ready to finish this off, цветок?"

"The fuck do you keep calling me? And what the fuck language are you speaking? I keep picturing you as some sort of Russian mafioso, and in Magnolia Springs, I just don't think that's the fucking case."

Chuckling at one of my many made-up stories, he answers my question. "It's Russian, and you're right about that part of your fantasies at least. It means flower."

"Why?" is all I'm able to say as my eyes meet his.

"All that ink running up your arms, Precious." I can feel his eyes rake over my body before he tries to go on, but I cut him off.

"The first time we met, you called me that, and I remember having a sweatshirt on."

"Why would you remember that so well, I wonder?"

"'Cause my mind has gone back there a time or two. I remember taking my sweatshirt off, because after tattooing you for a couple hours, I was hot as hell and needed to try and cool myself off." The blush that creeps to my face warms me again.

"The pictures on the wall, the one of you in the burlesque show. I'm sure that I must have seen the flowers there. It doesn't really matter because the name suits you very well."

Lowering my voice, I add, "More than you'd ever know."

The growl that I hear across the room does nothing to help distract my fantasies. "I can't wait for a chance to get in your clothes and see how much more ink you have when you're kneeling at my feet." Glancing toward my dress, he's quick to add, "And how much jewelry I'm sure you have hiding under those clothes. I'm betting you got some golden rings hanging from that pretty pussy of yours."

The smile that ghosts his face sends a bolt of heat right to my pussy, but his words snap me out of my haze. "Kneeling?"

His voice is low, barely above a whisper. "Yes, kneeling. Serving me in all the ways that I would like." Catching my eyes, he reaches out and places his hand on my thigh, a bare thigh at the moment, because he's swept my dress up and out of the way. "Don't deny that there is a submissive hiding behind all that huff and puff you got going on. Your eyes don't lie, цветок, and I for one look forward to dragging that out of you." He squeezes my thigh after moving his hand up a few more inches, so close to where I truly want him. "When you stop running, that is." And his hand is gone, moving again under his head, and my mind races with the pull he has on me.

Grabbing up some gloves, I get them on and dive right back into the ink, needing to focus my mind on something other than this gorgeous man laid out before me. It takes another two and a half hours to finish up, and I'm quick to clean up and get out of my room, but it seems that Adrik has other plans.

Standing up, he faces me while looking over his shoulder to get a good look in the mirror. "Your work is fucking amazing, цветок. I can't believe the detail that you've put into it. You are truly an artist." He moves quickly, turning around to grab my wrists. "Now Lady Justice is always with me, just like you will be, soon."

Trying my best to avoid his eyes, I drop my gaze, trying but failing desperately to get out of his hold.

"Your work is beyond anything that I could have thought possible. Don't think that I didn't notice you didn't meet all the details that I gave to you. I swore there were four things that I asked from you in this piece, and I'm only seeing three. Where is that last piece of the puzzle, my цветок?"

"That isn't something I'm comfortable doing as an artist, and I don't know why you would think that I or anyone ever would be," I say as nicely as I can as to why I wouldn't put my name into his ink. When he first brought it up, I thought it was a joke. Then he didn't mention it when it was left out of the sketch he'd approved. I thought my hunch was correct, that he hadn't really wanted it. Now, it seems that was incorrect.

"It's just something that I have most all my artists work into their pieces. But especially you, after the connection I felt with you when we met. You will be inking yourself onto my flesh at some point, цветок."

The look on my face must tell him exactly how I feel about the words he has just voiced.

"You, however, I see the fear in you. Don't run this time, цветок. I will hold it against you and that fucking ass of yours if you do." Smiling at his words, I'm glad he finds it pleasing, that I have pleased him by doing something I love so much. Another part of that submissive I thought wouldn't ever slip out again. Shaking my head from the thoughts, I'm quick to clean and wrap up his tattoo.

Grabbing up his shirt, he slips it over his head as I make my way out of the room.

"You're running again, цветок," is all I catch as I make my way into the office, locking the door behind me. Pulling up some fetish porn on my phone, I know that this will help to ease my racing thoughts, at least for a few minutes. Zoning out at the show, it must take me a few minutes to hear the knocking on the door. Cutting off the show, I stand up and unlock the door, only opening it a little bit to see Billie Jo on the other side. Swinging it wide, I grab up the punch she's brought with her before plopping myself down into the chair behind my desk.

"You're welcome, boss lady." She nods her head toward the punch that I'm now downing, straight from the pitcher I might add. "This is from that guy. Had me give him an envelope and paper to write you a note or some shit. Hope to hell there's a fat tip in there too, 'cause he sure as fuck didn't give me anything for you." Turning on her heel after tossing the envelope on the desk, she heads back toward the front. "I'm ready whenever you are," she calls out as she goes.

Grabbing up the envelope, I think better of opening it here, and shove it into my back pocket as I put away the papers and finish up my drink. Moving toward the front, I only have to nod at her before she's clicking the lights off and heading for the door as well.

"You wanna head over to the clubhouse with me, Billie Jo? Have a drink or two to unwind?"

"Nah, I'm gonna head home and catch some shut-eye. See ya in the morning, boss lady."

Five

Heading over to the clubhouse after this fucking day is exactly what I need. Stepping inside, Prez is behind the bar slingin', and I head straight up to it. "Can I get a punch, Prez?" I shove the stool out before plopping my ass into it. Rubbing my neck to relieve some of the tension from the hours spent slouched over that man today does little for me. The relief I felt from my new toy did more for giving me some relief than this shit attempt at a self-massage.

"Yeah, yeah. Looks like you had a rough session. I'm not even sure how that could be, seeing as how you just doodle on people for a living," Links heckles from a few seats down. Moving my head to her, I see Grimm at her feet, and call him over to me before she goes on. "Or were you demonstrating something out of that kink closet you got over there?" She chuckles.

"You jealous or something, Links? Your old man Monty Python not giving it to you good enough? Your garden need a little tending to?" Laughing out loud at my joke, I can't help but take it a step further. "You need some of that kink closet to help you and your man? I'll give you a stiff discount on whatever your heart, or vagina, desires." The laughter that spills from me at those words is loud, and startles Grimm as he makes his way toward me.

"Tits Ahoy" comes out in-between the giggles, which is echoed by Stiletto. But then the words she said strikes me, causing me to scowl. "Yeah, you finally feeling the itch of not wanting to be tied down to one dick?" I wag my eyebrows. "Well, not tied down in the way I like at least. You sure you don't need a little something outta that closet to spice it up a bit? 'Cause I don't know where this shit is coming from. Me and my doodles just made the club a grand today. How'd you do playing on that fucking computer of yours, Links? Fuck up any more purse hooks today?"

Rubbing Grimm behind the ear, I grab for the jar of treats from behind the bar and shake a couple out into my hand. Putting my hand down to his level, I let him have his fill before taking back up rubbing him behind the ears, cooing sweet words.

"Bloody hell, Titz, knock it off. For fuck's sake, stop feeding Grimm. I'm gonna start taking your share of club money to pay his vet bills." Looking around the table, she's quick to add, "Prez, she's only gotten worse the last few weeks since me and Roman have been together. I caught her pulling up a bench in Roman's back yard looking into my garden just two days ago when we were getting hot and heavy."

The smile that takes hold is so fucking wide with the memories of that night. Trying to plead my case might be useless, but it's fun nonetheless. "I might've had a few too many and knew that she would be spending time with that Queen Elizabeth lovin' dude. It just so happened that when I went strolling past, I heard a noise. You know the kind, and you know how I am."

Moving her eyes from me to Prez, she tries to plead with Rogue as she's putting my punch down in front of me. "Prez, come on, help me out here."

"You gotta be shittin' me. The club has nothing to do with this, and you sure as shit won't be cutting into funds for that. Don't make me remind you that she's raising those four little girls on her own, Links." Grabbing up her moonshine, she takes a swig before continuing. "The two of you are at each other constantly, and I ain't stepping in-between that shit. Work it out, because I for one am getting sick of this shit. I mean, you fight like sisters. We all know you love each other and would do anything for each other, but this shit is getting old." She turns and heads off in the direction of her old man, who's just made his way through the front door.

As I finish off my drink, I start to feel good before remembering the envelope. Pulling it out of my back pocket, I head over toward the back office. Opening the door, I step inside quietly, and the sight that greets me is something I should be turning away from. I know I should, but I don't. I can't fucking help that I like watching people fuck, and this here will be one hell of a show.

Prez is laid out flat on her desk, while her old man pounds into her from behind. The moans filling the room are something that any porn star would be proud of. Tilting my head to the side, I wonder if the weird motorcycle statue she keeps on her desk has been thrown to the floor, or if it's under her tits on the desk. Moving my head around, I try to figure out where that thing has gotten off to.

Not being able to stop the words that are coming outta my mouth, I say, "Hey, Prez, where's that motorcycle statue you always keep on your desk? It's not underneath you, is it? Fucking digging into your fluffy pillows, is it? I bet that shit would hurt like a motherfucker—" I'm cut off before I'm able to finish my thoughts.

"The fuck, Titz? Get the fuck outta here!" her old man hollers, pushing himself deeper into his woman, trying to keep his cock out of view. "What the fuck is wrong with her?"

Shrugging her shoulders in answer, Prez simply says how it is. These bitches know how I am. "It's her thing. She likes watching, or being watched, or anything remotely kinky." The smile that tugs wide is something I didn't expect from her. "You get used to it." She looks over at me. "Go up to your room, dumbass, or head back to the shop and get something out of that fucking closet of yours and take care of your shit. Or here's an idea, why don't you find yourself a man and get him to give you that cock you want so bad. Find the right guy to have you kneeling at his feet instead of that piece of shit ex-husband of yours. Maybe then you can stay the fuck out of here, or Stiletto's shop, or Link's garden when you don't have permission. You know the fucking rules, Titz."

Turning, I open the door before throwing over my shoulder, "Yeah, yeah. Okay, Prez. I'm heading back to the shop...I gotta go get something." I'm gonna need another go with that Hitachi after seeing Prez in that position, giving me that show.

Walking into the back door of the shop, I lock up after me and grab the pitcher of punch from the fridge as I go. Moving into my office, I grab the envelope out of my pocket and sit down at my desk. Pouring a glass of punch, I take a few big swigs before opening the envelope and pulling out the note from inside. As I do, five one hundred-dollar bills fall out onto my desk, causing a smile to pull at my lips. That money will really help in making it till the end of the month.

It's harder than hell being a single mom and having only one source of income to provide for those four girls I got at home. The running joke is that if only Titz could find a sugar daddy, all her dreams could come true, and nothing is closer from the truth. I mean, I love doing tattoos, and I wouldn't want to do anything else, but not having to put in twelve-hour days and working my fingers to the bone would be nice. Spending time with my kids, more than just getting them from daycare to school, or the next sitter, would be fucking nice.

Not being able to make ends meet has gotten me into trouble more than once. Fuck, like that one time I had to have Stiletto come down and use her powers of persuasion with Sheriff Hot Ass because I couldn't pay those parking fines. God damn, Sheriff Hot Ass and Clint always giving me fucking grief. That reminds me again, I've got to get a hold of the lawyer to make sure he can show up in court to help me fight the last ticket I got.

Pulling myself out of those thoughts, I open up the note tucked into the envelope with the cash, and my mouth hits the floor as I read.

Цветок,

Always running from me, it seems. I don't know why you are fighting this pull between us so much, but you will be mine. I will own every inch of that gorgeous body of yours, and your running is only serving to piss me off. It's pointless to try and fight it or run from me, and I'm not sure what has happened to you in the past to cause it. That is not me, though. You should be given any and everything you desire in life. The only worry you should have is how to please me each and every day.

I have never felt this way with the girls that have served me, and I knew the second you touched me that you were meant to be mine. It might take you a bit to stop fighting it, but it will happen, have no doubt. But for each day that it takes for that to happen, there will be consequences, for you.

Don't think I didn't hear you in that office the first time I was in the shop, using that fucking toy on yourself. I often think about that toy and how many times you have used it thinking about me. The times we have ran into each other in the street, have you used it? Or at night when you're alone, and your fingers glide over your body with those little moans that will forever be etched into my brain spilling from your lips? That shit stops now. I am the only one who will deal out pleasure to you from here on out. You'll do well to remember that, or the lessons I teach for that little discrepancy will bring those dirty little fantasies you have to fucking shame.

The next time I come to you, you will be on your knees for me, and I for one will be thanking the fucking heavens what you've never given someone exactly what you will be giving to me.

Your Everything,

A.S.

This man has it so wrong. I've been down that road before, and I sure as fuck won't go there again. I won't kneel to another man, give another man the power to control me, to take everything that is me and walk the fuck away. Well, he didn't walk away, I ran the fuck away and brought my girls somewhere safe. Somewhere I knew people would have our backs, and be my ride or dies, and that's exactly what the Dirty Bitches are—our family.

It took me years to get back to any sort of sanity after I left that dickhead ex of mine, and I won't do it again, no matter the feelings I'm having for him. Even if kneeling down at his feet is exactly what I want to do.

Six

Thirteen fucking days, and the thought of seeing him is driving me fucking insane. Today is the day, though, that I'll forget about him and get him the fuck out of my mind. I won't long to run into him on the street, drop my eyes for him, wait patiently for his praise to drive me wild. Speaking shit into reality has gotta work for some people, right? Why the fuck not me?

After my one session at the shop today, I have just enough time to head over to the store to pick up a few things so the girls can have a pow-wow tonight with the sitter, before I have to be to court at four. And God knows, Momma's gonna need some time to herself after the court case wraps up. Well, by myself, I mean with my Dirty Bitches.

I even dressed up fancy-like to impress the judge. I borrowed a pair of Stiletto's fancy heels and everything. She might not know about that, though, so I sure as fuck hope she doesn't show up at court. The pair with the red bottoms are just so fucking comfy, and they match the little black dress I picked out. They were too good to pass up. Checking myself in the mirror for the millionth time, I gotta say, my bazongas are looking damn fine if I do say so myself, and the heels serve to make my ass and thighs look fucking amazetits as well. Maybe Momma will get herself a little somethin' somethin' tonight.

Laughing at my joke, my mind wanders back to Adrik and the note that he left me. I've only seen him a couple times since his last session. I have, however, read and reread that note so much, the fold lines are getting frayed. Each time I've taken it out, I've cursed him the first minute and taken my Hitachi out and rubbed one out the next. My mind is so confused, wanting him this much, but only seeing him. Being in the same room with him and not even talking but a handful of times. It can't work like that, right? I mean, I'm sure love at first sight isn't a real fucking thing, but he has me feeling things I never thought I would again. And so much different, stronger, from the way I felt for Doug for the years that we were together.

"UGH!" rumbles out of me as I pull up to the shop. I see a Harley Heritage Classic sitting out front and wonder who the fuck's here. Maybe that Southern Lord Billie Jo is hooking up with got a new bike. He sure as shit needed it. Maybe I'll be walking into another show, and with that thought, my pace picks up and my mind starts raging as a smile pulls against the corners of my mouth.

Hoping that a strange bike outside the shop ends much the way it did the last time, I throw the kickstand down and sling my leg over, stopping myself when I see the black pumps hitting the ground. I know that I'm going to be in trouble if I scuff them, so I take extra care as I head right into the shop.

Stepping inside, seeing who that bike belongs to, forces a growl from me before I'm able to speak. Noticing Billie Jo behind the counter, I nod my head toward the back, and she takes the hint, scampering off to the office.

"Doug, what the fuck are you doing here?"

"Kitten, is that any way to greet your husband?" His voice drops as he moves toward me. "Your master." Stepping closer, yet only a foot or two between us, he smiles. "Your owner."

"You're none of those fucking things, Doug. I'm not a possession." The stress in me picks up, knowing that he's found out where I am, where our girls are, and has come here looking for something. What does that mean for me? "What the fuck do you want, Doug?"

"Tsk, tsk, Kitten. You know how I hate for you to speak that way. Your Momma raised you to be a much better woman than that, so I'm gonna have to ask that you respect her, and me in turn."

The butterfly's that had been floating through me with the thoughts of getting under Adrik, of being able to finally free my thoughts of him once I have him buried deep inside me, are gone now, replaced with a sickness that my ex has brought on. "Don't mention that woman to me. She's nothing to me, and neither are you. So tell me why the fuck you're here, and then get the fuck gone."

He doesn't bother stepping closer, or try to intimidate me, much like he used to. He raises his fist in the air, and I almost drop to my knees with fear and no other thought. That is, before the door chime sounds. I immediately feel his energy filling the room before I can even pull my eyes away from Doug to look at him. When I do, I see his rage, which is something that even I'm scared of.

"I would think better of hitting my цветок, you sorry fucking excuse of a man!" Nodding toward me, Adrik asks, "This the fucker that has you scared? Has you denying this thing between us?" Nodding toward Doug, I have to stop the nervous laughter that wants to spill from not only my anxiety and nerves, but the fear on Doug's face, or what I'm guess is piss that has just started running down his legs. Just the humor of the situation alone has me almost laughing as he adds, "This fucking small dick piece of shit who thinks that hitting a woman out of hate is something that's fucking acceptable?"

"Adrik" is all I can get out before I try to turn and explain our past to a man I know little about. "He's my ex, the father of my daughters."

Nodding in understanding, his eyes flare with shock. Adrik asks only one question. "He's hit you before?"

My eyes drop to the ground, ashamed of the woman that I was. I stayed too long and wasn't able to pull myself away from him for a long while after the abuse started—after the first time he hit me, the first time he forced himself on me, the first time he tied me to the bed with little but his own pleasure on his mind.

The sound of bone shattering and a high-pitched scream is the next thing that draws me out of my thoughts.

The growl that I hear sounds more like it should be coming from a bear in the woods instead of the man I now see pummeling my ex. I put my hand on his shoulder and simply say, "Please." All movement stops. When his eyes meet mine, I know that his rage is slowly subsiding.

"I'll call the sheriff," I hear Billie Jo call out from the hall, and nod toward her as I move to stand.

"You should go. I can handle Sheriff Hot Ass when he gets here."

Taking a step back, the look on his face is priceless, as the name registers with him. "Sheriff Hot Ass, you say? Is that something I should be worried about, цветок?" he asks, stepping over Doug and closing in on me.

"Um, no," I squeak out as he grabs me around the waist, pulling me into his body.

"No is damn right. What I wrote, I meant every fucking word of. Seeing the way this piece of shit treated you lets me know why you're running, but I for one won't be scared off from it." Reaching up, he tucks a few errant hairs behind my ear, before slowly running his hand down to my neck. "You're mine."

Kissing me breathless, I know in this second that the feelings I have been running from won't be held at bay. Jumping up, he catches me, thankfully, and I wrap my legs around his waist as he palms my ass.

Getting caught up in the kiss, I don't notice the chime before I hear a throat clearing behind me.

"Titz, could you climb down off of Mr. Smirnov and let me know what the hell is going on here?" Sheriff Jones says, shaking his head in disapproval. "It seems that you have an unconscious man on your shop floor. It even looks like he might have a broken bone or two from that fall he took. Mind explaining that to me?"

"Jeeze, Sheriff Jones, why'd it have to be you to respond to this shit? Wasn't Clint working today?"

"You know he doesn't like to be around you more than he has to be, Katarina. He got scared shitless the first time you flashed him your titties, and I'm sure it's only gone downhill with all the shit you've done to him since then." Looking at Adrik, and and then back at me, he goes on. "Anyway, it seems like he has a court case that he needs to be at later this afternoon. You know, a peeping tom case. So it seems that you're stuck with me."

The slap I feel against my ass keys me in on the fact that Adrik might not be too keen on the idea of me flashing my titties to the popo. Tilting my head up to his, I don't even bother explaining before looking away. If he only knew the other shit that I've done, he might not be so understanding.

"Sheriff, could we not do this now? This piece of shit lying on the floor here is my ex, and he was threatening me with physical violence when, uh, Adrik here, stepped up and protected me."

"Physical violence, huh?" Sheriff Jones whistles, looking from me to Adrik, then again to Doug, who has only now just started to rise up to his feet.

"That true, asshole? You trying to hit on this woman?"

"Nope. I wouldn't waste my time with her used-up pussy if she were the last woman on earth. I was just here trying to hash out some visitation with my daughters before this fucking piece of shit jumped me."

Looking between the two of us, it's only now that I realize Adrik has tucked me into his body, holding me close to him with an arm thrown over my shoulders.

As Doug takes it in, the anger only builds in his face, and his next words are like a punch to the gut. "I wanna press charges on the both of them, Sheriff."

Jones is quick to answer, and I for one am shocked at his words. "Nope. That ain't gonna be happening, Doug." Taking a step closer to Doug, his voice drops low. "What will be happening, though, is you're gonna get on that fucking bike of yours and go right back to where you fucking came from. It doesn't seem that anybody has missed you being outta their lives, and nobody wants you to be here in Magnolia Springs. I think you would do well to remember that and get the fuck gone."

The look of hatred I see on Doug's face as he nods and heads toward the door, lets me know that he's complying, but this is far from fucking over. His next words leave no doubt. "This ain't over, Kitten, you can fucking bet on that." And with that, the chimes ring out and he's gone. For now at least.

"Well, Katarina, it seems you have much more of a backstory than you've ever led me to believe," Sheriff Jones says, watching my ex walk through the door. "I knew that having four little girls on your own probably wasn't your first choice. But, that man right there, I can start to see why you're the way you are. Why you act and do the things you do."

"Oh, don't get all teary-eyed and shit, Sheriff. I'm still the same freak who walked in on you fucking Stiletto, and pulled up a chair to watch. That shit won't ever change, no matter how much you think you know about me."

He shakes his head. I know I'm being a bitch, but it's my go-to when I'm feeling like this—vulnerable. Shaking myself out of Adrik's grip, I head straight for my office, via the kitchen, to grab up the new pitcher of punch that I find there.

Nodding toward Billie Jo, I let her know it's safe to head back up front and get back to work. Pulling the door shut behind me, I forego the lock as I rush toward the phone. I dial the school first, then the daycare, wanting to make sure Doug isn't allowed in to see the girls if that's where he's heading. He never cared much for the kids, but I'm not sure how far he's willing to take this thing or why he's even come, and that scares me the most.

Hearing the door shut and lock, my head pops up to see Adrik resting against it. "You want to tell me about that guy I just fucking beat the hell out of for raising his hands to you?" Taking a deep breath before he goes on, I can tell that he's trying his best to remain calm. "Then you can follow that up with just how old you are to have four fucking daughters with said son of a bitch. Maybe you could fill me in a little bit about them, and why their mother seems to have left them out, or I haven't seen them with you the times I have run into you."

I literally don't know how to answer him, so I do something that neither of us expects. Slamming down the last of my pitcher of punch, I stand up, shoving the chair back to the wall as I go. Moving quickly, I drop down to my knees as I reach him, fumbling at the belt of his pants. Before I'm able to get it undone, his hands cover mine, stopping their movement.

"No, цветок, that's not how this is going to go. You are not going to use your body to get out of talking to me about this shit. I know we have only spent a little time together, but the feelings I have for you are rock-solid. I didn't believe it after that first day, but I felt the same these last weeks each time I have seen you. I haven't been able to keep my mind on anything except you, and that shit needs to be dealt with."

"Okay, we can talk, but it's gonna have to be later tonight."

"That's fine. I have an appointment to keep now, but you better not be running again, цветок."

"No, I just got somewhere that I gotta be as well, after a session, that is. Meet me at Killjoys around six and we can head somewhere to talk, clear up all this shit between us, okay?"

Stepping closer, he pulls me to him, bringing our bodies together. His breath is warm on my lips as he leans in. "Just one taste before I go then." And with those words, his mouth claims mine with a force that I have never known before. A force that causes my knees to buckle. I sure as shit never felt anything remotely close to that with Doug, that's for fucking sure.

Pulling back, he nips my bottom lip as he goes. "Until this evening then, цветок," he says before turning and making his way from the room.

Seven

Heading into the courthouse, I'm about fifteen minutes early, and know that I'll need to meet up with my lawyer before heading in. Seeing Clint walking toward a door, I head in that direction before Stiletto comes into view, stopping me dead in my tracks.

"Titz" she growls, drawing my attention away from Clint and toward her. "Those my fucking Louie's you got on? How the fuck did you even get into the house? Pryor would fucking die if he knew you crept in the house to steal my shoes. Jesus fucking Christ, girl, that's one of the reasons you're at court today." Shaking her head at me seems something that she's been doing more and more of lately. I used to think she was such a good time, but it seems that I might've been wrong.

"Calm your tits down. I just knew that these babies would look so good with this dress, and then I knew you were at the garage and I didn't wanna interrupt you to get them, so…"

"So you broke into the sheriff's house to get them?" comes a growl that I would recognize anywhere. Turning slowly, I stare at the shoes, and make a slow swipe up over his dress pants, crisp white shirt, dark blazer, and a tie that reminds me of fucking Christian Grey. Fuck my life!

"Adrik?" squeaks out as my mind is finally adding all the pieces up. What the sheriff said earlier about me climbing off of him…what did he call him? "Wait a second here. Your last name is Smirnov…you're the club's new lawyer?" And with that, his smile widens as my realization sets in.

"Did you know when you first came into the shop…when you *were* coming into the shop? Is that why you asked all about me to get some dirt on your new client? That why you were flirting with me, to try and figure me out? Trying to get me to fucking kneel down for you?" I'm in the courthouse about to lose my fucking shit with the club's new lawyer. God dammit!

"Цветок, watch how you speak to me. I won't have you disrespecting me." His voice drops low enough for only me to hear. "Especially here at the courthouse, my place of fucking business most days. Keep that fiery temper up and" pausing briefly, he points to my face, "these cheeks won't be the only pair turning a pretty shade of red." Trying to reach out and run a finger over my face, I move back quickly, almost causing myself to trip. Steadying myself, he goes on, dropping his hand back down to his side. "It may have been dishonest of me to head into your shop without letting you know who I really was, or why I was really there, but once I saw you, I knew that you were meant to be mine."

Trying to get my thoughts together, I waste too much time, and Adrik is speaking again before I can voice a word. "That you were the other half of my soul. That shit isn't something that I take lightly, and I would never have done something to betray you. The shit that I know of you only came from my father and the cases that he has worked on for the club." Laughing, he goes on. "Most of which, it seems, were for you, цветок."

"I can't help that the popo in this town don't seem to be too enthralled with me, or that the fire department puts those fucking fire hydrants in places that they shouldn't. I think they put that one in front of the shop on purpose, just to make some money off of me. I wonder if they need some new supplies, a new vehicle or something."

Just about then, Rogue comes walking up with Links to join our little party. It seems that both of them have noticed the small crowd gathering around me, and the looks on their faces are priceless.

"Oh shit, this is the guy she's been hung-up on this last month, isn't it? She never mentioned a name, but the few times I was with her in town and we would run into this guy, she would get all flustered, stumbling over her words and shit." Links' smile is wide. "Our little pervert finally found a man that can put her in her fucking place, and get her outta jail when Sheriff Pryor or Clint has had too much of her. The club lawyer, and she didn't even know it going in. No one could've been a better pick for you."

"Shut the fuck up, Links. Why don't you go home to fucking Sean Connery and go tend to your garden or some shit. Nobody needs you here for support."

Prez is quick to cut in. "Shut it, Titz. We all see you for just who you really are, underneath this rough and course woman. The angry act that you give everyone is getting old. Now isn't the time or the place for this shit. We've been here every time you've had court. That shit don't change, because we're a family." Glancing down at my feet, she shakes her head. "I can't fucking believe that you broke into the sheriff's house to steal a pair of shoes to wear to the court date for breaking into the garage and watching him and Stiletto fuck."

Looking around at us, the smile on Adrik's face grows even wider, if that's possible. "Oh, that shit is seriously what you're into? My, my, my, we will definitely have a good time together then, цветок."

Before I'm able to speak, the bailiff comes out and calls us into the courtroom. Adrik takes my arm as he turns to direct us inside. Leaning down, his breath is hot on my ear. "Don't say a fucking word, Katarina. This is what I get paid the big money for, and the less I have to deal with coming out of your sassy mouth, the easier time I'll have getting you off."

The giggle that erupts from my mouth gets me a death glare from him before I'm able to get myself under control. As the court is called to session and the judge is introduced, I keep my eyes pinned to the judge as he reads over the past complaints and my court history, before reading aloud the charges against me.

I do as Adrik has told me and let him do the talking, which is something that's so foreign to me, it almost hurts. As he speaks with the judge, his heavenly voice seems to shoot right to my core. The ache I feel for him has my legs slowly rubbing against each other, trying to get enough friction to relieve the tension. His big hand rests heavily on my thigh, getting them to stop their movement before the gavel bangs down. I lose myself to thoughts about this man next to me, to the way that he's consumed my life and thoughts these last weeks. The way that he stood up for me with Doug, with little knowledge about the situation.

Drawing myself out of my thoughts, I realize I don't even know what the fuck just went down here. Adrik is guiding me out of the courtroom, and weaving me into another room close by. I hear words exchanged between him and Rogue before the door shuts and the bolt slides closed. He's on me in seconds, and I know that this fight we've had between us is done the moment his lips land on mine. Consuming me, there's no question that I'll give this man everything that he asks or demands of me.

Towering over me, I find myself getting laid out on a table. I'm lost to him, to what he's doing to me. Pushing the dress up my thighs, his fingers find the scrap of black panties soaked, before ripping them from my body. He makes no qualms about pushing two fingers deep inside me before grabbing up one of my breasts roughly with his other hand.

"I told you time and again that you would be mine. That each time you ran you would be punished. And you ran from me many times, цветок. So many times that I've lost track, it seems." Moving his fingers inside of me, I'm not sure what to say or how to answer him, so I choose to stay quiet, but he must see the wheels spinning. "Smart move, but there will be one thing that I need an answer from you about, цветок."

Shaking myself out of the lust-filled haze he's put me in, I speak low, "What's that, Adrik?"

"You won't be pulling anymore shit that lands you in trouble with my place of work, you hear me? I won't have my woman in court, defending her against charges that were easily avoided. You won't show disrespect to me in this, do you understand me?"

Never the one to easily follow orders, I say, "Now, by easily avoided, what exactly do you—"

His fingers are pulled from me, and the slap that lands on my pussy is the first shock to my system. A chair is moved out and away from the table, and then I'm being picked up roughly, turned over onto his lap, feeling the air on my ass as my dress is flipped up. Wasting no time, he lands ten swats on my ass before I can register what's going on. I should be offended at what's happening, but what I find myself being is turned on.

My ex never dared to do this sort of thing. His punishments were truly abuse, and I learned quickly to fall in line. This, the way that Adrik is making me feel, is completely different, and I want nothing more than to fall to my knees for him.

"цветок, answer me, and stop with the sass."

"Yes, sir. I won't be caught up by the popo's again, doing something that I enjoy doing."

"Good girl," he growls, running the fingers of his hand over and down my ass cheek. Moving them lower, he doesn't stop until he finds the moisture that's seeping from my body, running down the inside of my thighs. Rubbing it crudely, I'm not sure if he's trying to rub it into my flesh or if he's trying to draw more out of me.

"Adrik…" His hand slides up slowly, reaching the exact place that I need him the most. The pressure he applies isn't enough, and the chuckle that falls from his lips tells me he knows just what he's doing.

"Are you finally admitting that you will be mine, цветок? That you will do what I want, when I want, where I want? That you will kneel down to me and serve me for the rest of your days? That you will let me be the one to take the troubles and worries off your shoulders? That I will be the one to give you your every pleasure and desire?" Running his free hand over my back, he grabs one of my ass cheeks and squeezes hard. "That you will give me your everything?"

Knowing that's what he wants, there's only one answer I could possibly give. "Yes, Master." And with those two words, I know that my life is forever changed.

Eight

After the courthouse today, I wasn't sure how the night would go. I know that Adrik and I need to talk, and we need to learn more about each other. But, I find myself only wanting to find a dark corner and let him have his way with me.

He takes me to the diner in town. It's not the best way to celebrate, but when you're in Magnolia Springs, you don't have many options, so Mama's Kitchen it is. Grabbing a booth at the back, Adrik waits for me to sit before joining me on my side of the booth.

"Really? These booths are tiny, and I'm not sure if you know this about yourself, but you by no means are a small man."

"I do indeed know that about myself. But, I also know that if I sit on this side of the booth with you, I'll be able to do this." Placing a hand on my thigh, he runs it up slowly toward my pussy. Grabbing my thigh tight, he tugs it closer to him, giving himself easier access.

Moving his fingers through me, I find it almost impossible to keep my sanity about me as the waitress comes strolling up to the table. She takes our orders, only after Adrik makes sure to hear each and every special twice while pumping his fingers in and out of me.

As the waitress walks away, he draws his fingers out of me and brings them to his lips. Licking them off slowly, he doesn't break eye contact with me the whole time. I don't know what he's doing to me. All I know is that I want more.

After dinner, we ended up at Killjoys, right on time to meet up with my Dirty Bitches.

We've been here going on three hours, and the drinks haven't stopped flowing to celebrate not only the court win, but also as Prez so nicely puts it, "That Titz has finally found someone to put her in her place." What the fuck ever.

Speaking of the man, he must be reading my thoughts. My gaze lands on his cock, but his growl does little to stop my perusal. My tongue shoots out of my mouth, and I run it slowly along my bottom lip before taking my eyes from his pants.

"цветок, stop those thoughts or my cock will be the last thing you get tonight. We are out celebrating, and I'm getting to know these women who are your family. Would you take that from me?"

"No, but don't you think we could just sneak back in a dark corner or the bathroom, and I could get a taste of what's to come?"

"Oh, цветок, you will learn." His voice lowers so only I can hear. "You don't lead this shit, Precious. You will learn that very quickly. We won't do anything that I don't want to have happen, and fucking you in a bar bathroom isn't in the cards for you tonight."

The pout that consumes my face has Links laughing out loud from the next table over. "Fuck yeah. Someone that can make that crass mouth of hers shut up." Glancing from me to Adrik, she adds, "Thank you so much for coming into our lives. Maybe I won't have to see so much of her titties now."

Sticking my tongue out at her is only the first thing that I think of. Glancing around to see that we're close to needing drinks, I make a mental note to bring back a bunch of snacks for Grimm to piss her off.

Rogue laughs at the comment, and needs to add something as well. "Maybe you could keep her from pulling up a chair and watching when we're with our men? She really enjoys that shit. Maybe you could find a place that actually has that as an option instead of her method?"

"Yes, yes, I have already reached out to a club that I know of in Birmingham and added her to my account."

My eyes widen with the thought, and I can't keep my mouth quiet. "Fuck yeah. That's what I'm talkin' about. I'm gonna be getting all kinky up in a BDSM club and none of you bitches are invited."

"цветок," he growls out in a warning, and I frown with the reprimand. Taking another swig of my drink, I slam the cup down on the table and head up to the bar to grab another round for the table. The hands that I feel on my hips as I begin my order aren't ones that I'm used to, and certainly aren't those of Adrik.

Turning slowly, I try to shove the guy back a bit before speaking with him. That soon isn't needed, though, as I see Adrik coming up behind him. Wasting no time, he throws the man away from me, jumping on him as he lands.

"What the fuck do you think you're doing, boy?" are the only words I hear Adrik speak as someone pulls me out of the way. The sight I see before me is something that I try to get my hands around. Adrik making sure that I'm safe, no matter who's around or what's going on, and it brings me joy, peace, and even hope.

When he finishes talking with the kid, he comes back and wraps his arms around me before placing his lips to my ear. "цветок, are you okay? Did he hurt you?"

"No, Adrik, I'm fine. He was only trying to hit on me. The shit happens all the time, so you're gonna have to get used to it."

"No, that is one thing I won't ever get used to." His arms loosen their hold and glide down to my hips. "Your body isn't yours to give away any longer. It's mine. And I don't share anything that's mine."

His head lowers, and I wait for him to bring his lips close to mine. The wait is torture as he slowly moves in and gives me a soft, gentle kiss. I try to get more from him, moving my hands toward his cock, but he's pulling away before the kiss can deepen, or I can get my hands on him.

"No, Precious, I told you that this isn't yours to lead. I will decide each step as we take it. You won't force my hand or get your way."

I pout, but he just swats my ass before turning to the bar. Grabbing up our drinks, he throws down a fifty on the bar before returning to our tables.

The night continues on until the early morning, when Adrik follows me home, leaving me with only a chaste kiss before walking away.

Bringing home the man that you'd already promised yourself to for the rest of your fucking days is weird. Having four little girls at home, gawking as you do so, is even more unusual. Having my sisters from the Dirty Bitches surrounding us as well puts even more uneasiness to it. It seems that each of them knew that he was going to be the man who could put me in my place and give me exactly what it is that I've been looking for.

But with him next to me, I feel almost at peace. The time we've taken to get to know each other, and testing our limits and patience, has proven that we are indeed meant to be together. The way he can command not only my thoughts and mind, but my body, is something that I have only ever wished and dreamt of.

After that courtroom appearance, the one that Adrik got me off of with no conviction, no jail time, and no fine, the heat between us exploded. The room that he pulled me into only served to start the fire that has continued to burn each day. We waited these two months before bringing him into the girls' lives. Knowing that when we finally did, there would be no question of our future together.

He's made sure that Doug is out of the picture, and I'm not entirely sure how much on the up-and-up it was. But, I know better than to question him in that sort of thing. He only let me know that Doug wouldn't be dropping by again. That when we become a family, he promised to not put up any fight when and if the girls decided to have Adrik adopt them. That his back payments of support would be coming, and would interest added onto them.

Today is that day, the day that my girls will finally meet the man that's captured my heart. They've heard me talk of him over these past few months, and each know that I'm ready for the next step. For him to become a member of our family, an old man to me, and a father figure to them. They haven't had anyone except me and my sisters in their lives since Doug left, and I'm not sure how they'll react to Adrik, but I'm hopeful.

Seeing his truck pull up out front of the house, I make my way toward the door, but am beaten to it, not only by Violet, but Jasmin, Dahlia, and Rose as well. They head outside with little worry about the stranger that's making his way out of his vehicle. Stiletto, Rogue, and Links are all in the yard with their men, working to setup the yard games, coolers, and tents.

Seeing Adrik in tight blue jeans and a T-shirt, I know this is my laid-back guy, not the man I first met, trying to figure me out. Not the man that I know wears suits and heads off to an office to do his job. Not the man that wears leathers and has me on my knees, serving him as much as he possibly can. Not the man that has done more than anyone else, trying to rid me of the horrific past I've been dealt.

This version of my man is quickly becoming one of my favorites, one that I'm getting more and more accustomed to. This version of him as a provider, as the family man, the man who stole my heart. This version, who's pulling gifts out of the back of his truck. Gifts wrapped up in ribbons and bows, with balloons attached to them. Gifts that have each of my daughters squealing out with glee in turn as they open them.

Moving slowly toward the sight, I see my sisters each embracing their men, and know that this thing that we have built here in Magnolia Springs is something that we can be proud of. Coming to a stop, I see the trinkets, candies, and toys that Adrik has brought for my daughters. The happiness I see in them is something that's been a long time coming, and I can't be happier to see the joy return to their eyes.

Noticing me coming to a stop close by him, Adrik comes to me with a gleam in his eye. Without waiting, and with little care for the folks around us, he drops to a knee, pulling a wrapped package from behind his back as he does. The ribbons and bows, it seems, do not only belong to my daughters on this day.

"цветок, you own me, heart and soul. I know you feel the same way about me, I don't even need to ask. But I will, for the sake of your family, your daughters, and the other children that will soon join our family, and of course your sisters." Snapping open the box, I see the most gorgeous ring and collar set, and am instantly hit with the feels.

"Katarina Orlovis, you will marry me, and there isn't much to say about it." He looks over to our friends and family that are gathered around us. "You were born to be my baby, and baby I was made to be your man." Not being able to speak, I only nod my head as he raises up, putting first the ring on my finger, then the collar around my neck, followed lastly by a kiss on my lips, branding me as his forever.

THE END

Avelyn Paige is a born and raised Indiana Internationally bestselling author. While she may be a Hoosier by birth, she is a Boilermaker by choice. Boiler Up! She resides in a sleepy little town in Indiana with her husband and three crazy pets.

Find more information about Avelyn at:

http://www.authoravelynpaige.com

Winter Travers is a devoted wife, mother, and aunt turned author who was born and raised in Wisconsin. After a brief stint in South Carolina following her heart to chase the man who is now her hubby, they retreated back up North to the changing seasons, and to the place they now call home.

Winter spends her days writing happily ever afters, and her nights being a karate mom hauling her kid to practices and tournaments. She also has an addiction to anything MC related, her dog Thunder, and Mexican food! (Tamales!)

Find more information about Winter at: www.wintertravers.com

Geri Glenn writes alpha males. She's best known for writing motorcycle romance, including the internationally bestselling series, the Kings of Korruption MC.

She lives in the Thousand Islands with her hubby, two young girls, one big dog and one terrier that thinks he's a Doberman. Before she began writing contemporary romance, Geri worked at several different occupations. She's been a pharmacy assistant, a 911 dispatcher, and a caregiver in a nursing home. She can say without a doubt though, that her favorite job is the one she does now–writing romance that leaves an impact.

She loves homemade cookies, copious amounts of coffee and Diet Coke by the case. You can connect with Geri on her website http://geriglenn.com where you can sign up for her newsletter to find out more about her less than glamorous life, and what she's working on now.

GM Scherbert writes erotic romance. She's best known for her Devil's Iron MC series and her skills with a flogger. She's quirky, unique, has a filthy mind, is hard to hate but harder to love.

GM lives in Milwaukee with her husband and four daughters, their dog and three cats. By day, she is a devoted mother and a teacher for students on the Autism spectrum. By night, she can found reading or writing stories that would make a porn star blush.

If you like romance with lots of twists and darker themes, GM Scherbert may just become your new favourite author.

Find more information about GM at:

https://www.facebook.com/Authorgmscherbert

Facebook: https://goo.gl/7nzrYD

Facebook Group: https://bit.ly/2rLCgU5

Twitter: www.twitter.com/dirtybitchesmc

Instagram: www.instagram.com/dirtybitchesmc

Website: www.dirtybitchesmc.com

Join Our Newsletter: http://eepurl.com/dtns4T

Apply to be part of a future season of the Dirty Bitches:

https://goo.gl/forms/xYcRZeWsrHptt6ue2

Made in the USA
Columbia, SC
18 July 2018